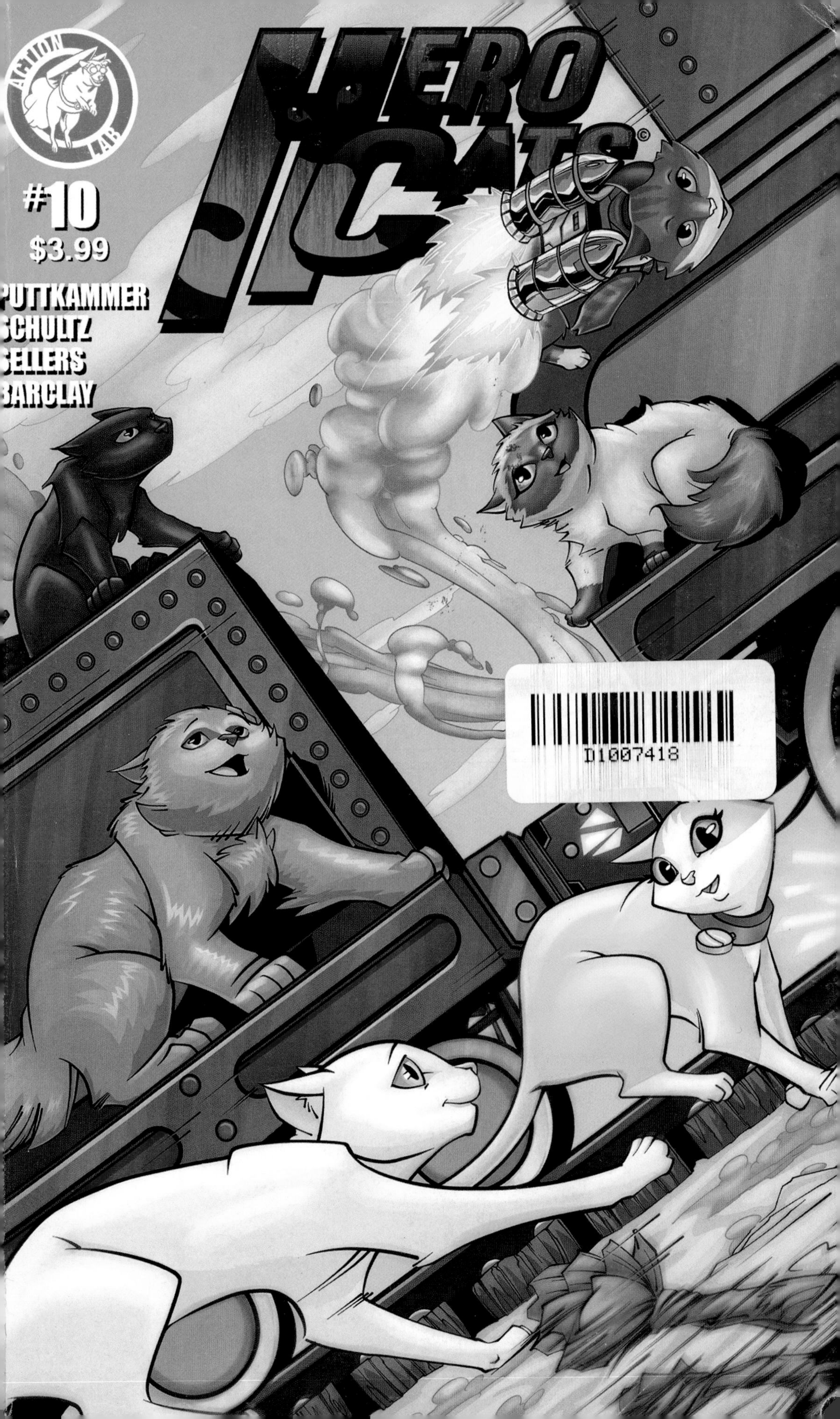
ACTION LAB
HERO CATS ©
#10
$3.99
PUTTKAMMER
SCHULTZ
SELLERS
BARCLAY

FROM ALL-AGES TO MATURE READERS
ACTION LAB HAS YOU COVERED.

 **Appropriate for everyone.**

 **Appropriate for age 9 and up. Absent of profanity or adult content.**

 **Suggested for 12 and Up. Comics with this rating are comparable to a PG-13 movie rating. Recommended for our teen and young adult readers.**

 **Appropriate for older teens. Similar to Teen, but featuring more mature themes and/or more graphic imagery.**

 **Contains extreme violence and some nudity. Basically the Rated-R of comics.**

FIND YOUR NEW FAVORITE COMICS.

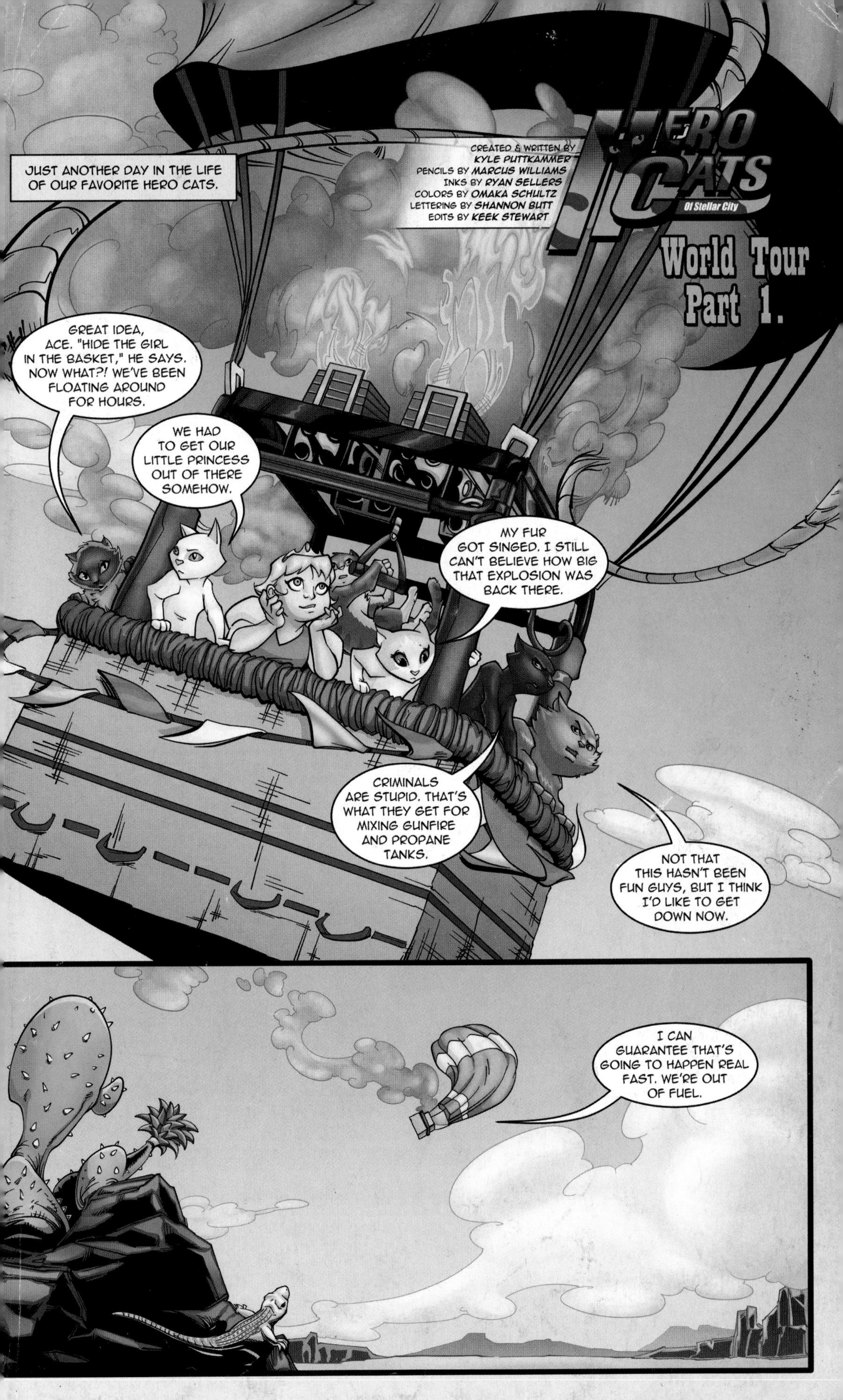

HERO CATS
Of Stellar City
World Tour Part 1.
CREATED & WRITTEN BY KYLE PUTTKAMMER
PENCILS BY MARCUS WILLIAMS
INKS BY RYAN SELLERS
COLORS BY OMAKA SCHULTZ
LETTERING BY SHANNON BUTT
EDITS BY KEEK STEWART
JUST ANOTHER DAY IN THE LIFE OF OUR FAVORITE HERO CATS.
GREAT IDEA, ACE. "HIDE THE GIRL IN THE BASKET," HE SAYS. NOW WHAT?! WE'VE BEEN FLOATING AROUND FOR HOURS.
WE HAD TO GET OUR LITTLE PRINCESS OUT OF THERE SOMEHOW.
MY FUR GOT SINGED. I STILL CAN'T BELIEVE HOW BIG THAT EXPLOSION WAS BACK THERE.
CRIMINALS ARE STUPID. THAT'S WHAT THEY GET FOR MIXING GUNFIRE AND PROPANE TANKS.
NOT THAT THIS HASN'T BEEN FUN GUYS, BUT I THINK I'D LIKE TO GET DOWN NOW.
I CAN GUARANTEE THAT'S GOING TO HAPPEN REAL FAST. WE'RE OUT OF FUEL.

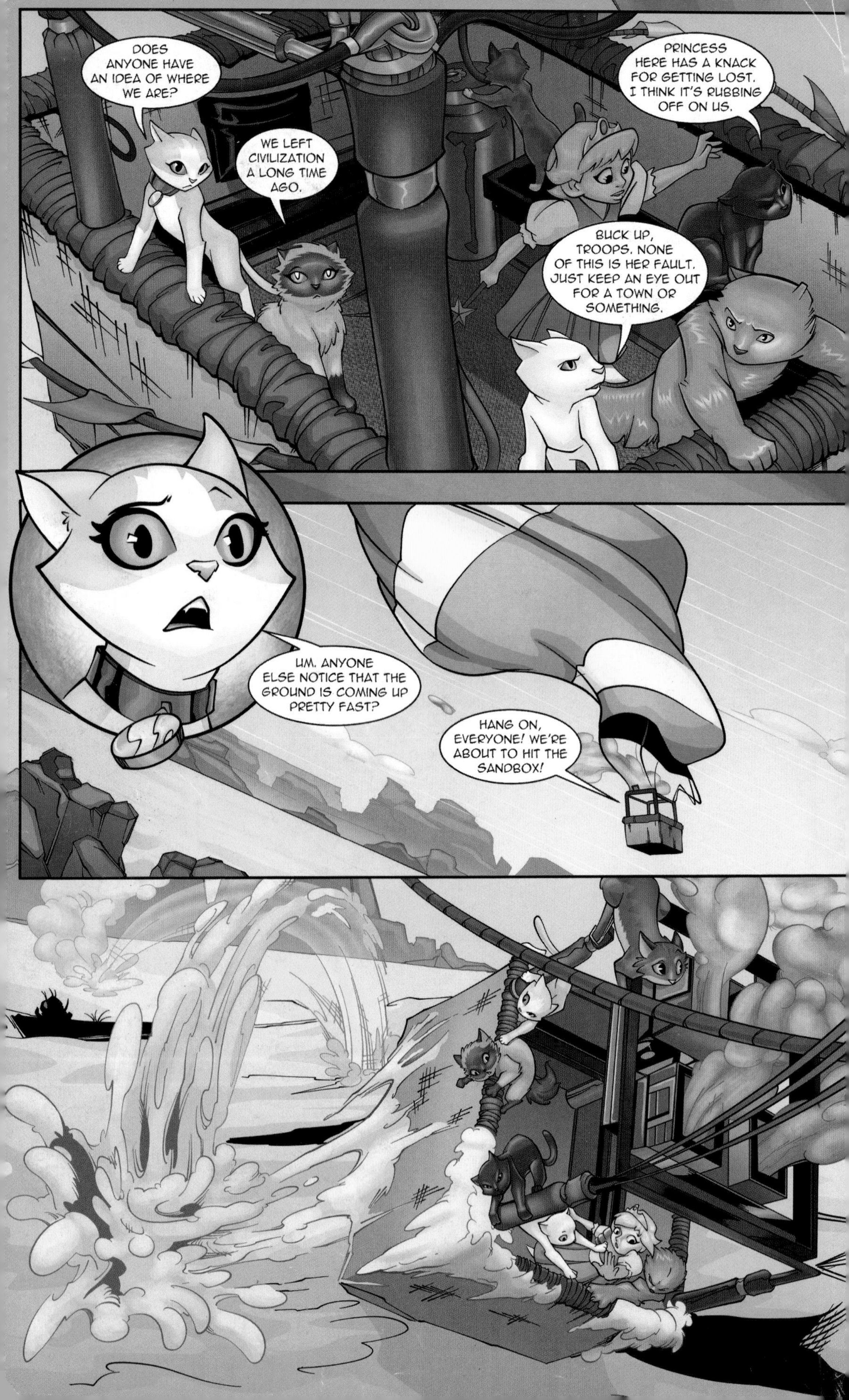
DOES ANYONE HAVE AN IDEA OF WHERE WE ARE?
WE LEFT CIVILIZATION A LONG TIME AGO.
PRINCESS HERE HAS A KNACK FOR GETTING LOST. I THINK IT'S RUBBING OFF ON US.
BUCK UP, TROOPS. NONE OF THIS IS HER FAULT. JUST KEEP AN EYE OUT FOR A TOWN OR SOMETHING.
UM. ANYONE ELSE NOTICE THAT THE GROUND IS COMING UP PRETTY FAST?
HANG ON, EVERYONE! WE'RE ABOUT TO HIT THE SANDBOX!

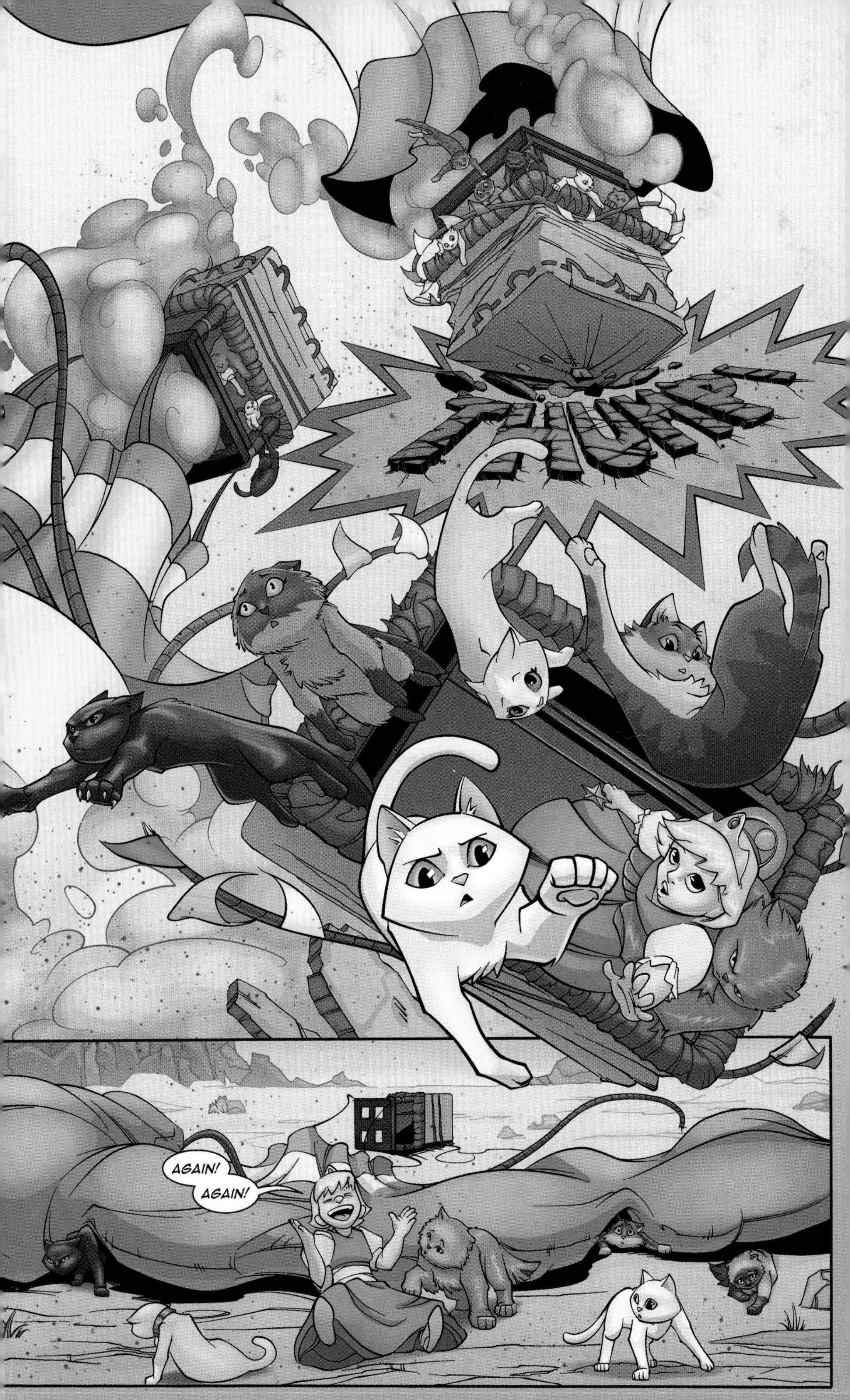
THUMP!
AGAIN! AGAIN!

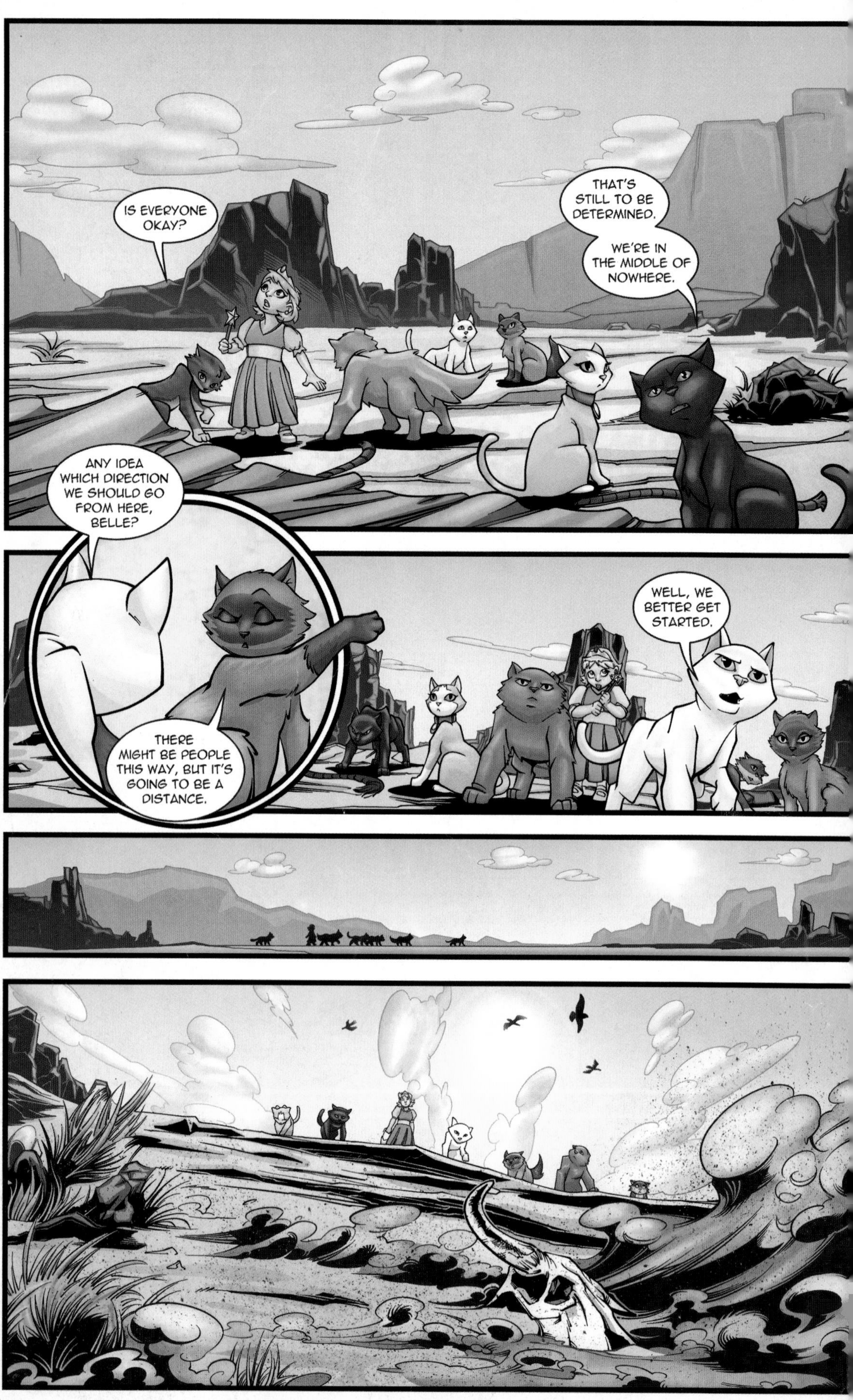
IS EVERYONE OKAY?
THAT'S STILL TO BE DETERMINED.
WE'RE IN THE MIDDLE OF NOWHERE.
ANY IDEA WHICH DIRECTION WE SHOULD GO FROM HERE, BELLE?
THERE MIGHT BE PEOPLE THIS WAY, BUT IT'S GOING TO BE A DISTANCE.
WELL, WE BETTER GET STARTED.

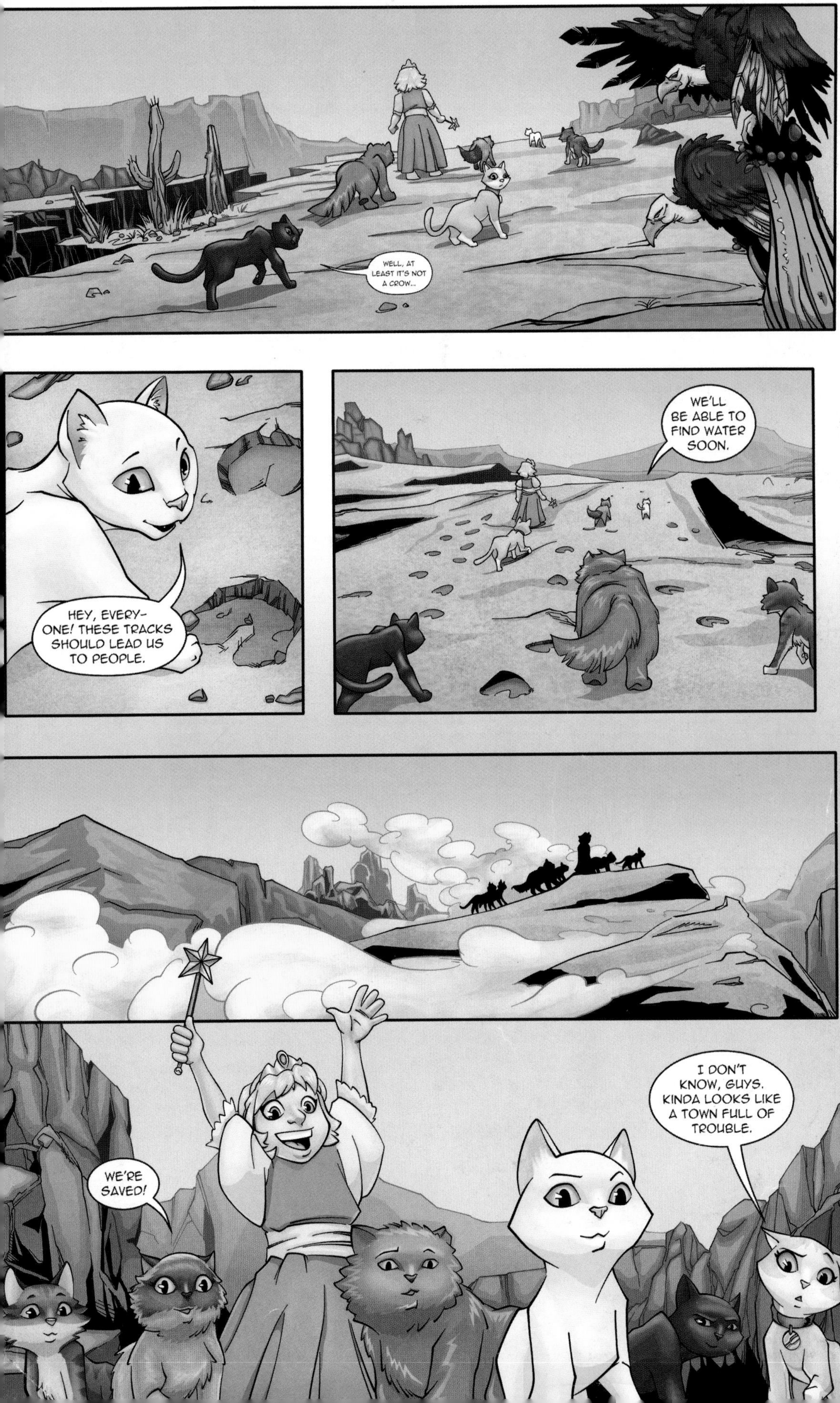
WELL, AT LEAST IT'S NOT A CROW...
HEY, EVERY-ONE! THESE TRACKS SHOULD LEAD US TO PEOPLE.
WE'LL BE ABLE TO FIND WATER SOON.
WE'RE SAVED!
I DON'T KNOW, GUYS. KINDA LOOKS LIKE A TOWN FULL OF TROUBLE.

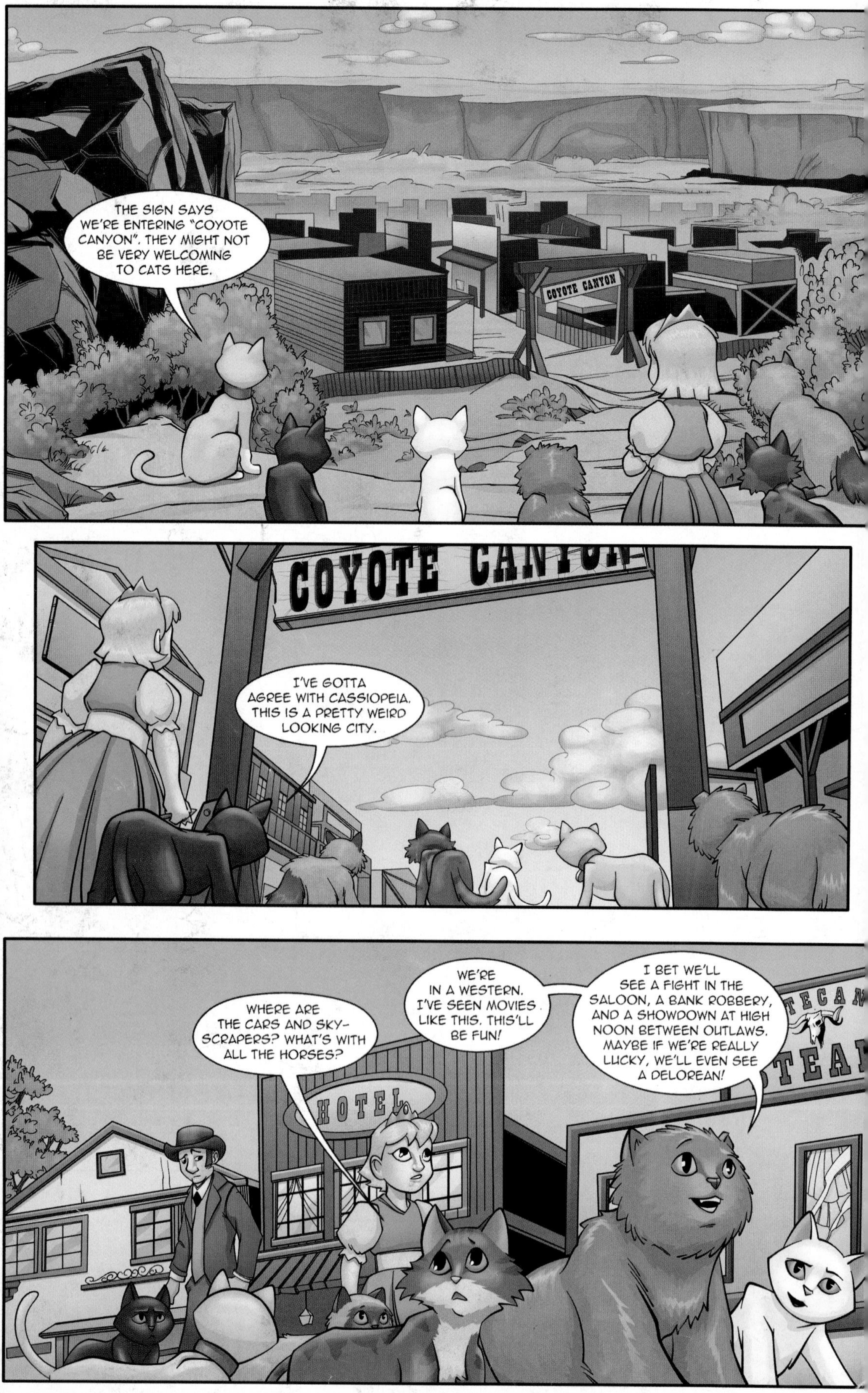
THE SIGN SAYS WE'RE ENTERING "COYOTE CANYON". THEY MIGHT NOT BE VERY WELCOMING TO CATS HERE.
COYOTE CANYON
I'VE GOTTA AGREE WITH CASSIOPEIA. THIS IS A PRETTY WEIRD LOOKING CITY.
WHERE ARE THE CARS AND SKY-SCRAPERS? WHAT'S WITH ALL THE HORSES?
WE'RE IN A WESTERN. I'VE SEEN MOVIES LIKE THIS. THIS'LL BE FUN!
I BET WE'LL SEE A FIGHT IN THE SALOON, A BANK ROBBERY, AND A SHOWDOWN AT HIGH NOON BETWEEN OUTLAWS. MAYBE IF WE'RE REALLY LUCKY, WE'LL EVEN SEE A DELOREAN!
HOTEL

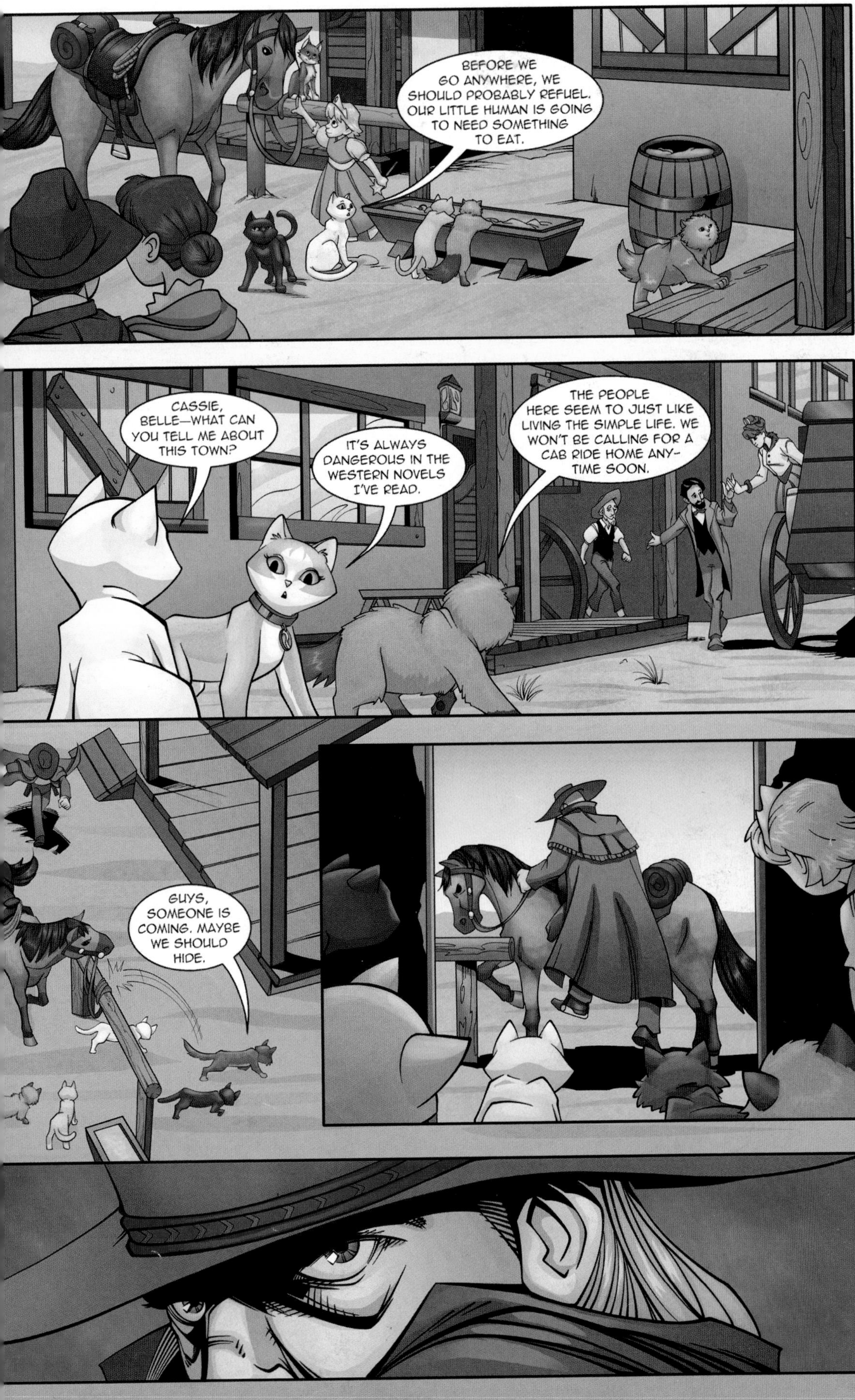
BEFORE WE GO ANYWHERE, WE SHOULD PROBABLY REFUEL. OUR LITTLE HUMAN IS GOING TO NEED SOMETHING TO EAT.
CASSIE, BELLE—WHAT CAN YOU TELL ME ABOUT THIS TOWN?
IT'S ALWAYS DANGEROUS IN THE WESTERN NOVELS I'VE READ.
THE PEOPLE HERE SEEM TO JUST LIKE LIVING THE SIMPLE LIFE. WE WON'T BE CALLING FOR A CAB RIDE HOME ANY-TIME SOON.
GUYS, SOMEONE IS COMING. MAYBE WE SHOULD HIDE.

I FOUND FOOD FOR OUR LITTLE PRINCESS.

I DIDN'T MISS ANYTHING WHILE I WAS GONE, DID I?

WHERE DID YOU GET THE BREAD?

FROM THE SALOON.

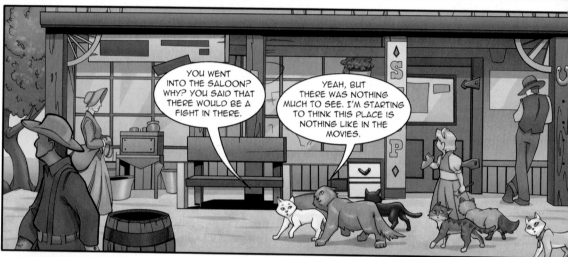

YOU WENT INTO THE SALOON? WHY? YOU SAID THAT THERE WOULD BE A FIGHT IN THERE.

YEAH, BUT THERE WAS NOTHING MUCH TO SEE. I'M STARTING TO THINK THIS PLACE IS NOTHING LIKE IN THE MOVIES.

MAYBE IF I GOT MYSELF A HAT.

WHADDYA THINK, PARTNER?

WE'RE NOT GETTING YOU A HAT, ROCCO. WE HAVE TO GET PRINCESS BACK TO STELLAR CITY. HER PARENTS ARE PROBABLY WORRIED SICK ABOUT HER.

WE'VE GOT NO BUSINESS IN COYOTE CANYON AND WE'D BEST BE MOSEYING ALONG.

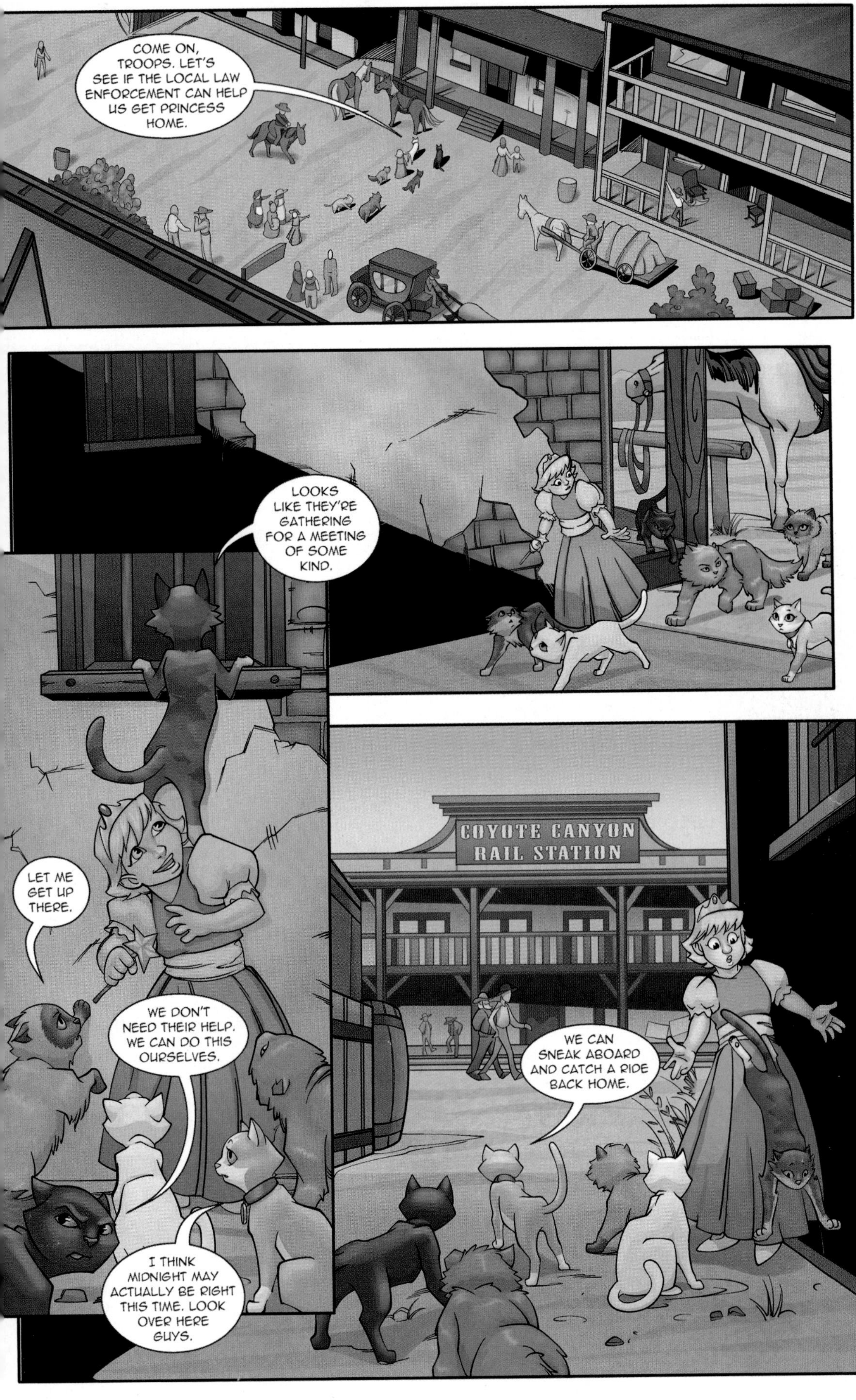
COME ON, TROOPS. LET'S SEE IF THE LOCAL LAW ENFORCEMENT CAN HELP US GET PRINCESS HOME.
LOOKS LIKE THEY'RE GATHERING FOR A MEETING OF SOME KIND.
LET ME GET UP THERE.
WE DON'T NEED THEIR HELP. WE CAN DO THIS OURSELVES.
I THINK MIDNIGHT MAY ACTUALLY BE RIGHT THIS TIME. LOOK OVER HERE GUYS.
COYOTE CANYON RAIL STATION
WE CAN SNEAK ABOARD AND CATCH A RIDE BACK HOME.

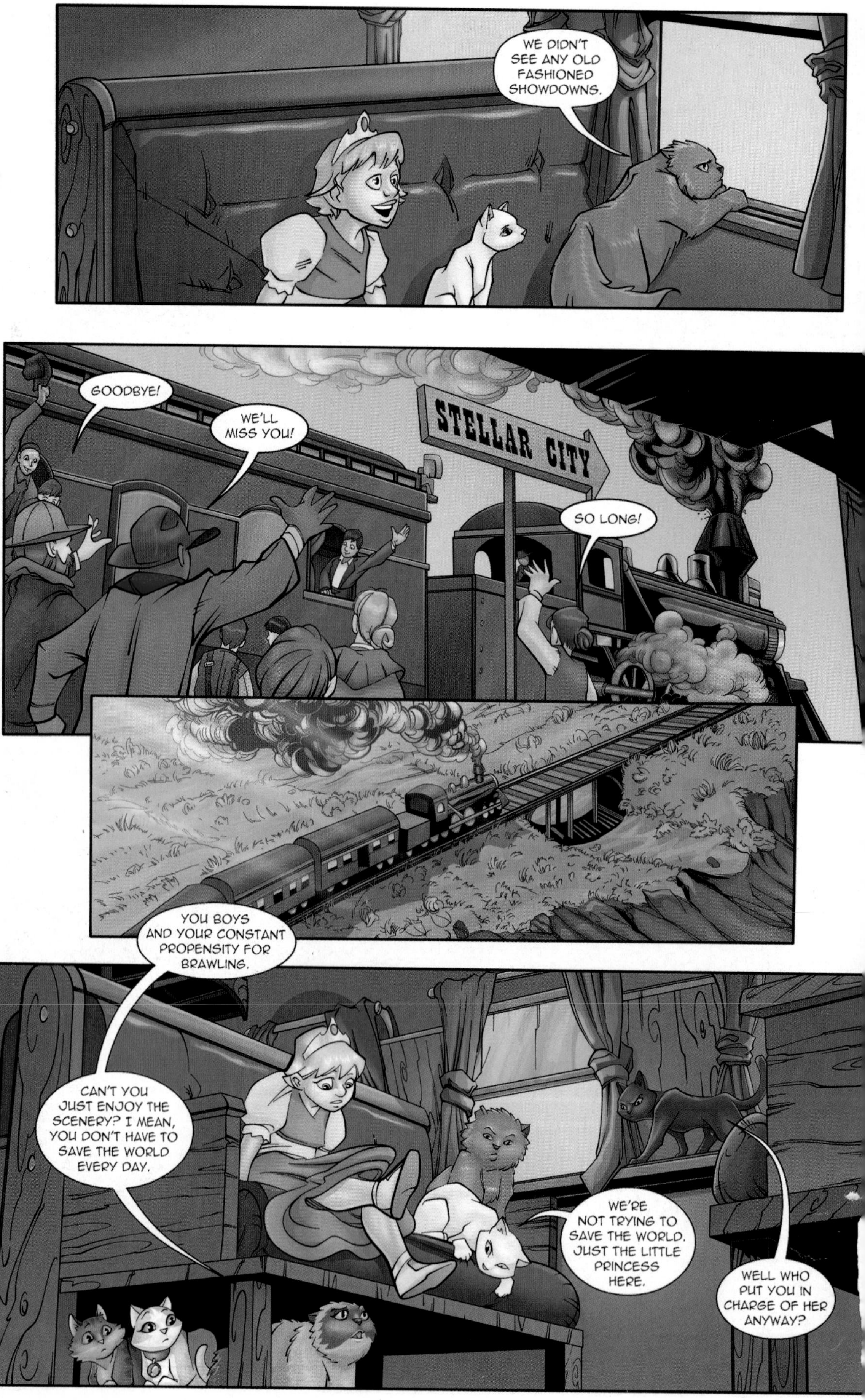
WE DIDN'T SEE ANY OLD FASHIONED SHOWDOWNS.
GOODBYE!
WE'LL MISS YOU!
STELLAR CITY
SO LONG!
YOU BOYS AND YOUR CONSTANT PROPENSITY FOR BRAWLING.
CAN'T YOU JUST ENJOY THE SCENERY? I MEAN, YOU DON'T HAVE TO SAVE THE WORLD EVERY DAY.
WE'RE NOT TRYING TO SAVE THE WORLD. JUST THE LITTLE PRINCESS HERE.
WELL WHO PUT YOU IN CHARGE OF HER ANYWAY?

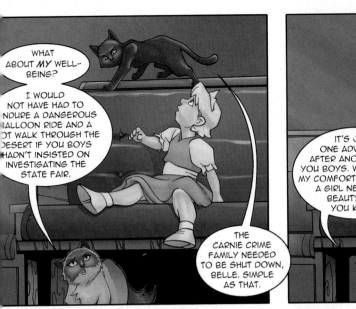

WHAT ABOUT *MY* WELL-BEING?

I WOULD NOT HAVE HAD TO ENDURE A DANGEROUS BALLOON RIDE AND A HOT WALK THROUGH THE DESERT IF YOU BOYS HADN'T INSISTED ON INVESTIGATING THE STATE FAIR.

THE CARNIE CRIME FAMILY NEEDED TO BE SHUT DOWN, BELLE. SIMPLE AS THAT.

IT'S JUST ONE ADVENTURE AFTER ANOTHER WITH YOU BOYS. WELL, I MISS MY COMFORTABLE PORCH. A GIRL NEEDS HER BEAUTY REST YOU KNOW.

NOW IS THE PERFECT TIME FOR A NAP, BELLE. THERE'S NOTHING MORE RELAXING THAN A TRAIN RIDE.

LET'S JUST GET SETTLED IN AND KEEP A LOW PROFILE.

WE HAVE A LONG TRAIN RIDE BACK HOME.

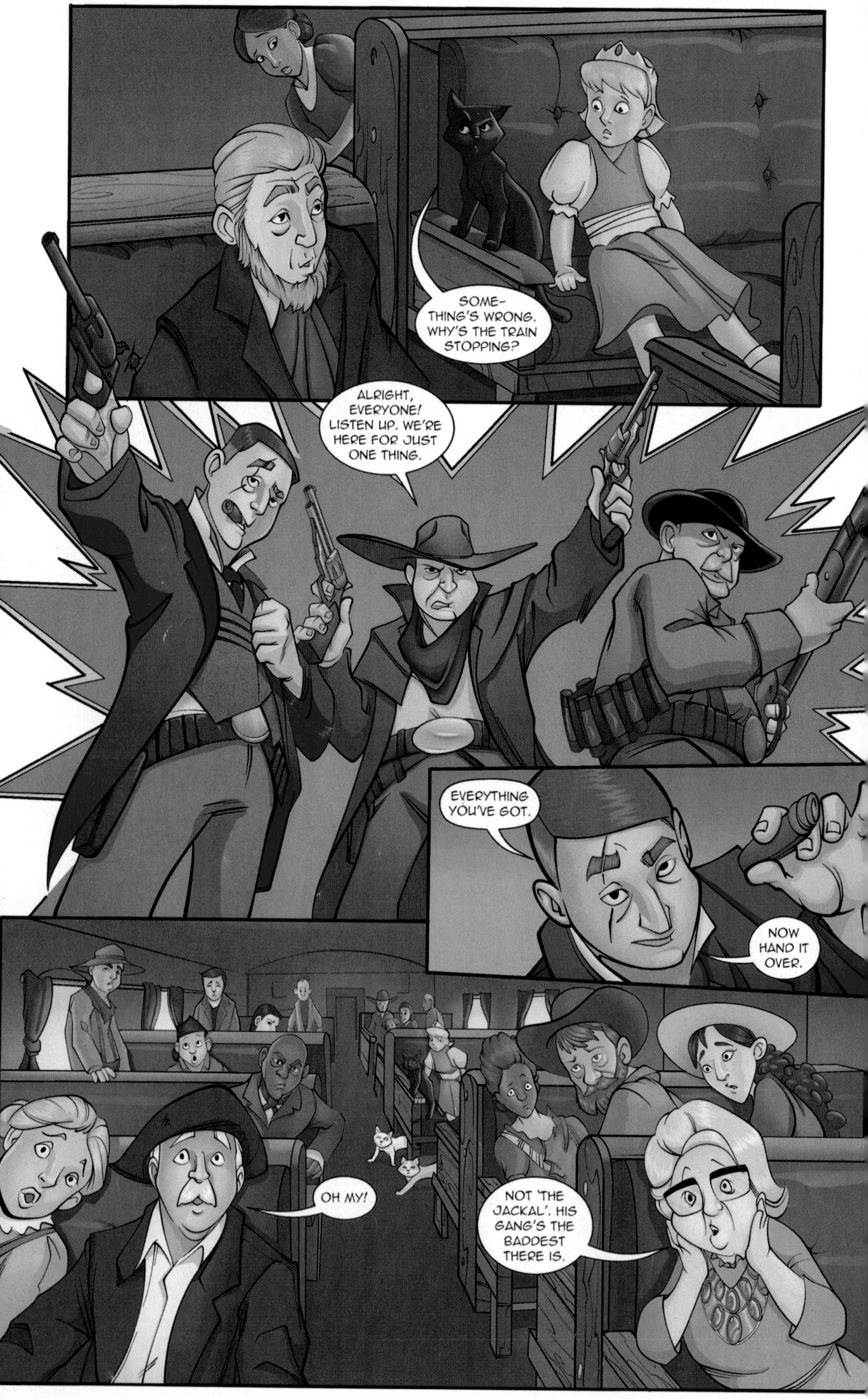
SOME-
THING'S WRONG.
WHY'S THE TRAIN
STOPPING?
ALRIGHT,
EVERYONE!
LISTEN UP. WE'RE
HERE FOR JUST
ONE THING.
EVERYTHING
YOU'VE GOT.
NOW
HAND IT
OVER.
OH MY!
NOT 'THE
JACKAL'. HIS
GANG'S THE
BADDEST
THERE IS.

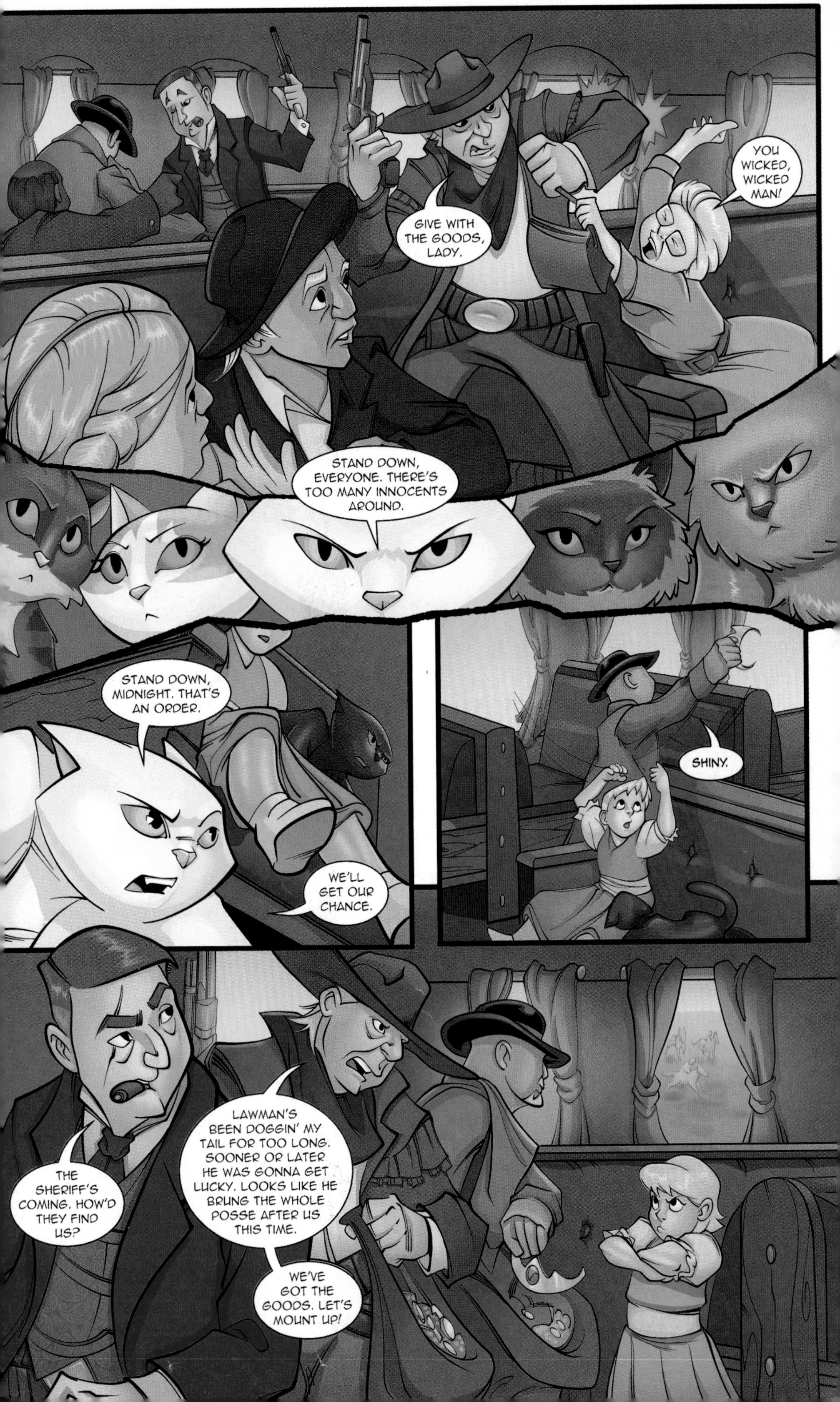
GIVE WITH THE GOODS, LADY.
YOU WICKED, WICKED MAN!
STAND DOWN, EVERYONE. THERE'S TOO MANY INNOCENTS AROUND.
STAND DOWN, MIDNIGHT. THAT'S AN ORDER.
WE'LL GET OUR CHANCE.
SHINY.
THE SHERIFF'S COMING. HOW'D THEY FIND US?
LAWMAN'S BEEN DOGGIN' MY TAIL FOR TOO LONG. SOONER OR LATER HE WAS GONNA GET LUCKY. LOOKS LIKE HE BRUNG THE WHOLE POSSE AFTER US THIS TIME.
WE'VE GOT THE GOODS. LET'S MOUNT UP!

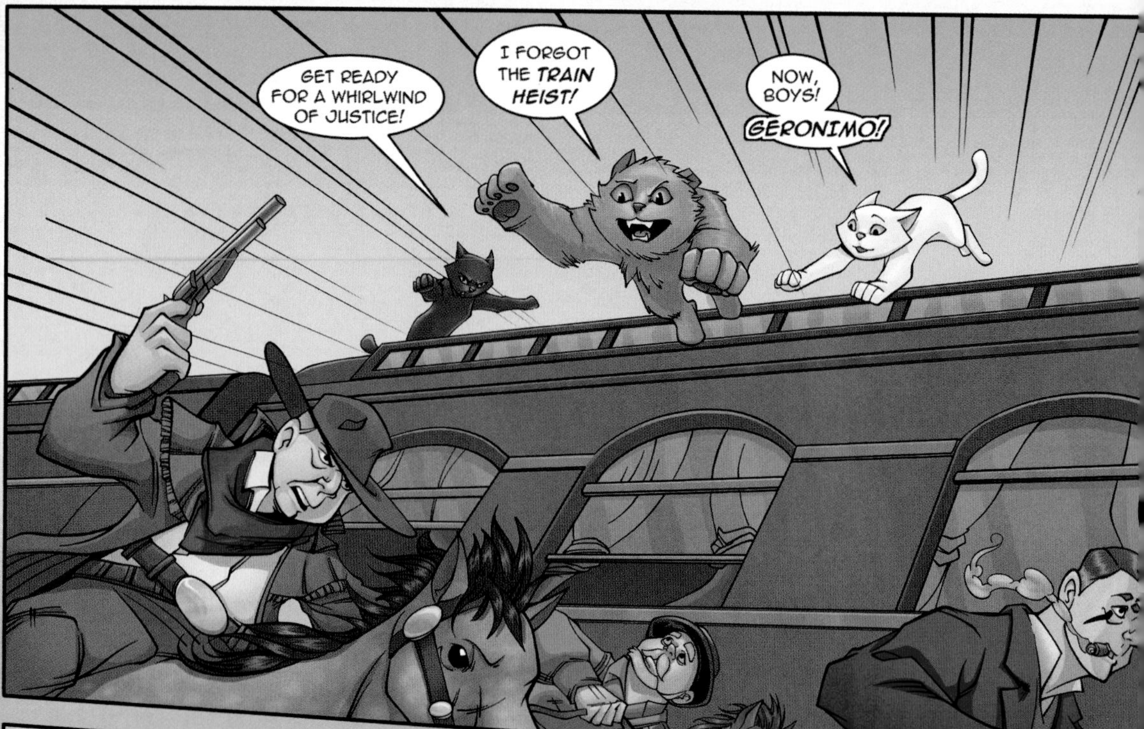
GET READY FOR A WHIRLWIND OF JUSTICE!
I FORGOT THE TRAIN HEIST!
NOW, BOYS!
GERONIMO!!

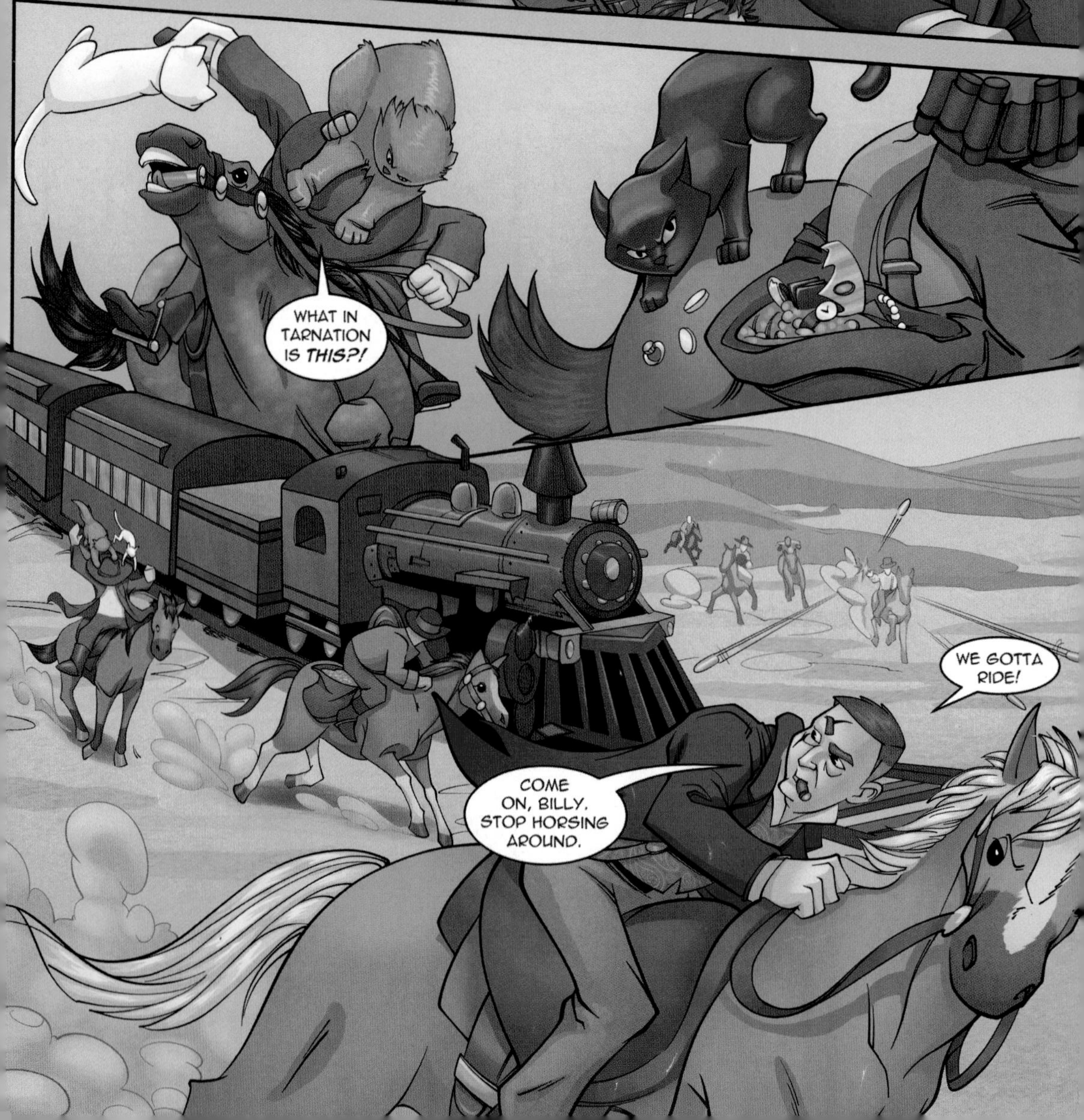
WHAT IN TARNATION IS THIS?!
WE GOTTA RIDE!
COME ON, BILLY. STOP HORSING AROUND.

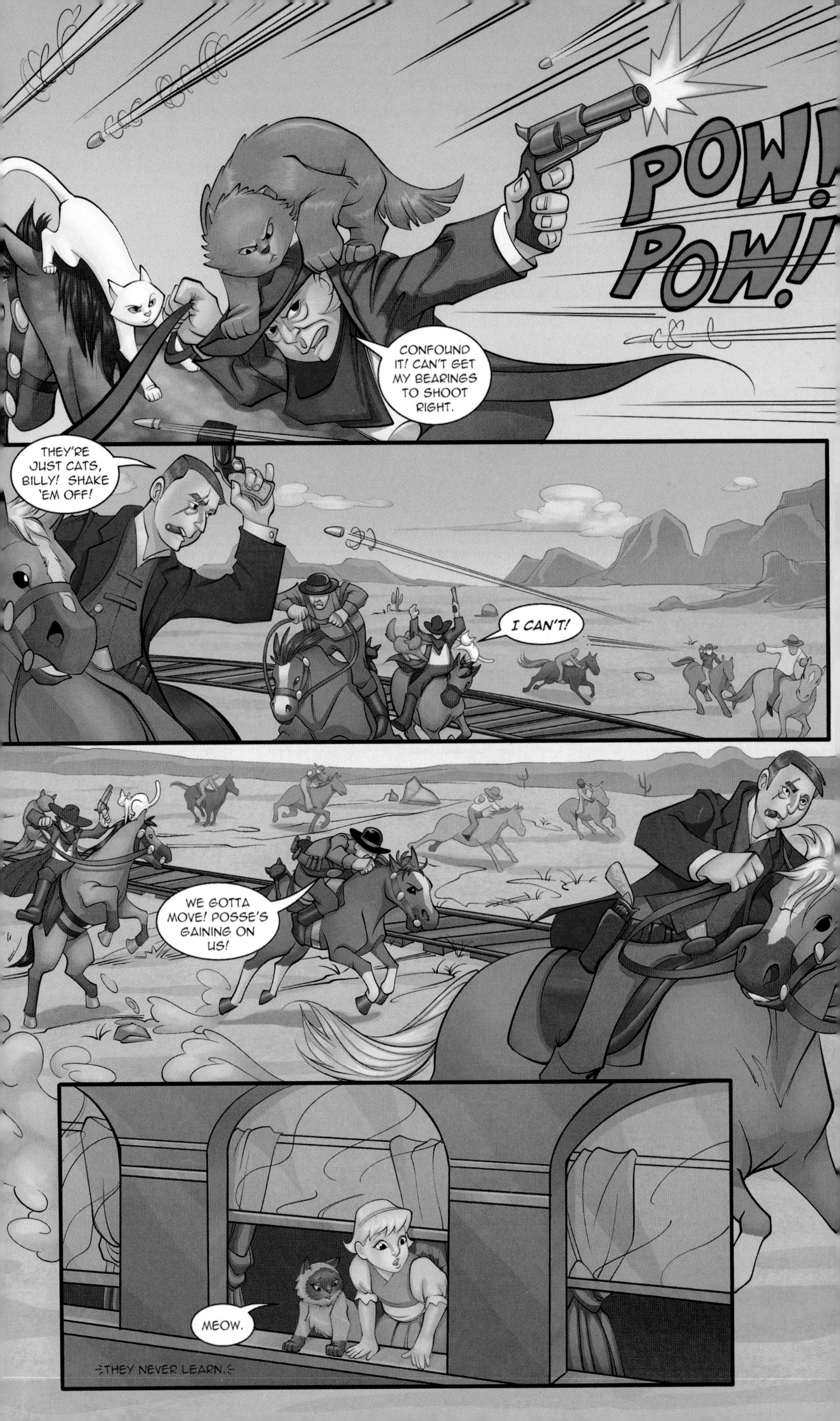
POW!
POW!
CONFOUND IT! CAN'T GET MY BEARINGS TO SHOOT RIGHT.
THEY'RE JUST CATS, BILLY! SHAKE 'EM OFF!
I CAN'T!
WE GOTTA MOVE! POSSE'S GAINING ON US!
MEOW.
THEY NEVER LEARN.

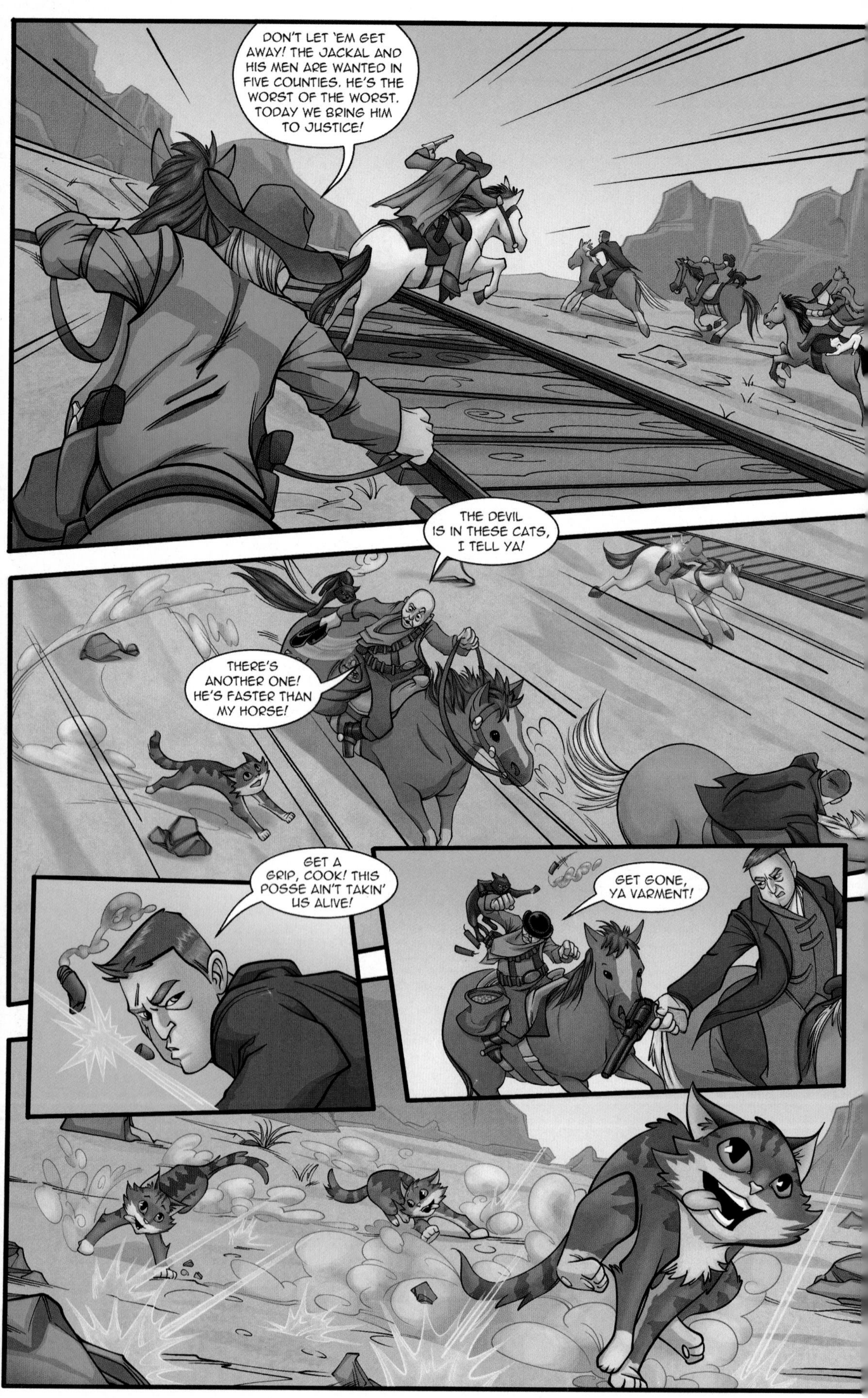
DON'T LET 'EM GET AWAY! THE JACKAL AND HIS MEN ARE WANTED IN FIVE COUNTIES. HE'S THE WORST OF THE WORST. TODAY WE BRING HIM TO JUSTICE!
THE DEVIL IS IN THESE CATS, I TELL YA!
THERE'S ANOTHER ONE! HE'S FASTER THAN MY HORSE!
GET A GRIP, COOK! THIS POSSE AIN'T TAKIN' US ALIVE!
GET GONE, YA VARMENT!

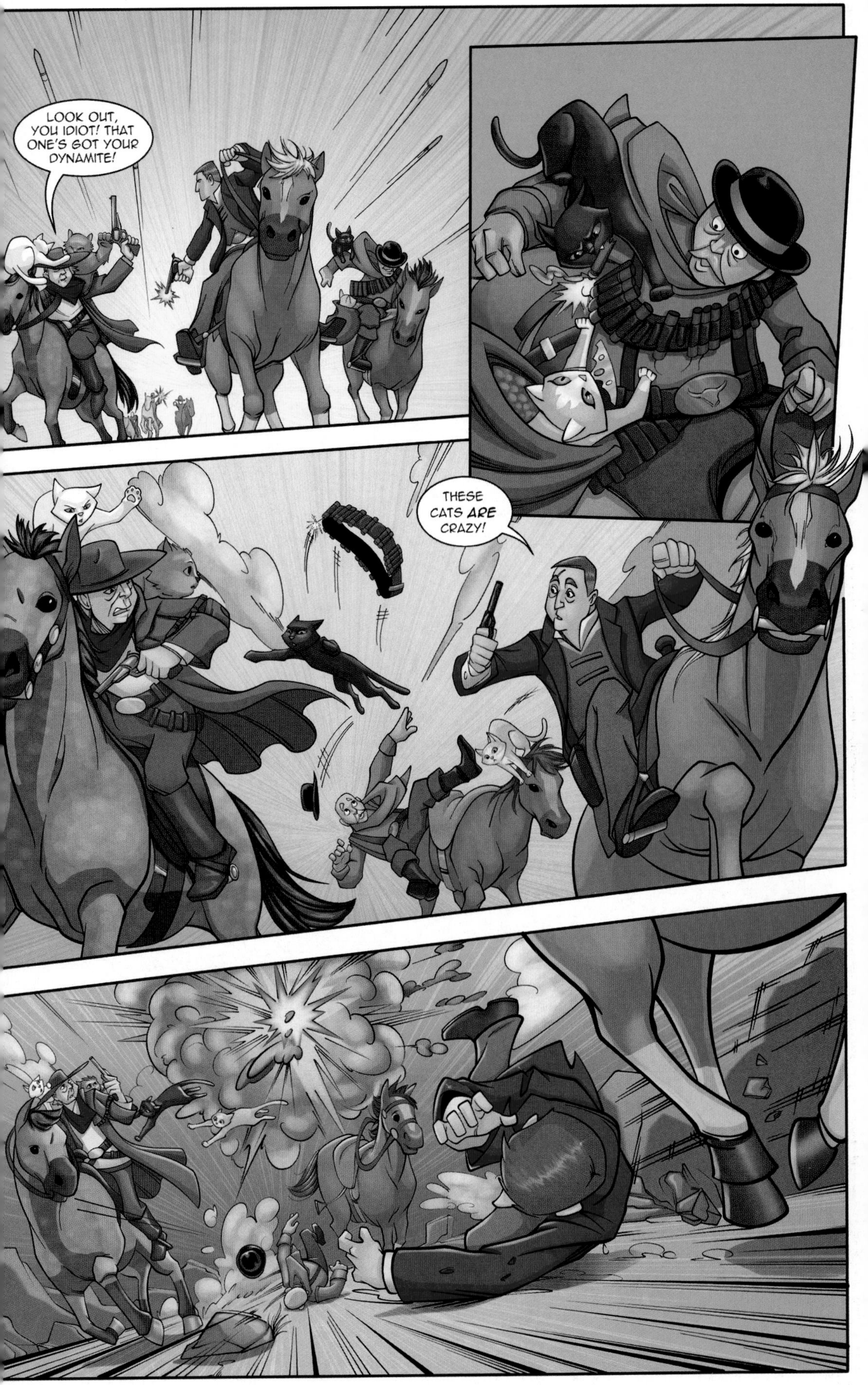
LOOK OUT, YOU IDIOT! THAT ONE'S GOT YOUR DYNAMITE!
THESE CATS **ARE** CRAZY!

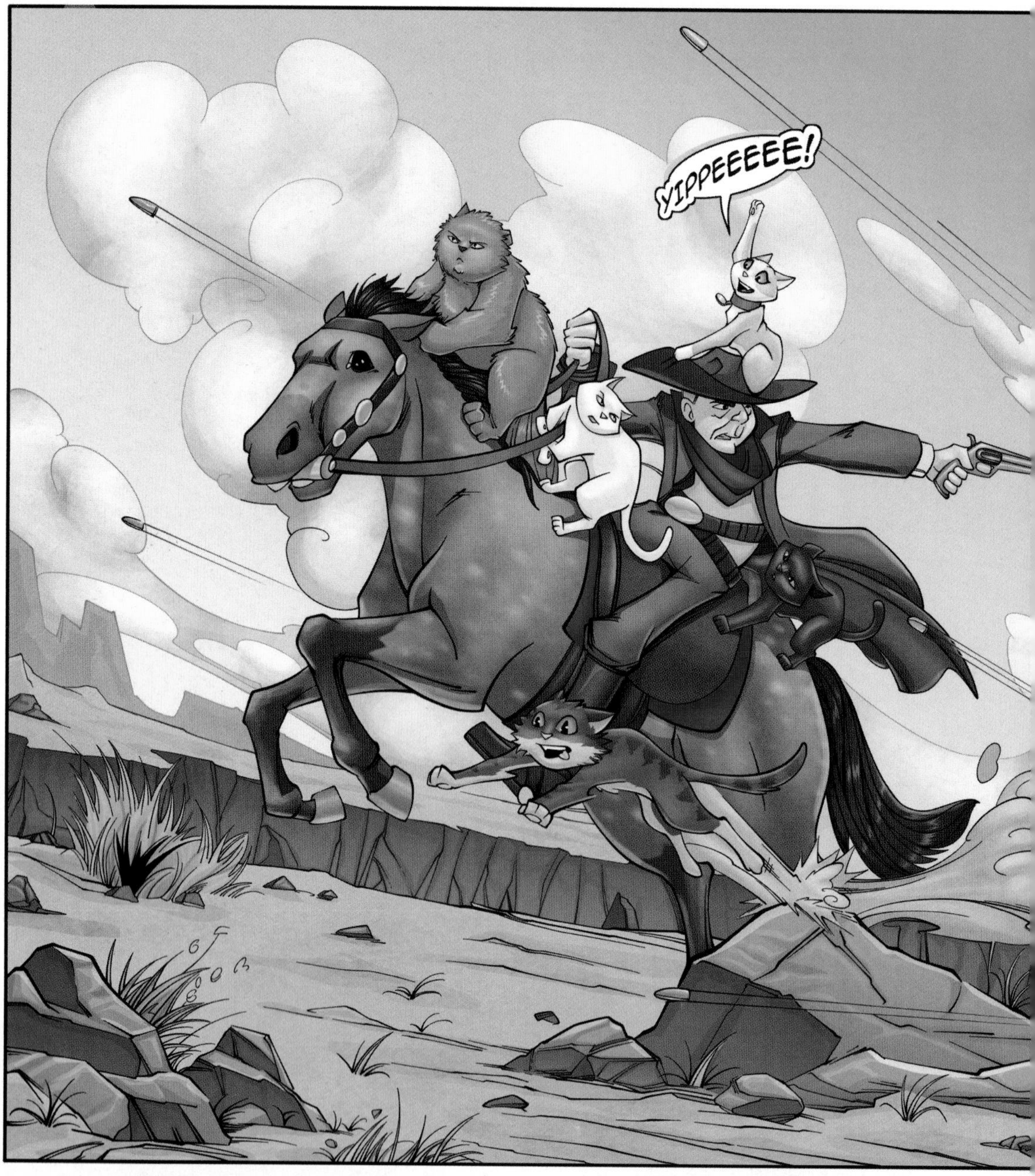
YIPPEEEEE!

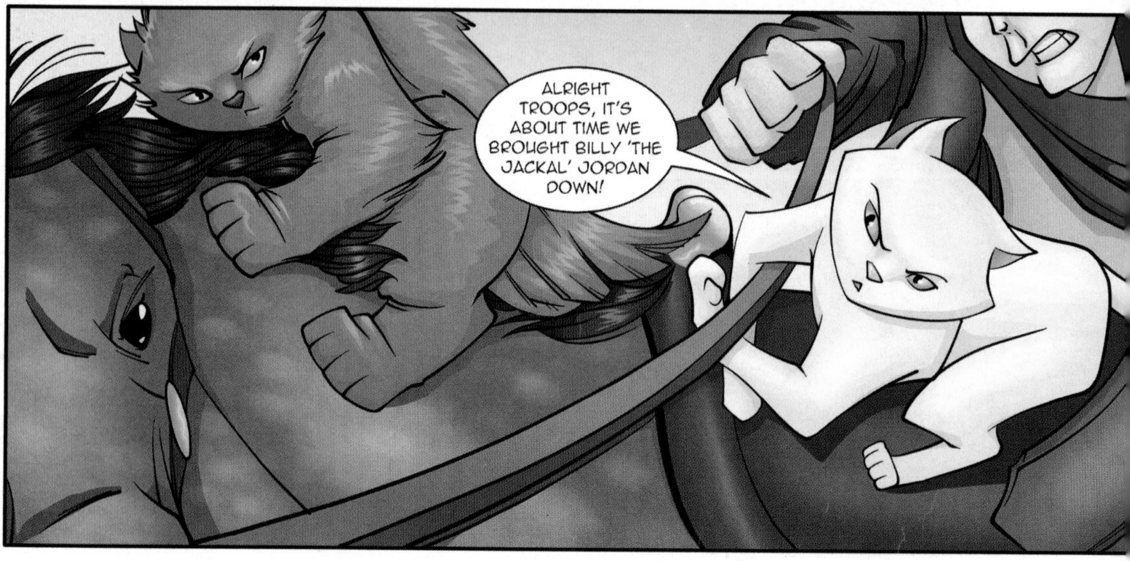
ALRIGHT TROOPS, IT'S ABOUT TIME WE BROUGHT BILLY 'THE JACKAL' JORDAN DOWN!

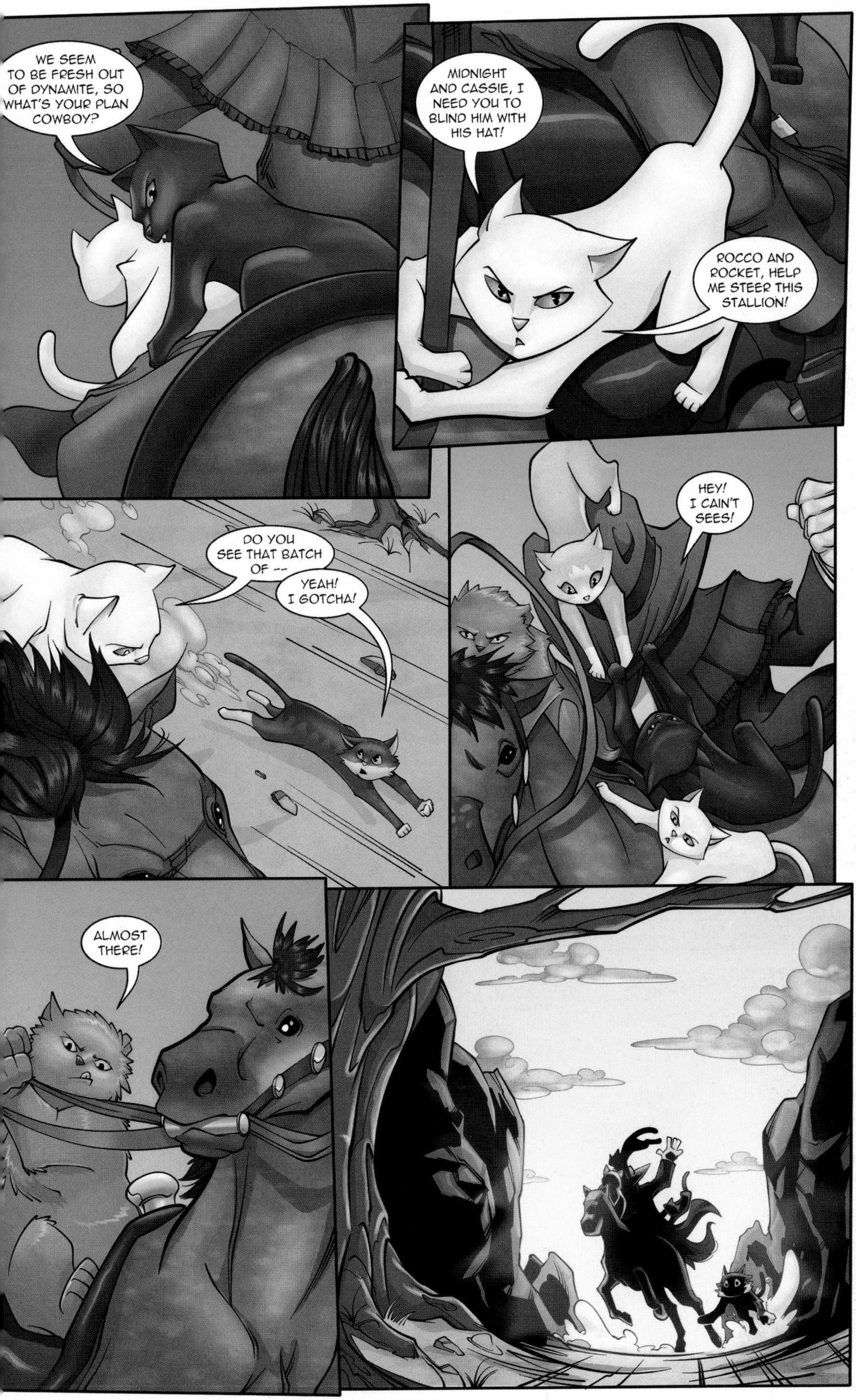
WE SEEM TO BE FRESH OUT OF DYNAMITE, SO WHAT'S YOUR PLAN COWBOY?
MIDNIGHT AND CASSIE, I NEED YOU TO BLIND HIM WITH HIS HAT!
ROCCO AND ROCKET, HELP ME STEER THIS STALLION!
DO YOU SEE THAT BATCH OF --
YEAH! I GOTCHA!
HEY! I CAIN'T SEES!
ALMOST THERE!

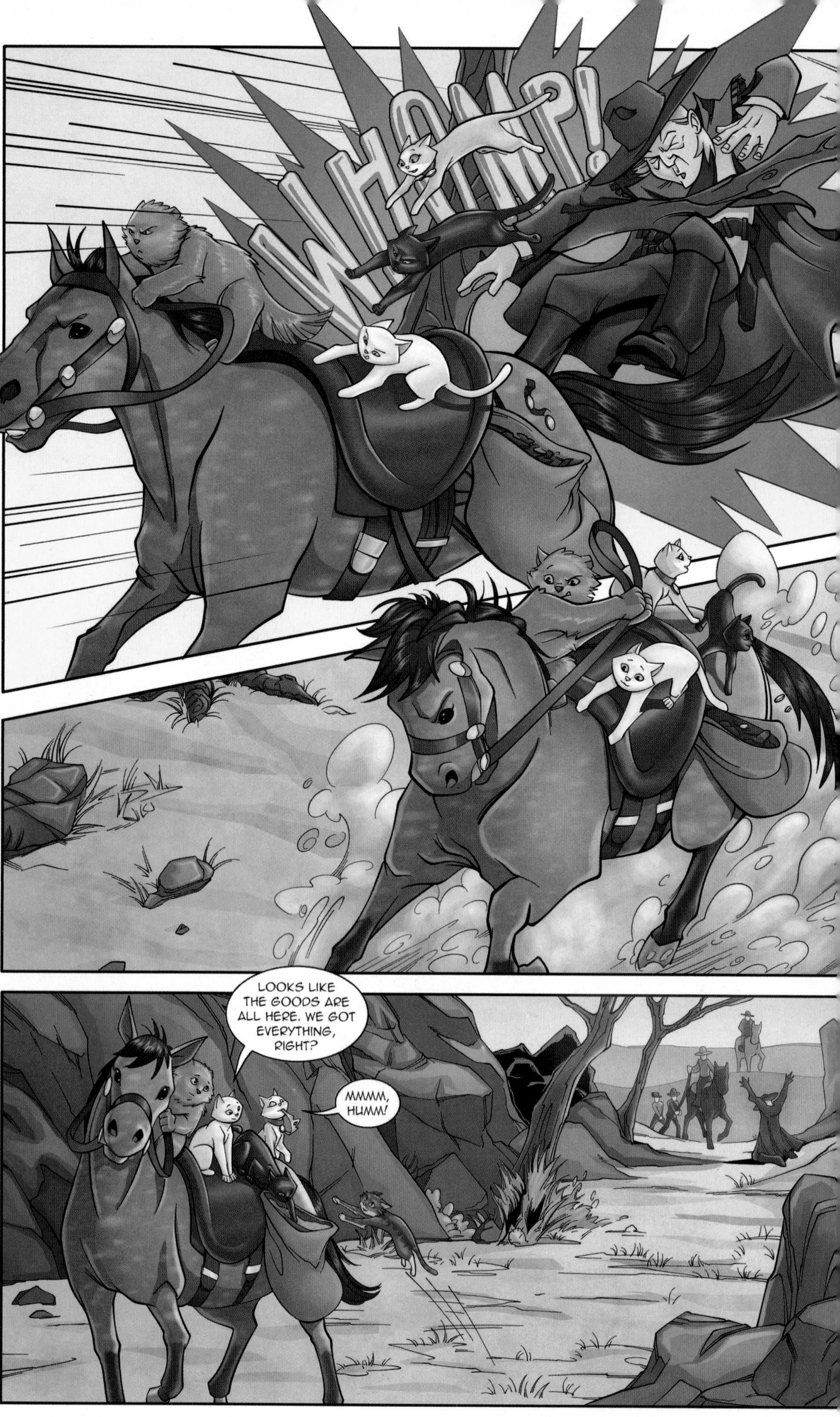
WHOMP!
LOOKS LIKE THE GOODS ARE ALL HERE. WE GOT EVERYTHING, RIGHT?
MMMM, HUMM!

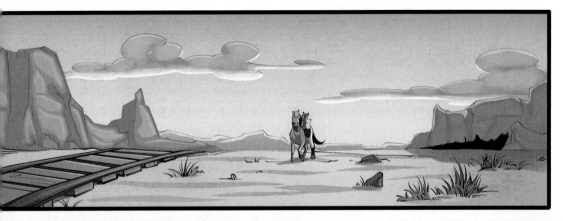

WELL, HOWDY YOUNG LADIES!

Y'ALL LOOK LIKE YOU COULD USE A RIDE BACK TO THE BIG CITY.

YES INDEED, GOOD SIR. I THINK WE'VE HAD *JUST* ABOUT ENOUGH TRAIN RIDES FOR THE DAY. DO YA THINK YOU COULD BE OF ASSISTANCE?

IT WOULD BE OUR HONOR.

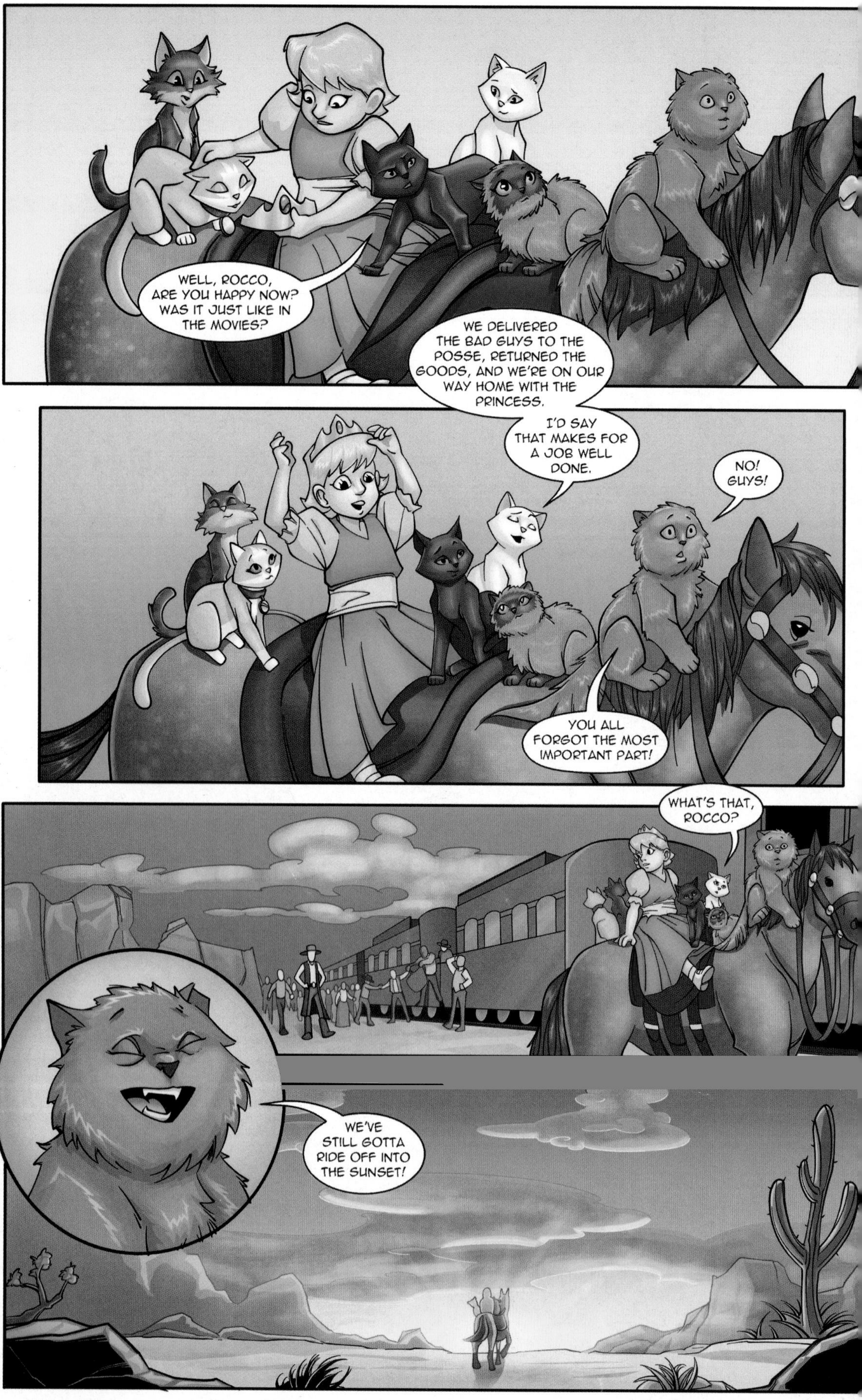

WELL, ROCCO, ARE YOU HAPPY NOW? WAS IT JUST LIKE IN THE MOVIES?
WE DELIVERED THE BAD GUYS TO THE POSSE, RETURNED THE GOODS, AND WE'RE ON OUR WAY HOME WITH THE PRINCESS.
I'D SAY THAT MAKES FOR A JOB WELL DONE.
NO! GUYS!
YOU ALL FORGOT THE MOST IMPORTANT PART!
WHAT'S THAT, ROCCO?
WE'VE STILL GOTTA RIDE OFF INTO THE SUNSET!

OUTLAW HERO CHAT

YOU'D BEST BE CAREFUL!

COYOTE CANYON IS SAFE FOR NOW, THANKS TO THE HERO CATS, BUT THAT DON'T MEAN THERE AIN'T OTHER OUTLAWS OUT THERE.

TAKE THE RENEGADES PICTURED BELOW FOR EXAMPLE. THEY'LL STIR UP NOTHIN' BUT TROUBLE IF THEY COME RIDIN' INTO YOUR TOWN.

APPREHENDED

THE LEADER OF THIS PARTICULAR GANG CALLS HIMSELF "STAGECOACH" KYLE. HE'S CONSTANTLY CRACKIN' THE WHIP AND TAKIN' HIS GANG ON A WILD RIDE ALL ACROSS THE COUNTRY. IF YA CATCH HIM IN JUST THE RIGHT MOOD, HE'LL TELL YOU HIS STORIES.

OMAKA SCHULTZ· RYAN SELLERS· KYLE PUTTKAMMER· JULIE BARCLAY

OMAKA "THE ARTIST" HAS GOT A KNACK FOR THE PEN AND PAPER. THIS IS ONE SKETCHY FELLOW.

"ROWDY" RYAN IS A SHARP-SHOOTING SON OF A GUN WHO'S HEART IS SO DARK IT BLEEDS BLACK.

JULIE "THE SINGER" BARCLAY ROUNDS OUT THE GANG. SHE'S SO COLORFUL, THE SUNSET GETS JEALOUS.

THIS GANG'S TAKEN TO TELLIN' TALL TALES AND BREAKIN' ALL KINDS OF HEARTS ALONG THE WAY.

BEST BEWARE!

HEROCHAT

THE DASTARDLY TWO SCAR AND
COOK MET THEIR MATCH WHEN
THEY CROSSED PATHS WITH THE
HERO CATS.

WHAT ARE THOSE ROUGH-AND-TUMBLE
CATS UP TO NOW? IT SEEMS
ANDREA PUTTKAMMER HAS CAPTURED
THE TEAM ENJOYING A LITTLE
DOWN TIME ON THE FRONT PORCH.

ANDREA PUTTKAMMER

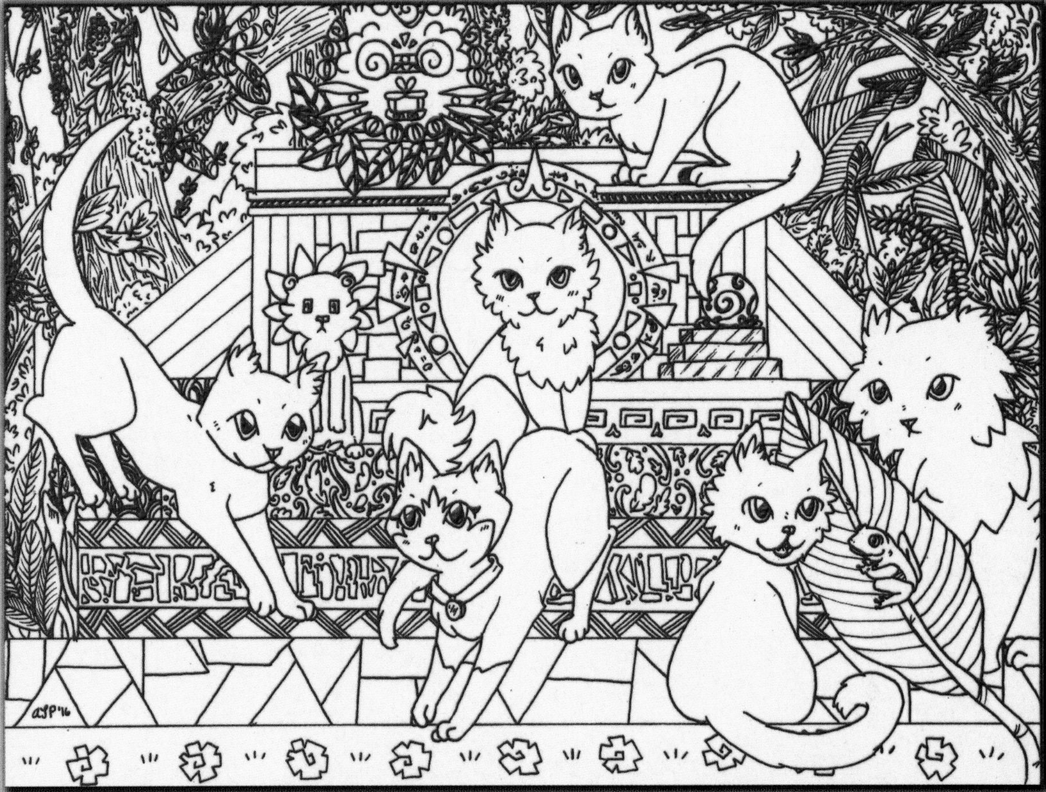

ANNA PUTTKAMMER

THE TEAM SETS OUT ON YET ANOTHER ESCAPADE.
THIS TIME THEY'RE OFF TO THE JUNGLE.
PERHAPS THEY'LL FIND SOME ANCIENT TREASURE
OR FEROCIOUS BEAST. WHICH WILL IT BE?!

UP NEXT
JUNGLE CATS

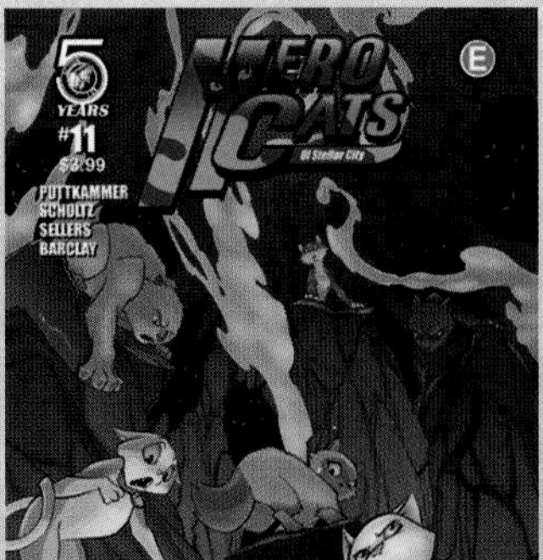
5 YEARS
HERO CATS
Of Stellar City
E
#11
$3.99
PUTTKAMMER
SCHOLTZ
SELLERS
BARCLAY

Bryan Seaton - Publisher
Dave Dwonch - President
Shawn Gabborin - Editor in Chief
Jamal Igle - Director of Marketing
Jim Dietz - Social Media Director
Jeremy Whitley - Education Outreach Director
Chad Cicconi & Colleen Boyd - Associate Editors

Credit Correction for Hero Cats issue 9, Brandon Page provided the internal inks.

Herocats over Stellar City #10, May 2016

Printed in Canada.

First Printing

CHECK OUT OUR NEW WEBSITE AT WWW.HEROCATSONLINE.COM

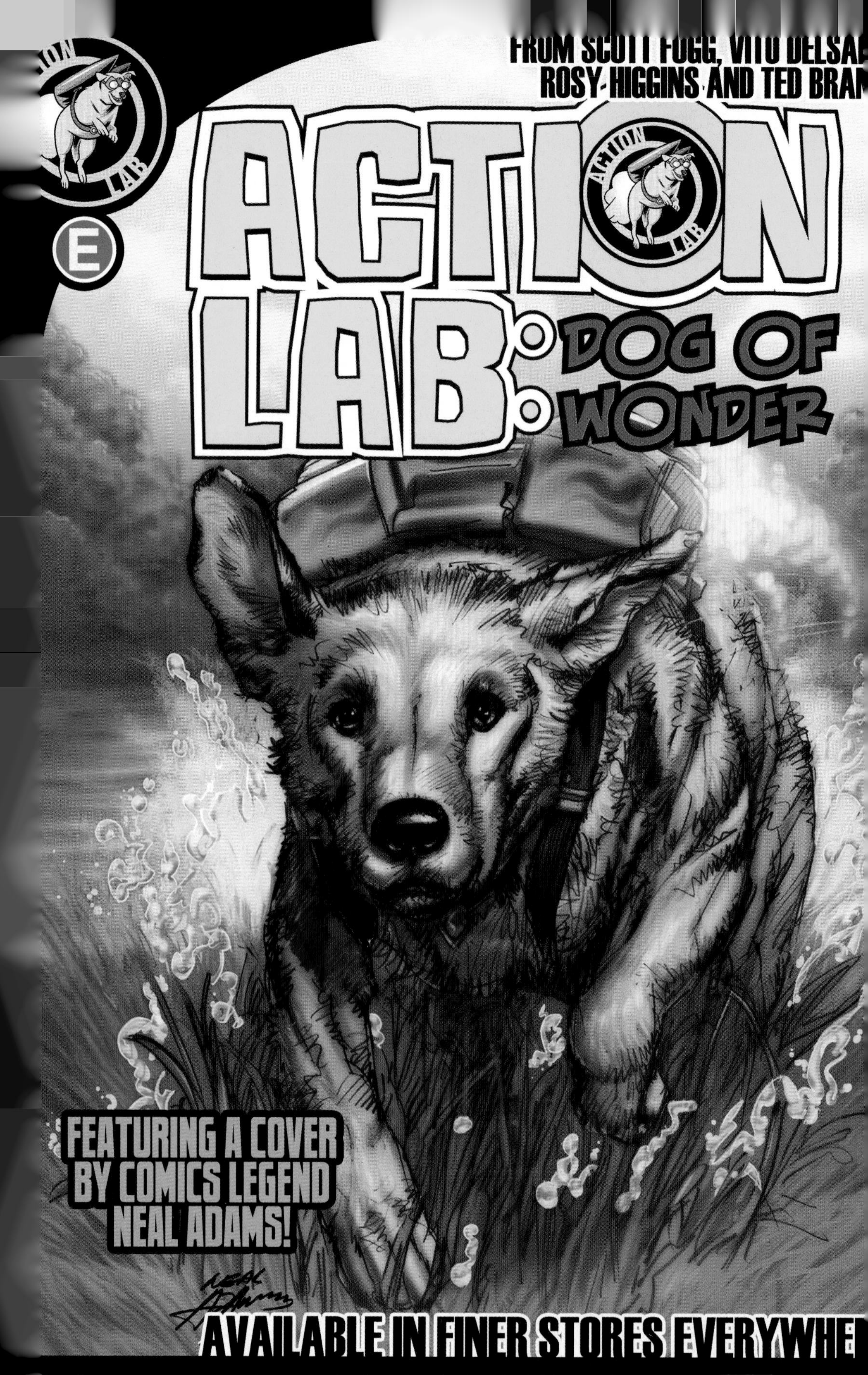
FROM SCOTT FOGG, VITO DELSA
ROSY HIGGINS AND TED BRA
ACTION LAB
E
ACTION LAB: DOG OF WONDER
FEATURING A COVER BY COMICS LEGEND NEAL ADAMS!
AVAILABLE IN FINER STORES EVERYWHE

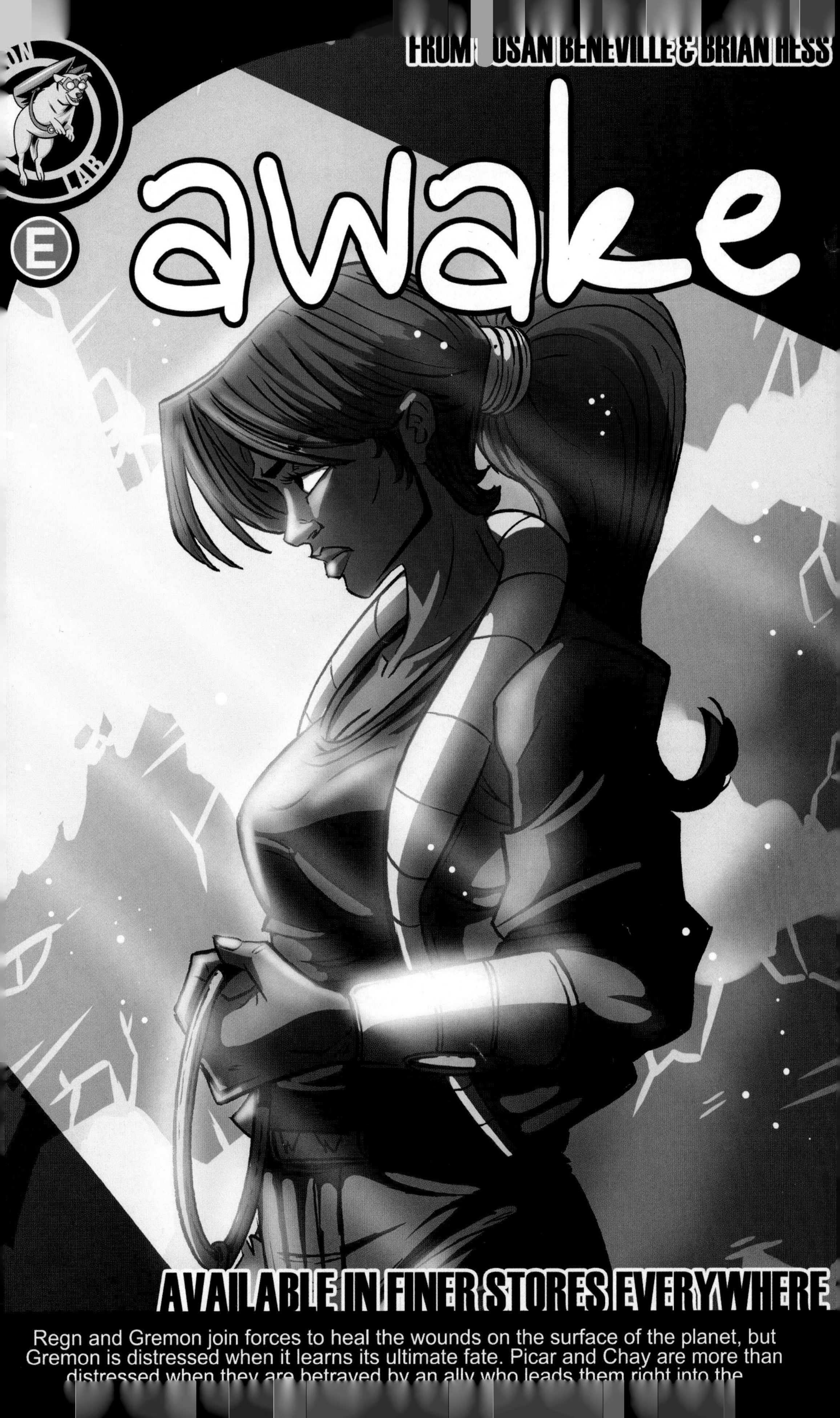
FROM USAN BENEVILLE & BRIAN HESS
E
awake
AVAILABLE IN FINER STORES EVERYWHERE
Regn and Gremon join forces to heal the wounds on the surface of the planet, but Gremon is distressed when it learns its ultimate fate. Picar and Chay are more than distressed when they are betrayed by an ally who leads them right into the

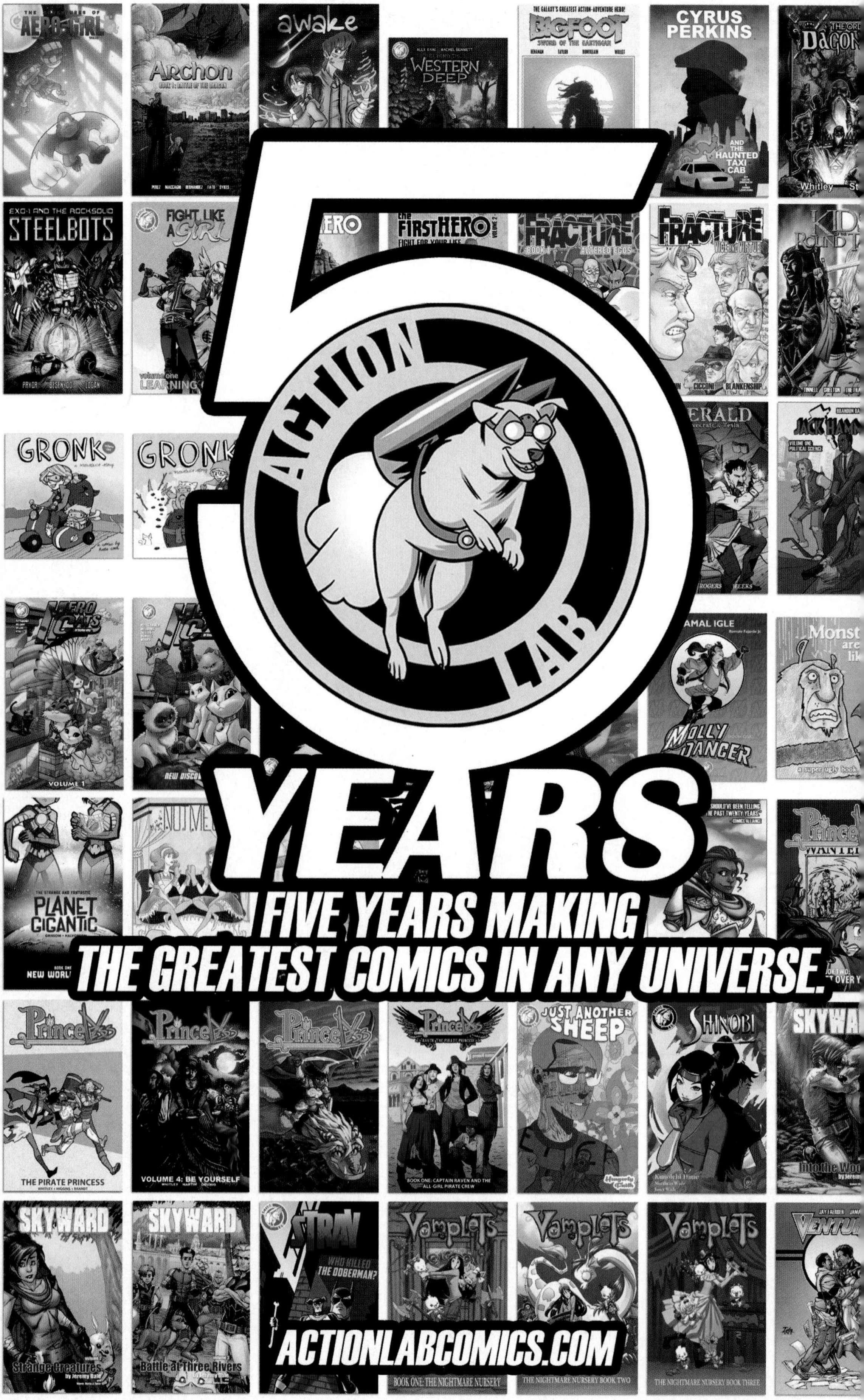
ACTION LAB
5
YEARS
FIVE YEARS MAKING
THE GREATEST COMICS IN ANY UNIVERSE.
ACTIONLABCOMICS.COM

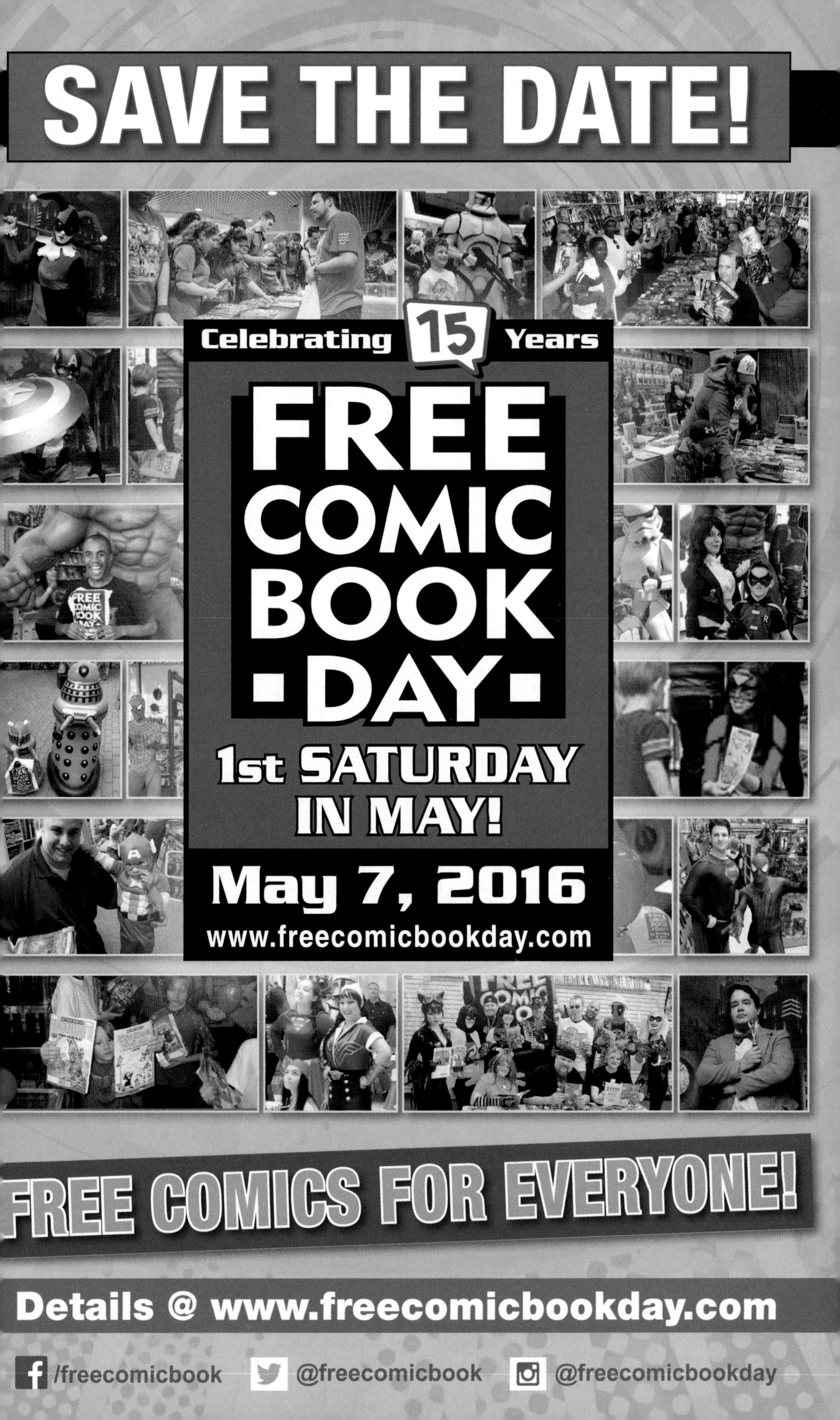
SAVE THE DATE!
Celebrating 15 Years
FREE COMIC BOOK DAY
1st SATURDAY IN MAY!
May 7, 2016
www.freecomicbookday.com
FREE COMICS FOR EVERYONE!
Details @ www.freecomicbookday.com
/freecomicbook
@freecomicbook
@freecomicbookday

READ MORE NOW

ACTIONLABCOMICS.COM

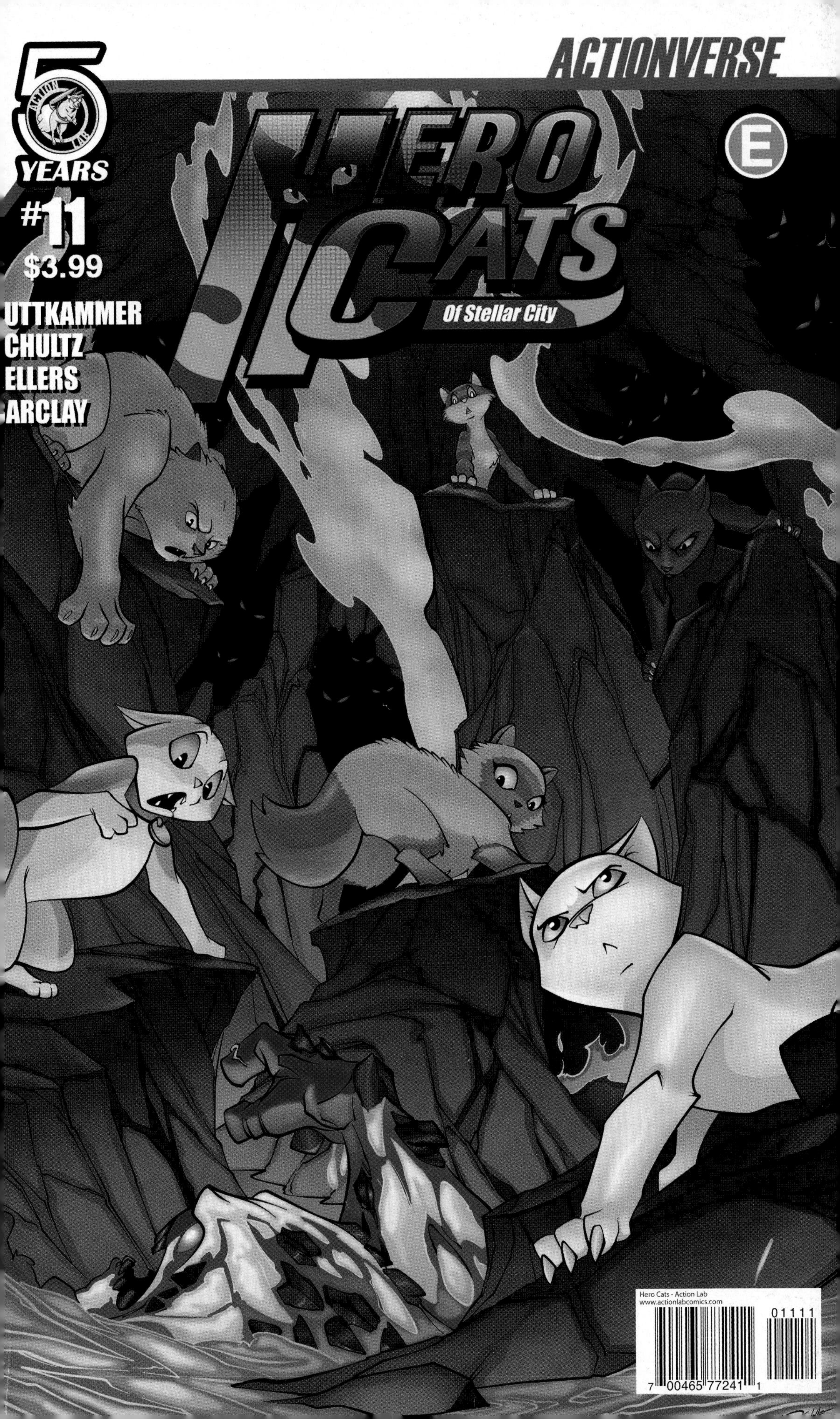

ACTIONVERSE
5 YEARS
ACTION LAB
HERO CATS
Of Stellar City
E
#11
$3.99
UTTKAMMER
CHULTZ
ELLERS
ARCLAY
Hero Cats - Action Lab
www.actionlabcomics.com

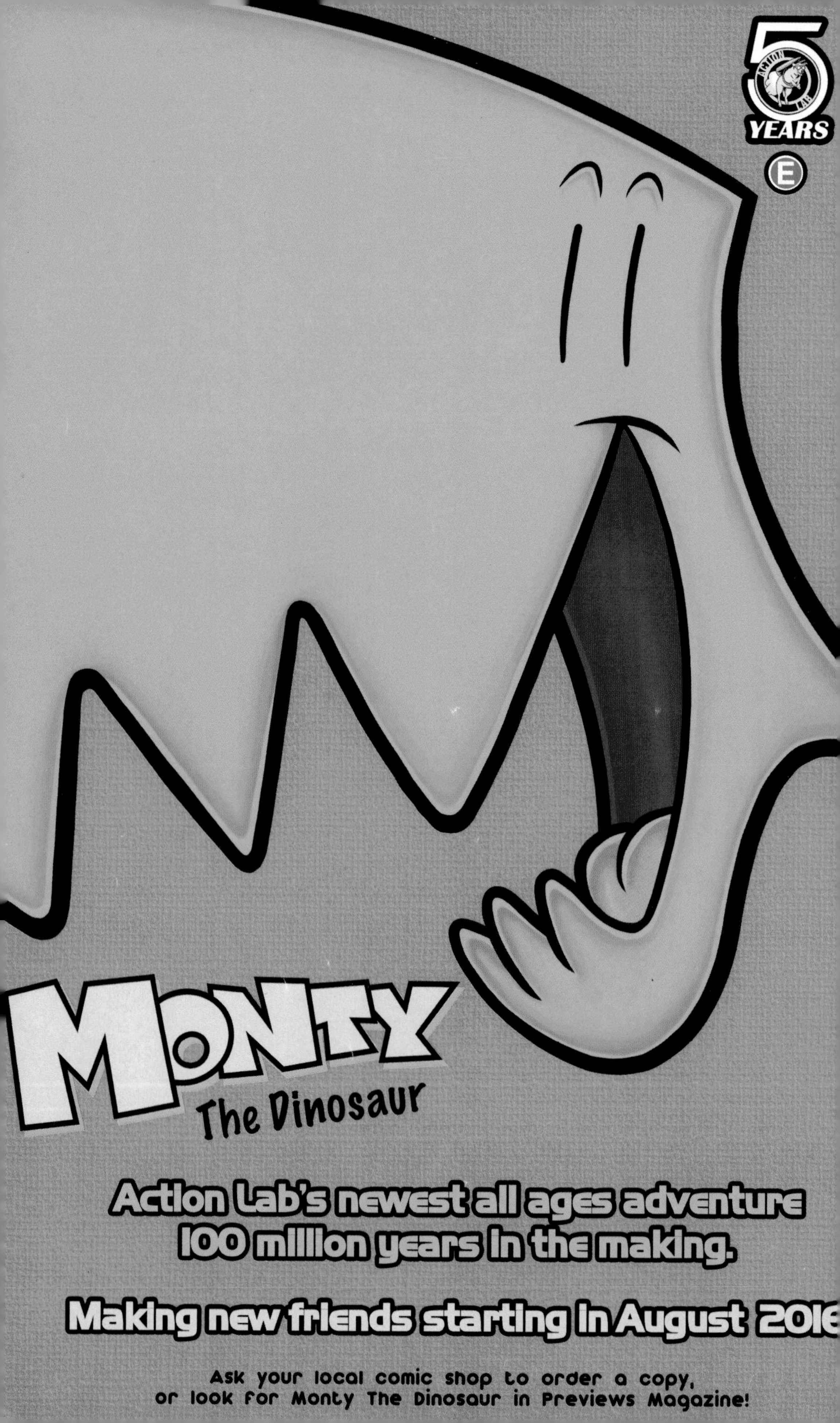
5 YEARS
E
MONTY
The Dinosaur
Action Lab's newest all ages adventure
100 million years in the making.
Making new friends starting in August 2016
Ask your local comic shop to order a copy,
or look for Monty The Dinosaur in Previews Magazine!

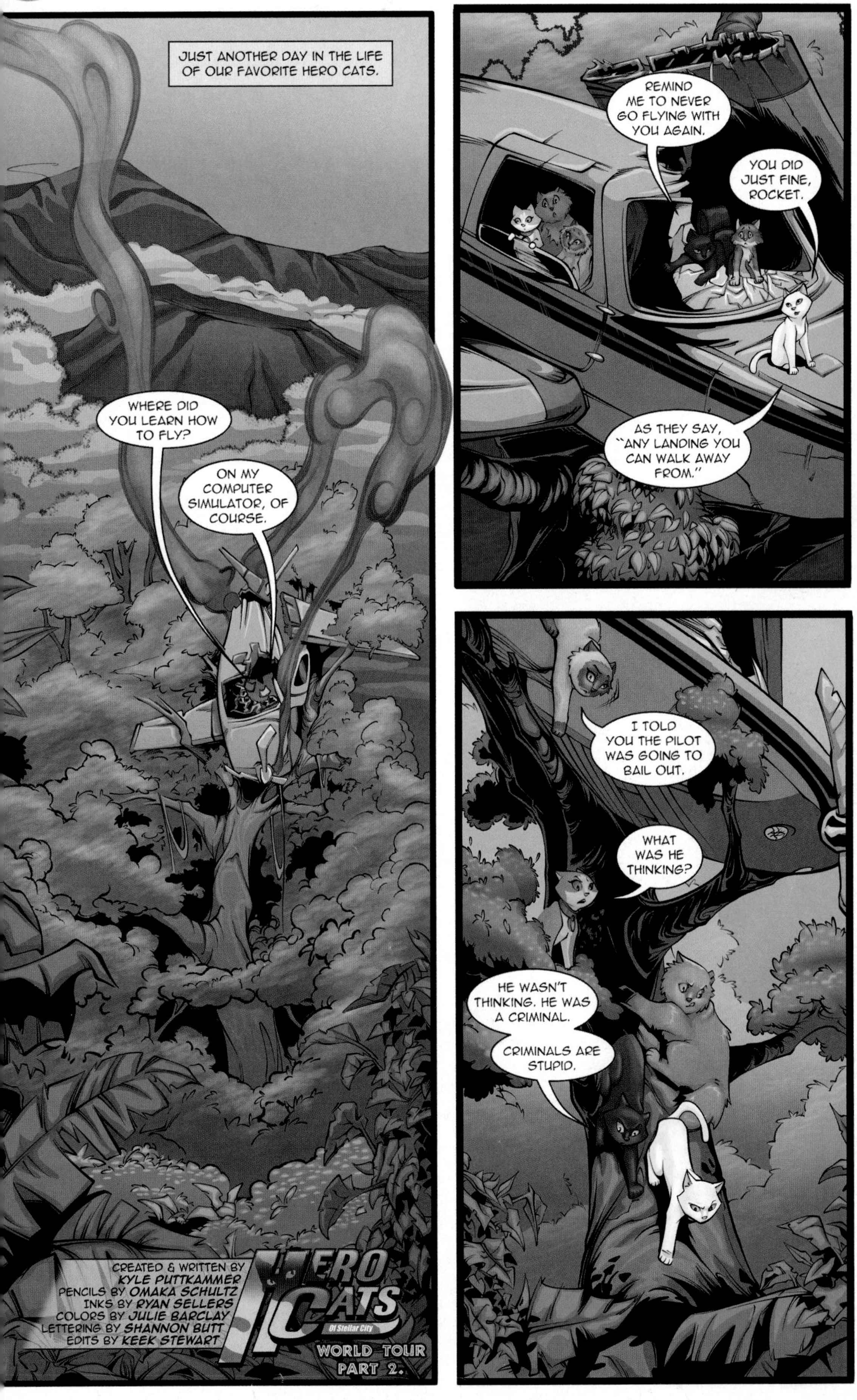
JUST ANOTHER DAY IN THE LIFE OF OUR FAVORITE HERO CATS.
WHERE DID YOU LEARN HOW TO FLY?
ON MY COMPUTER SIMULATOR, OF COURSE.
CREATED & WRITTEN BY KYLE PUTTKAMMER
PENCILS BY OMAKA SCHULTZ
INKS BY RYAN SELLERS
COLORS BY JULIE BARCLAY
LETTERING BY SHANNON BUTT
EDITS BY KEEK STEWART
HERO CATS
Of Stellar City
WORLD TOUR PART 2.
REMIND ME TO NEVER GO FLYING WITH YOU AGAIN.
YOU DID JUST FINE, ROCKET.
AS THEY SAY, "ANY LANDING YOU CAN WALK AWAY FROM."
I TOLD YOU THE PILOT WAS GOING TO BAIL OUT.
WHAT WAS HE THINKING?
HE WASN'T THINKING. HE WAS A CRIMINAL.
CRIMINALS ARE STUPID.

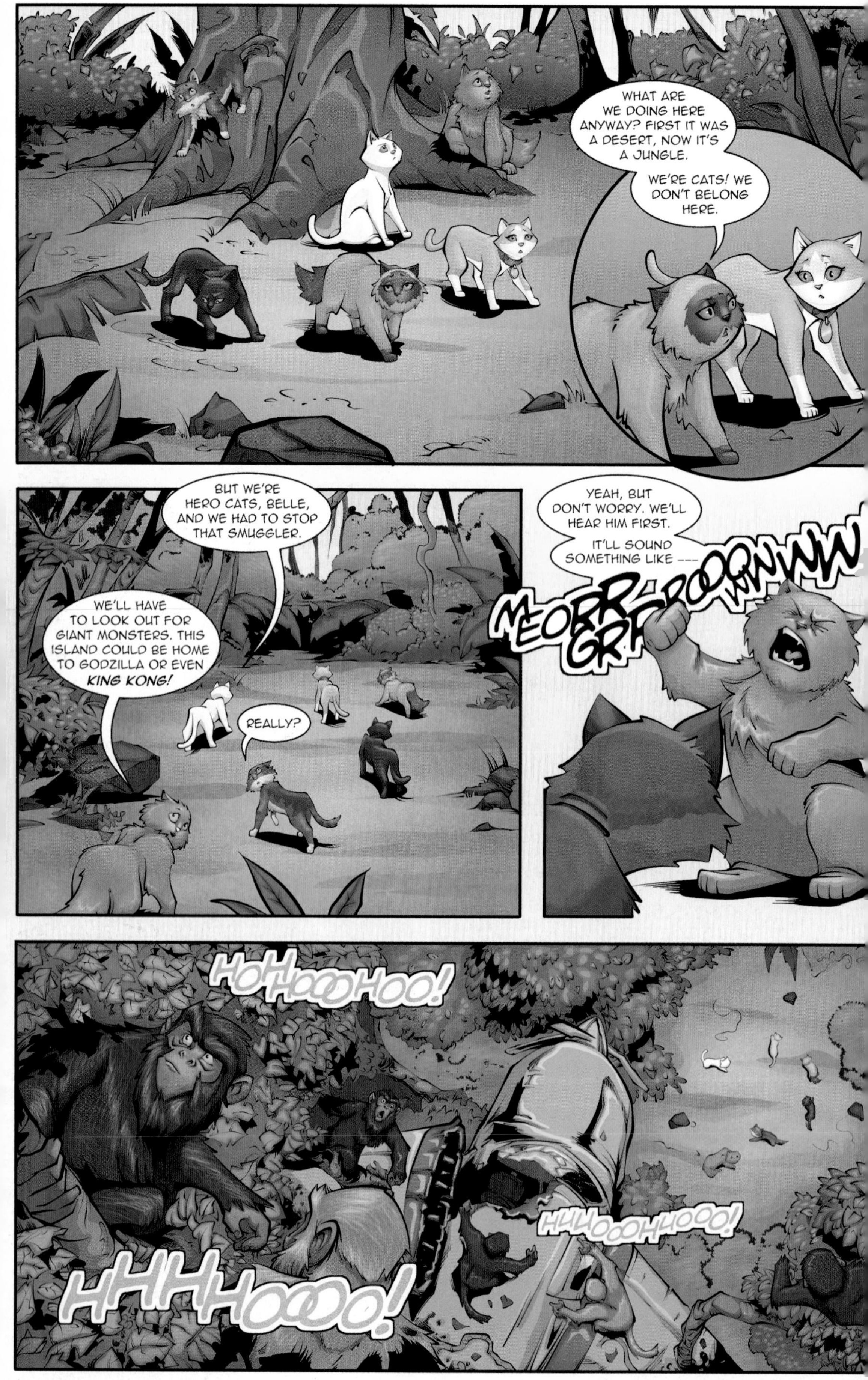
WHAT ARE WE DOING HERE ANYWAY? FIRST IT WAS A DESERT, NOW IT'S A JUNGLE.
WE'RE CATS! WE DON'T BELONG HERE.
BUT WE'RE HERO CATS, BELLE, AND WE HAD TO STOP THAT SMUGGLER.
WE'LL HAVE TO LOOK OUT FOR GIANT MONSTERS. THIS ISLAND COULD BE HOME TO GODZILLA OR EVEN KING KONG!
REALLY?
YEAH, BUT DON'T WORRY. WE'LL HEAR HIM FIRST.
IT'LL SOUND SOMETHING LIKE ---
MEORR-GRROOOWWWW
HOHHOOOHOO!
HUUOOOHHOOO!
HHHHOOOO!

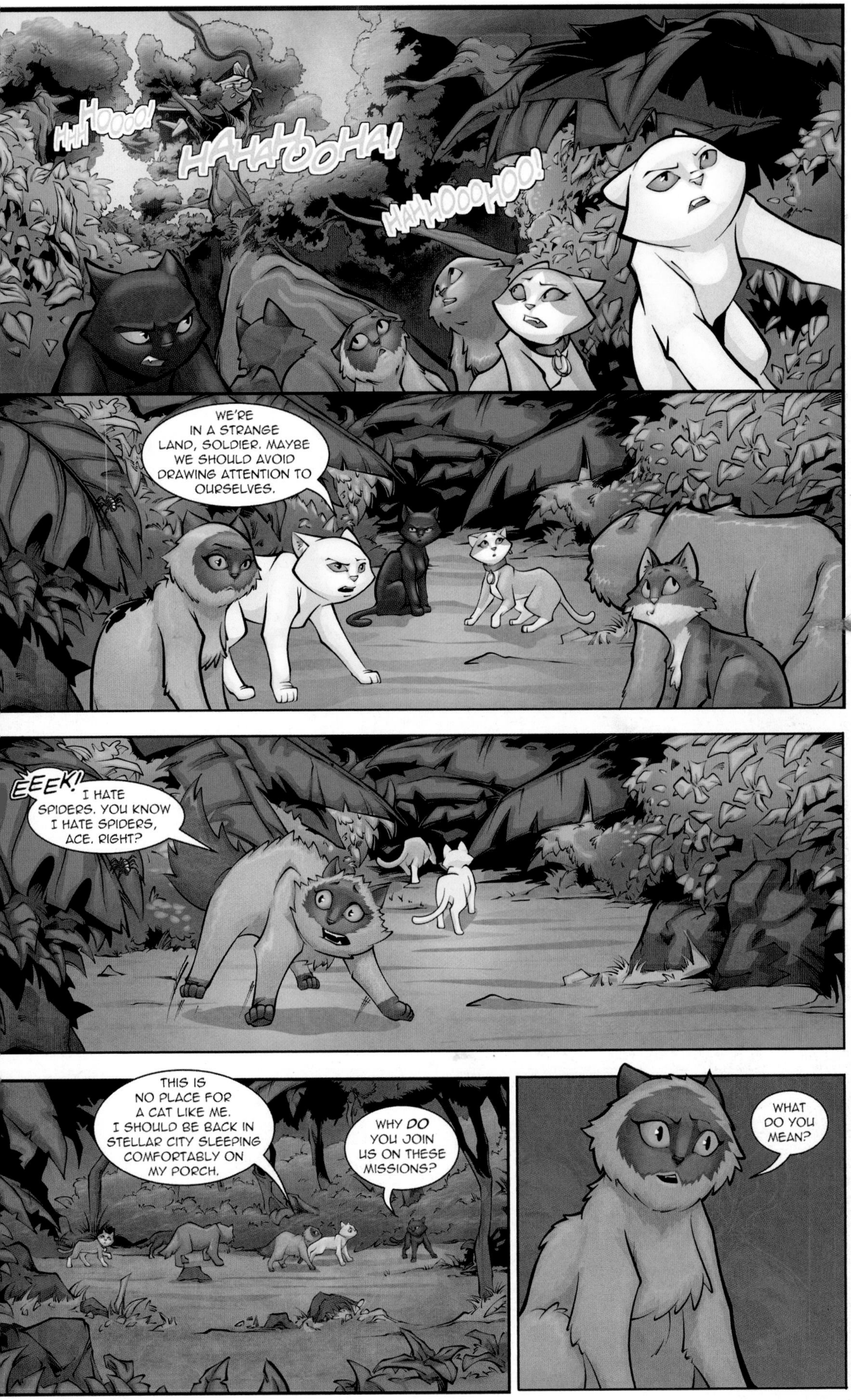
HHHHOOOO!
HAHAHOOHA!
HAHHOOOHOO!
WE'RE IN A STRANGE LAND, SOLDIER. MAYBE WE SHOULD AVOID DRAWING ATTENTION TO OURSELVES.
EEEK!
I HATE SPIDERS. YOU KNOW I HATE SPIDERS, ACE. RIGHT?
THIS IS NO PLACE FOR A CAT LIKE ME. I SHOULD BE BACK IN STELLAR CITY SLEEPING COMFORTABLY ON MY PORCH.
WHY *DO* YOU JOIN US ON THESE MISSIONS?
WHAT DO YOU MEAN?

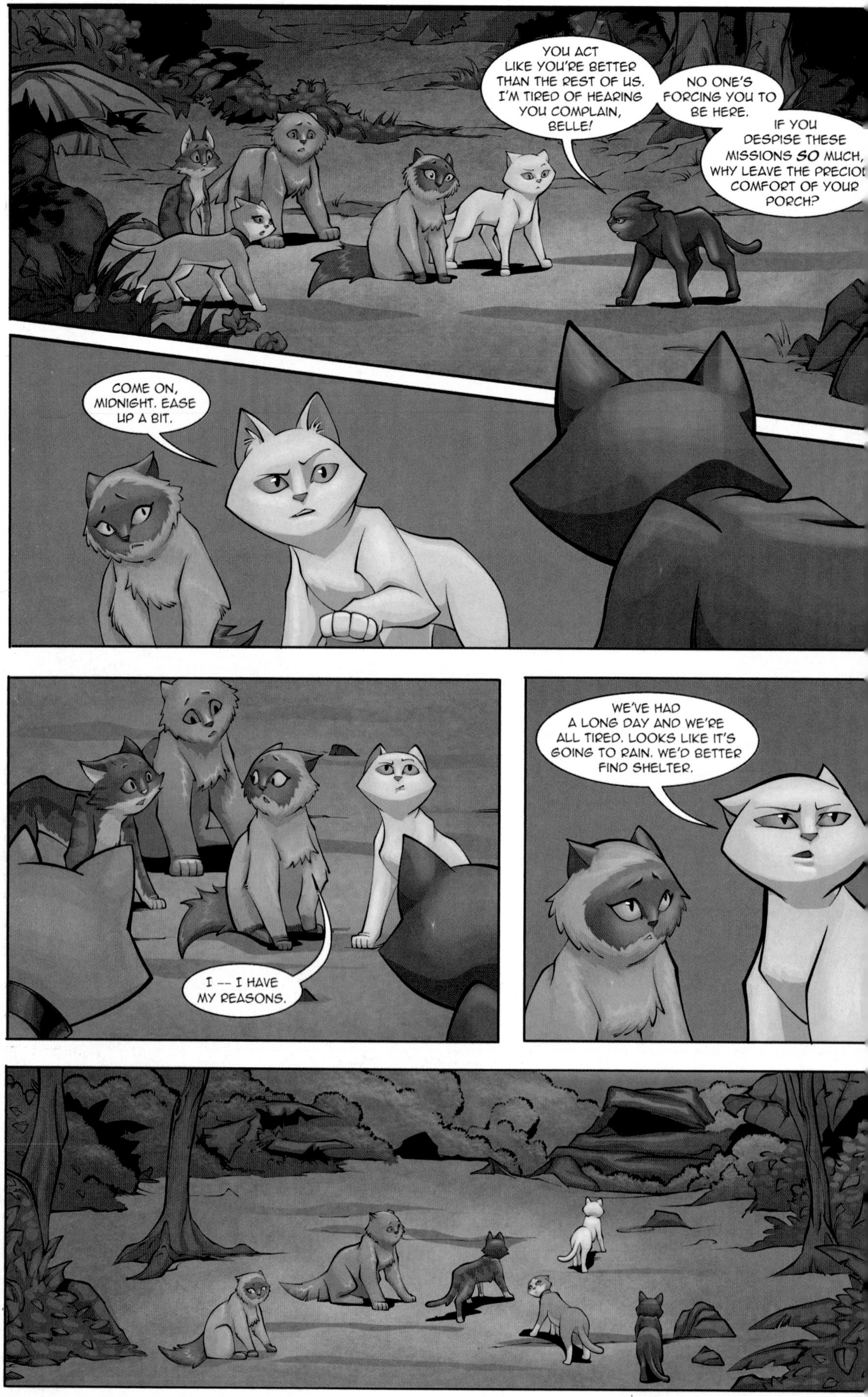
YOU ACT LIKE YOU'RE BETTER THAN THE REST OF US. I'M TIRED OF HEARING YOU COMPLAIN, BELLE!
NO ONE'S FORCING YOU TO BE HERE.
IF YOU DESPISE THESE MISSIONS SO MUCH, WHY LEAVE THE PRECIO COMFORT OF YOUR PORCH?
COME ON, MIDNIGHT. EASE UP A BIT.
I -- I HAVE MY REASONS.
WE'VE HAD A LONG DAY AND WE'RE ALL TIRED. LOOKS LIKE IT'S GOING TO RAIN. WE'D BETTER FIND SHELTER.

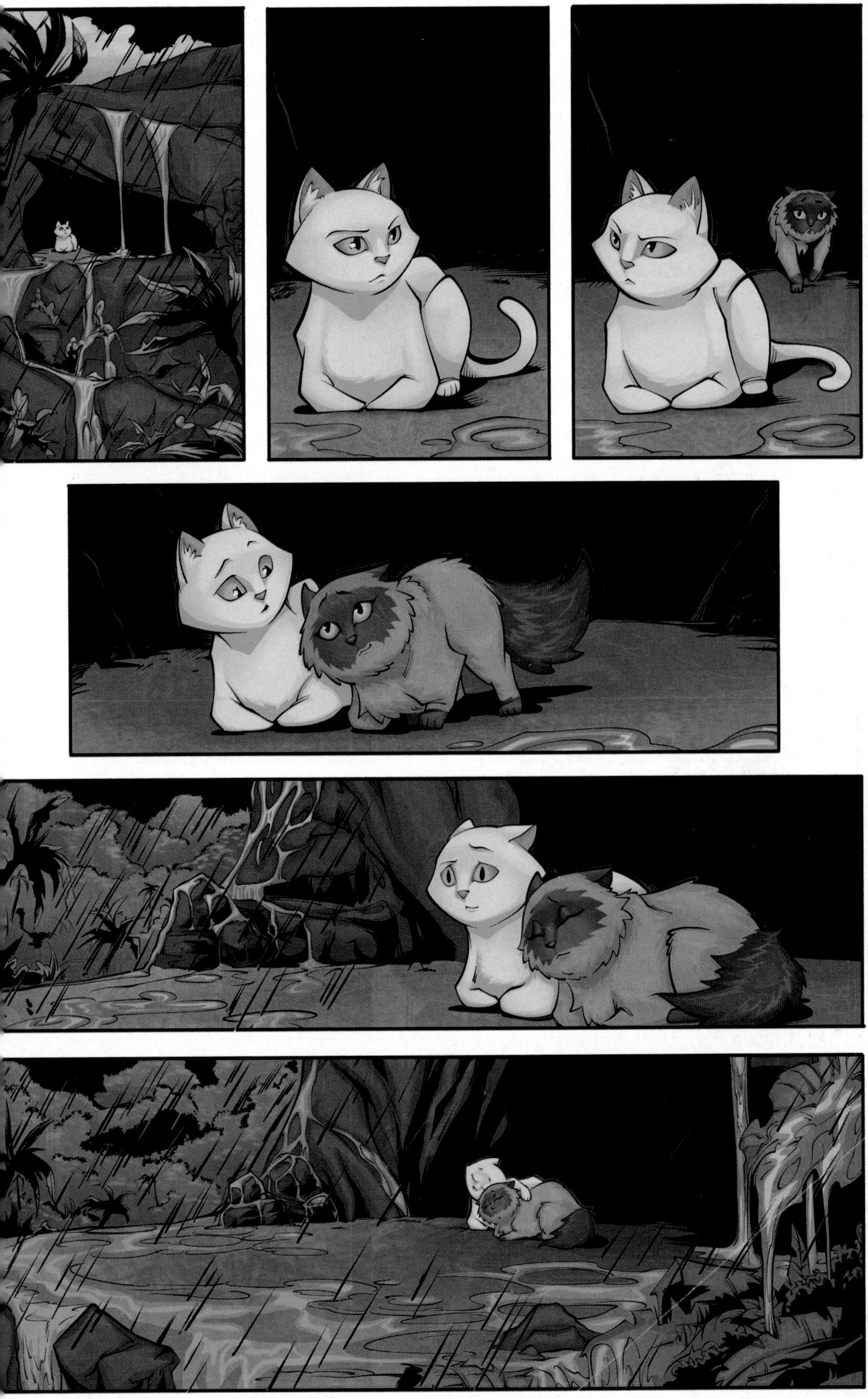

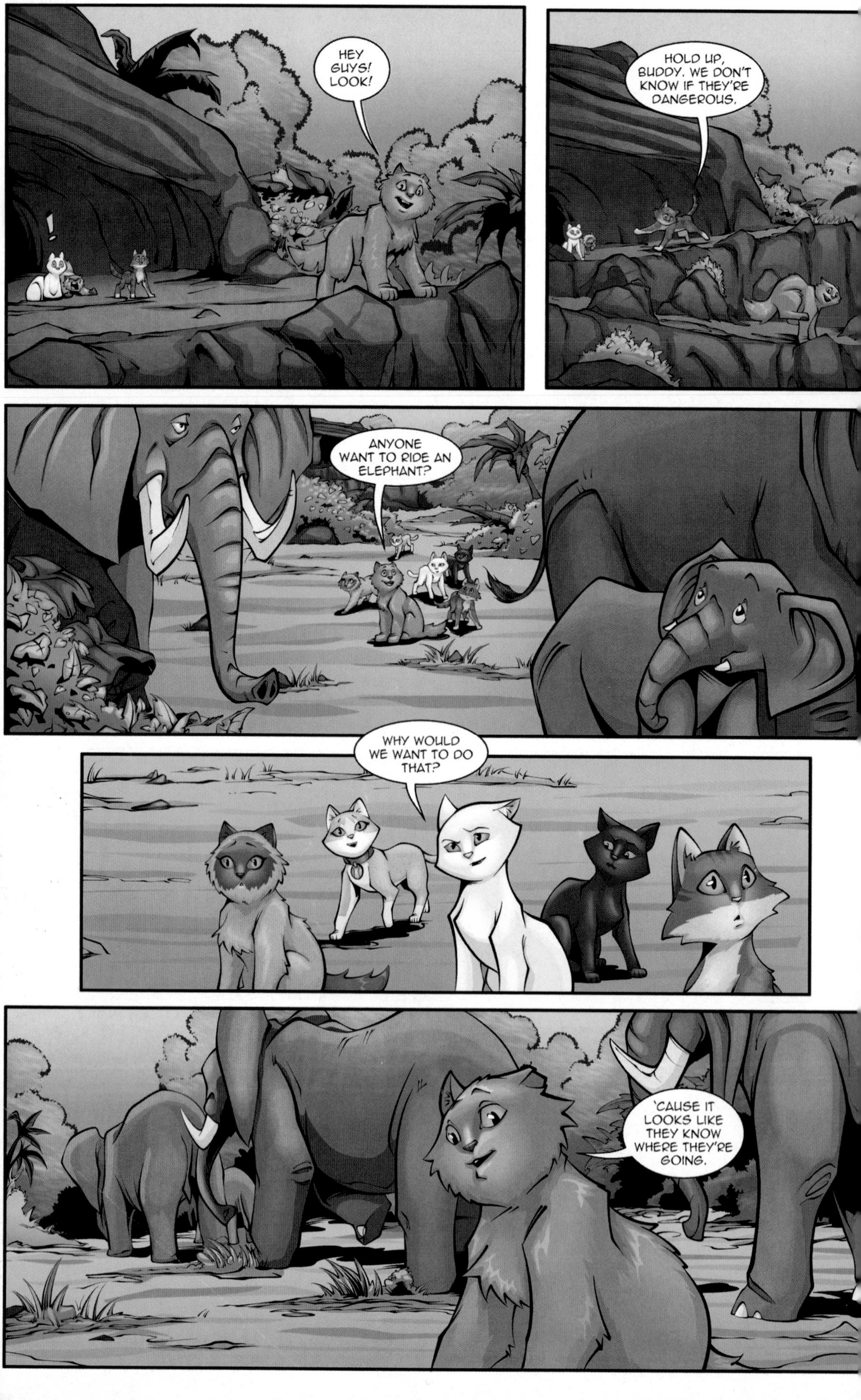
HEY GUYS! LOOK!
HOLD UP, BUDDY. WE DON'T KNOW IF THEY'RE DANGEROUS.
ANYONE WANT TO RIDE AN ELEPHANT?
WHY WOULD WE WANT TO DO THAT?
'CAUSE IT LOOKS LIKE THEY KNOW WHERE THEY'RE GOING.

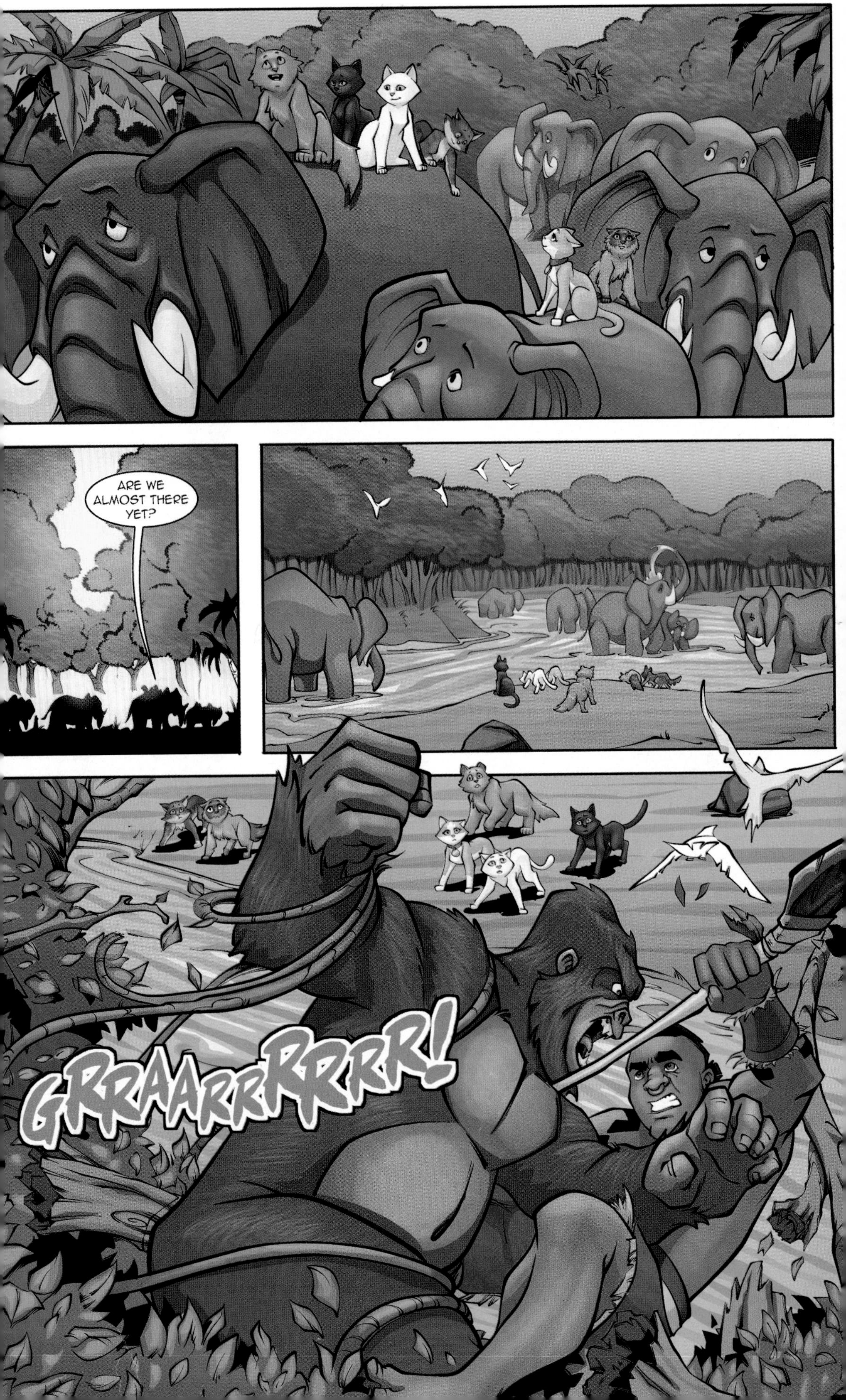
ARE WE ALMOST THERE YET?
GRRAARRRRRR!

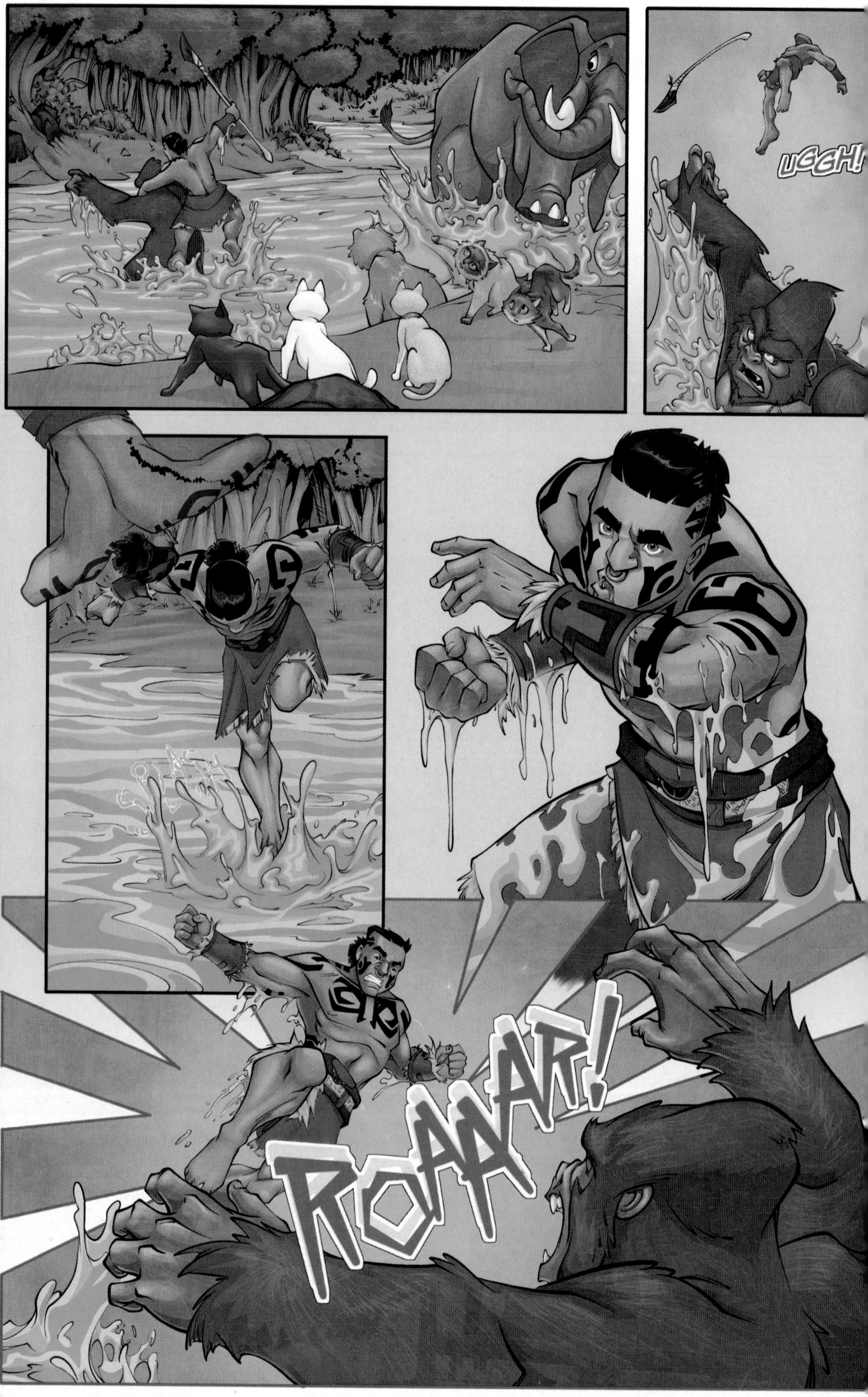
UGGH!
SPLASH
ROAAAR!

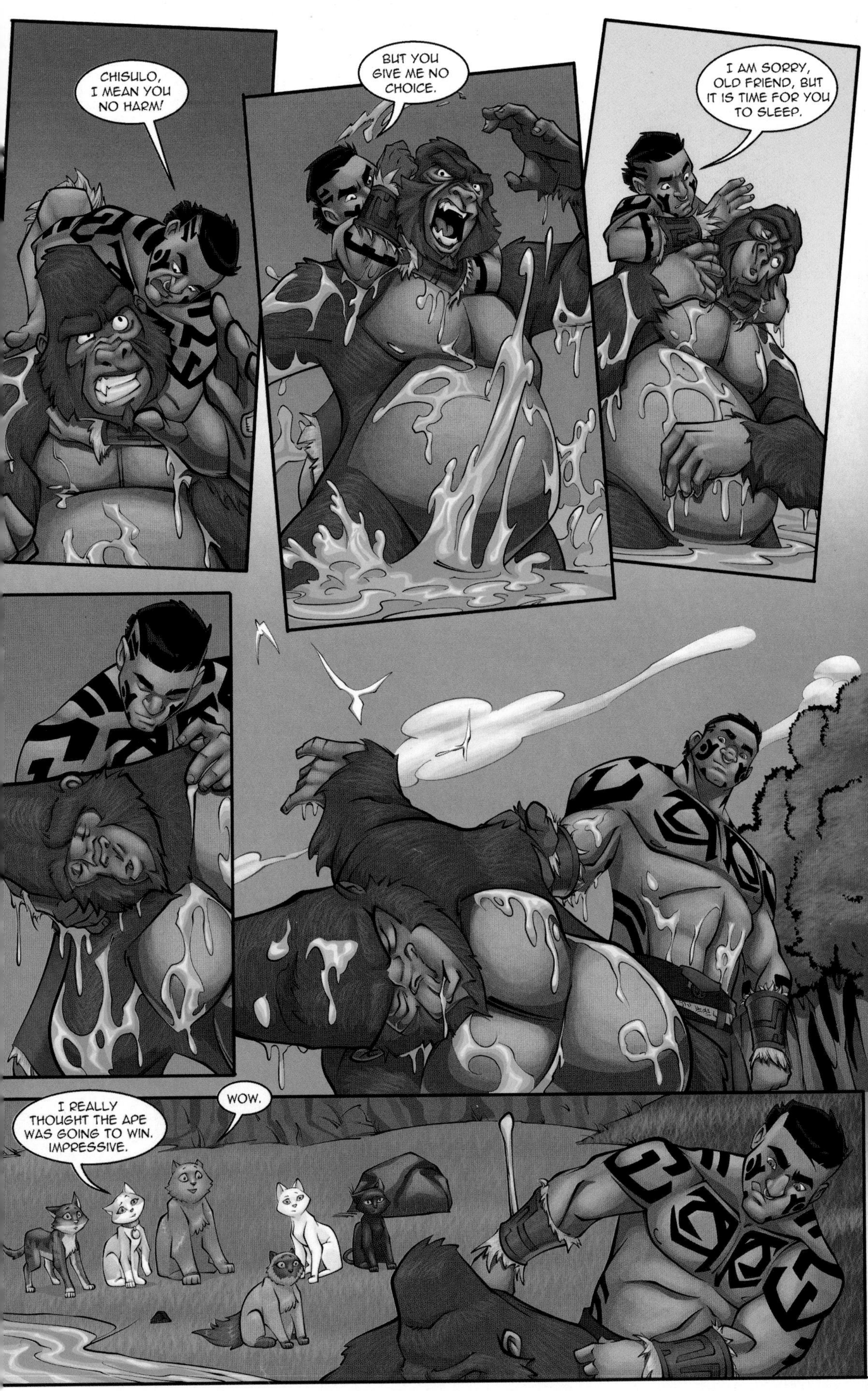
CHISULO, I MEAN YOU NO HARM!
BUT YOU GIVE ME NO CHOICE.
I AM SORRY, OLD FRIEND, BUT IT IS TIME FOR YOU TO SLEEP.
I REALLY THOUGHT THE APE WAS GOING TO WIN. IMPRESSIVE.
WOW.

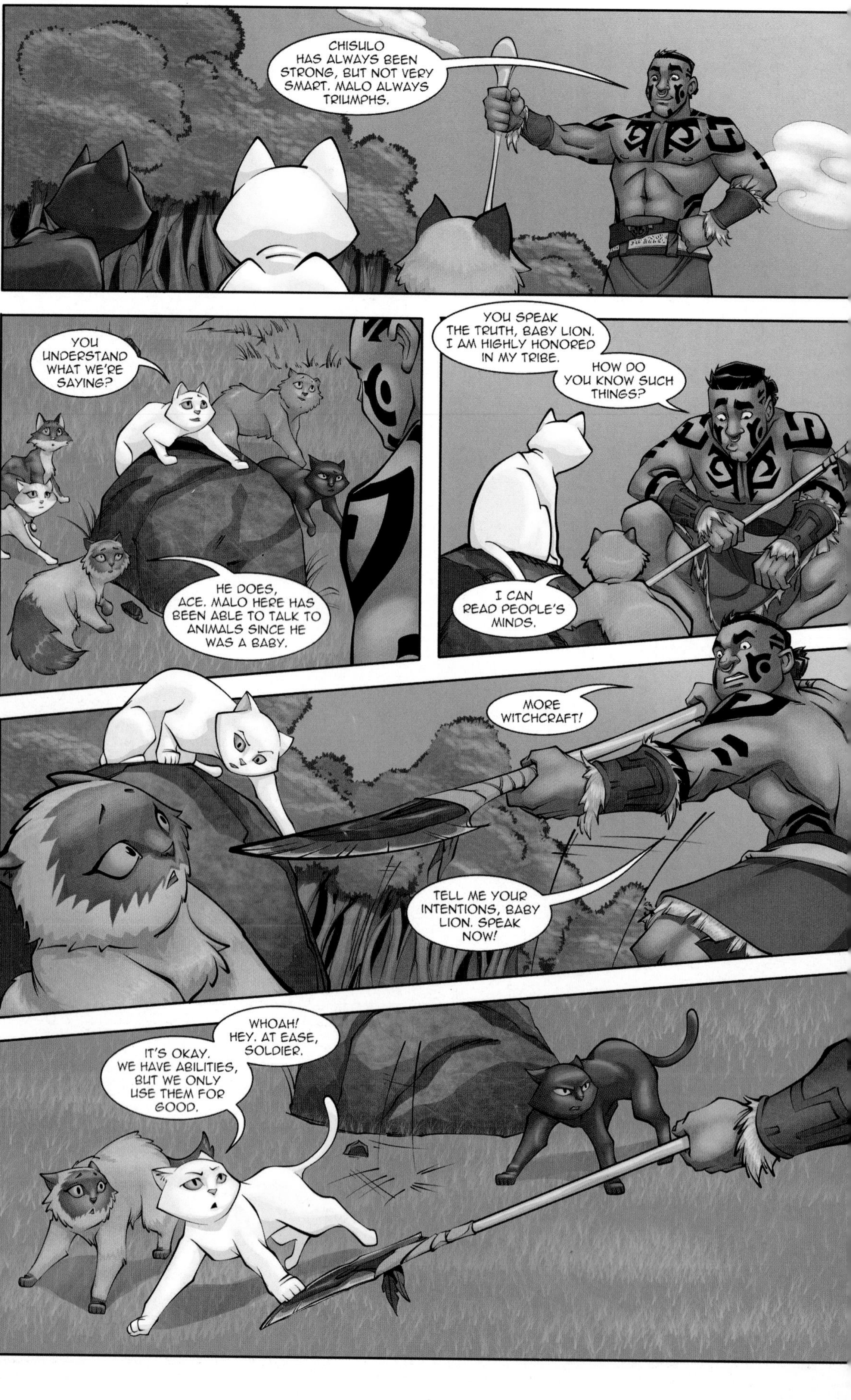
CHISULO HAS ALWAYS BEEN STRONG, BUT NOT VERY SMART. MALO ALWAYS TRIUMPHS.
YOU UNDERSTAND WHAT WE'RE SAYING?
HE DOES, ACE. MALO HERE HAS BEEN ABLE TO TALK TO ANIMALS SINCE HE WAS A BABY.
YOU SPEAK THE TRUTH, BABY LION. I AM HIGHLY HONORED IN MY TRIBE.
HOW DO YOU KNOW SUCH THINGS?
I CAN READ PEOPLE'S MINDS.
MORE WITCHCRAFT!
TELL ME YOUR INTENTIONS, BABY LION. SPEAK NOW!
WHOAH! HEY. AT EASE, SOLDIER.
IT'S OKAY. WE HAVE ABILITIES, BUT WE ONLY USE THEM FOR GOOD.

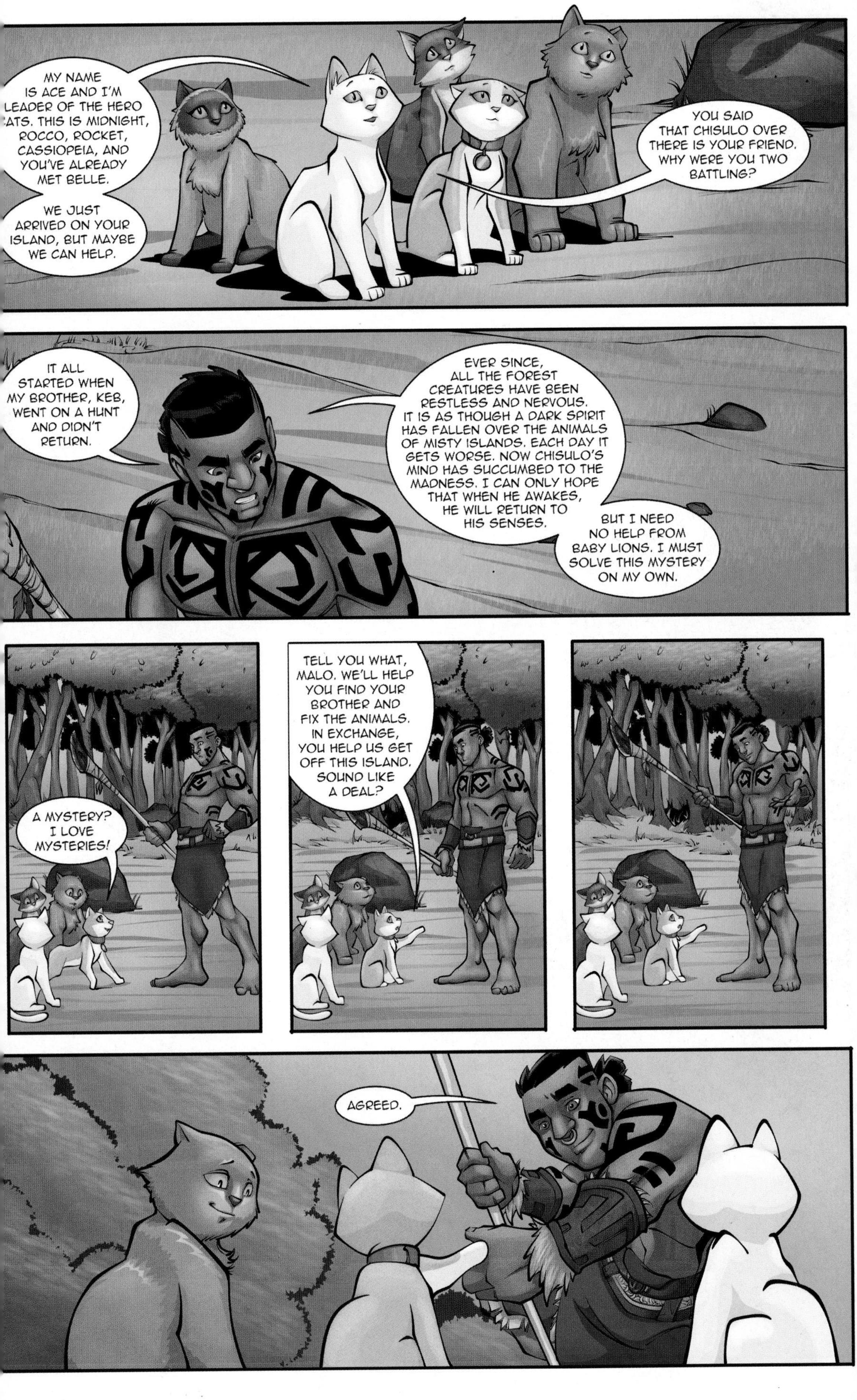
MY NAME IS ACE AND I'M LEADER OF THE HERO CATS. THIS IS MIDNIGHT, ROCCO, ROCKET, CASSIOPEIA, AND YOU'VE ALREADY MET BELLE.
WE JUST ARRIVED ON YOUR ISLAND, BUT MAYBE WE CAN HELP.
YOU SAID THAT CHISULO OVER THERE IS YOUR FRIEND. WHY WERE YOU TWO BATTLING?
IT ALL STARTED WHEN MY BROTHER, KEB, WENT ON A HUNT AND DIDN'T RETURN.
EVER SINCE, ALL THE FOREST CREATURES HAVE BEEN RESTLESS AND NERVOUS. IT IS AS THOUGH A DARK SPIRIT HAS FALLEN OVER THE ANIMALS OF MISTY ISLANDS. EACH DAY IT GETS WORSE. NOW CHISULO'S MIND HAS SUCCUMBED TO THE MADNESS. I CAN ONLY HOPE THAT WHEN HE AWAKES, HE WILL RETURN TO HIS SENSES.
BUT I NEED NO HELP FROM BABY LIONS. I MUST SOLVE THIS MYSTERY ON MY OWN.
A MYSTERY? I LOVE MYSTERIES!
TELL YOU WHAT, MALO. WE'LL HELP YOU FIND YOUR BROTHER AND FIX THE ANIMALS. IN EXCHANGE, YOU HELP US GET OFF THIS ISLAND. SOUND LIKE A DEAL?
AGREED.

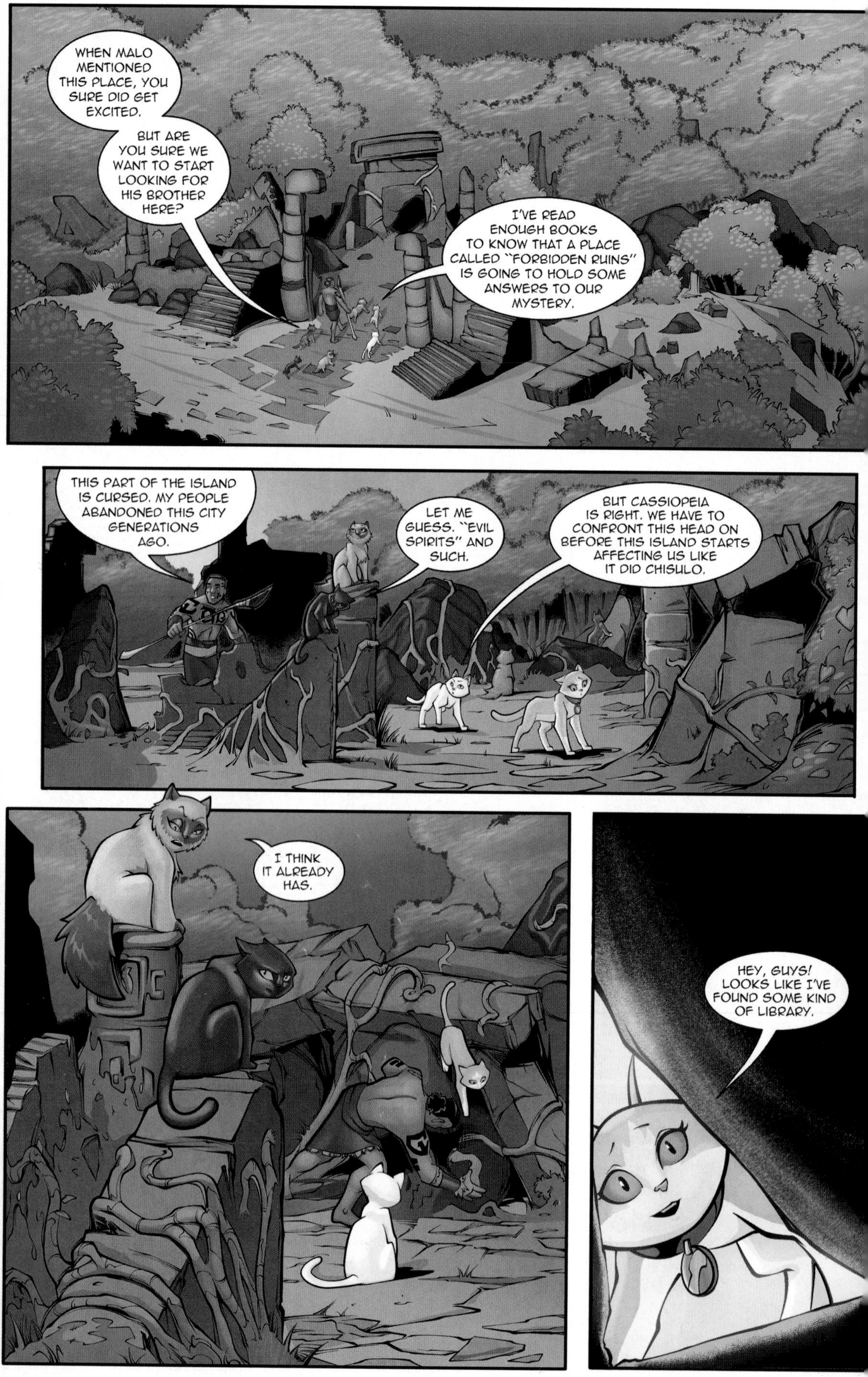
WHEN MALO MENTIONED THIS PLACE, YOU SURE DID GET EXCITED.
BUT ARE YOU SURE WE WANT TO START LOOKING FOR HIS BROTHER HERE?
I'VE READ ENOUGH BOOKS TO KNOW THAT A PLACE CALLED "FORBIDDEN RUINS" IS GOING TO HOLD SOME ANSWERS TO OUR MYSTERY.
THIS PART OF THE ISLAND IS CURSED. MY PEOPLE ABANDONED THIS CITY GENERATIONS AGO.
LET ME GUESS. "EVIL SPIRITS" AND SUCH.
BUT CASSIOPEIA IS RIGHT. WE HAVE TO CONFRONT THIS HEAD ON BEFORE THIS ISLAND STARTS AFFECTING US LIKE IT DID CHISULO.
I THINK IT ALREADY HAS.
HEY, GUYS! LOOKS LIKE I'VE FOUND SOME KIND OF LIBRARY.

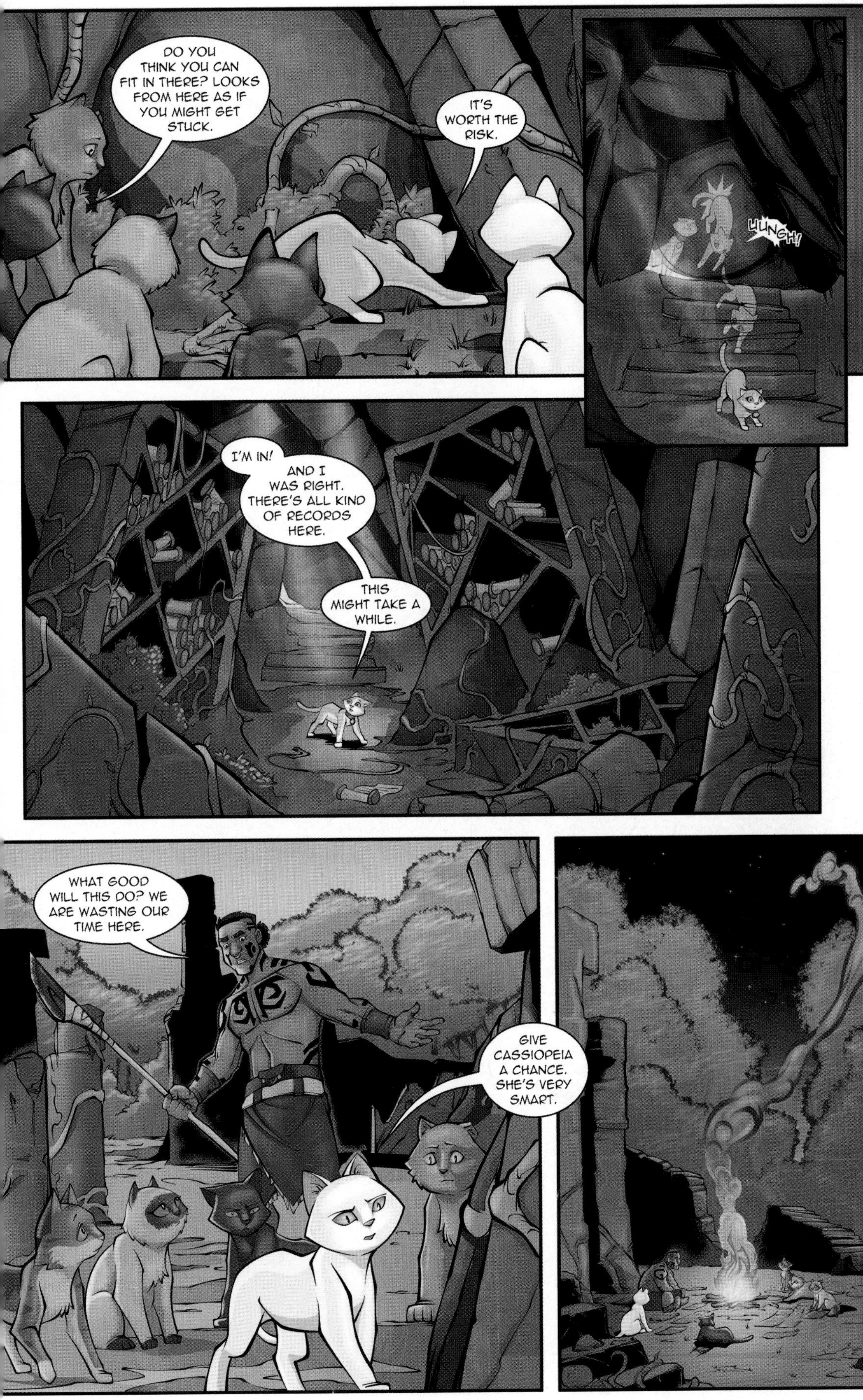
DO YOU THINK YOU CAN FIT IN THERE? LOOKS FROM HERE AS IF YOU MIGHT GET STUCK.
IT'S WORTH THE RISK.
UUNGH!
I'M IN!
AND I WAS RIGHT. THERE'S ALL KIND OF RECORDS HERE.
THIS MIGHT TAKE A WHILE.
WHAT GOOD WILL THIS DO? WE ARE WASTING OUR TIME HERE.
GIVE CASSIOPEIA A CHANCE. SHE'S VERY SMART.

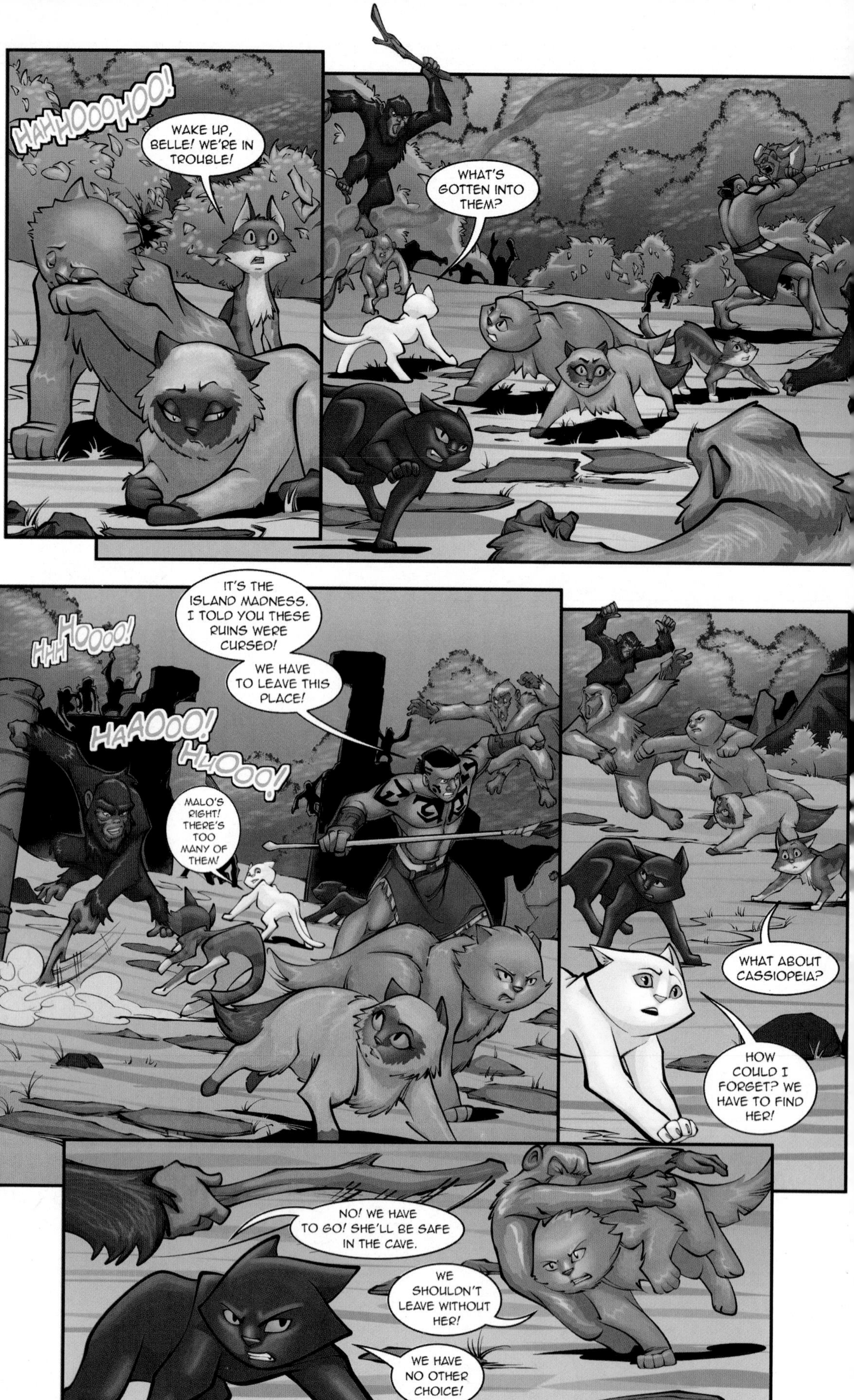
HAHHOOOHOO!
WAKE UP, BELLE! WE'RE IN TROUBLE!
WHAT'S GOTTEN INTO THEM?
HHHHOOOO!
IT'S THE ISLAND MADNESS. I TOLD YOU THESE RUINS WERE CURSED!
WE HAVE TO LEAVE THIS PLACE!
HAAOOO!
HUOOO!
MALO'S RIGHT! THERE'S TOO MANY OF THEM!
WHAT ABOUT CASSIOPEIA?
HOW COULD I FORGET? WE HAVE TO FIND HER!
NO! WE HAVE TO GO! SHE'LL BE SAFE IN THE CAVE.
WE SHOULDN'T LEAVE WITHOUT HER!
WE HAVE NO OTHER CHOICE!

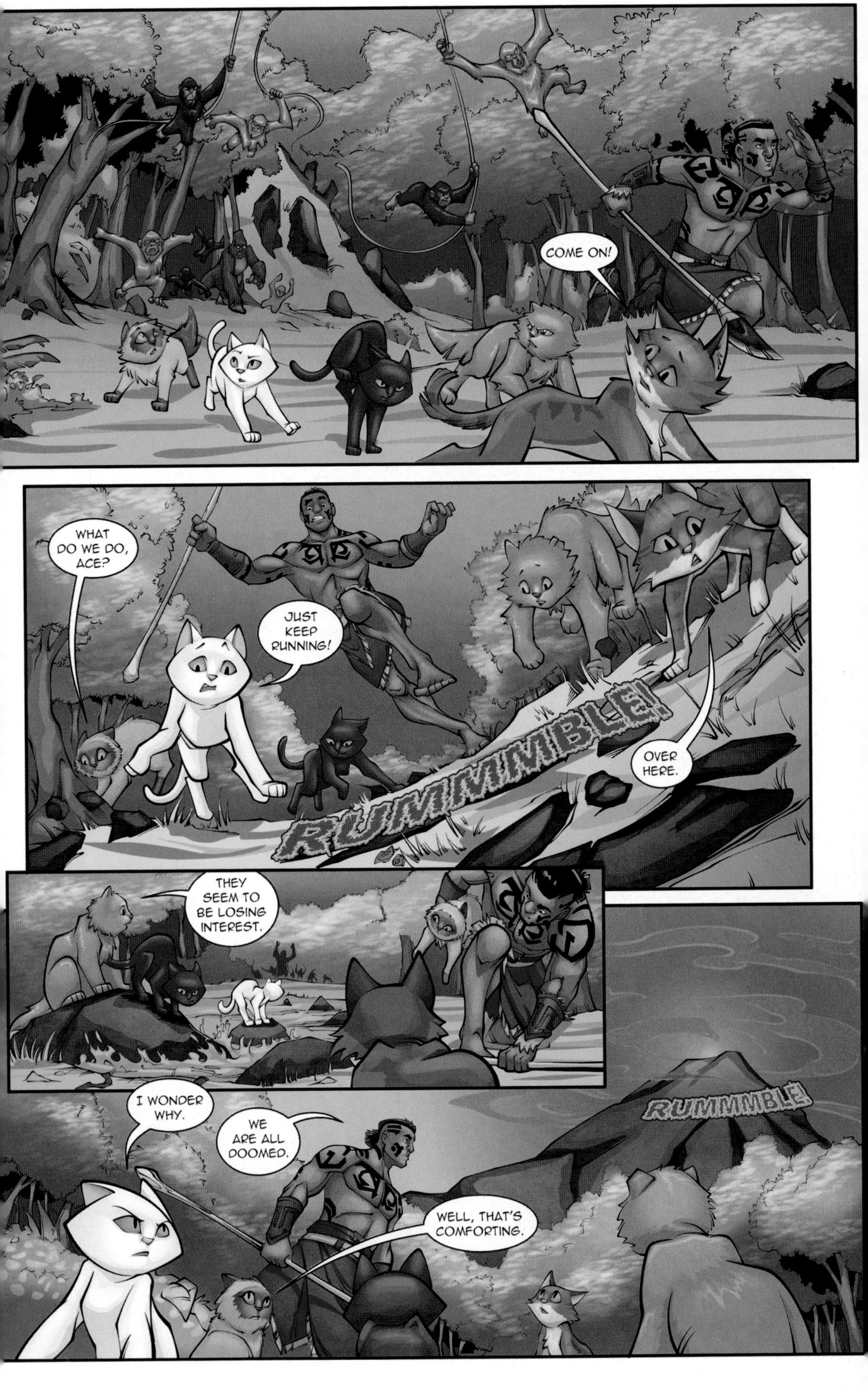
COME ON!
WHAT DO WE DO, ACE?
JUST KEEP RUNNING!
RUMMMMBLE!
OVER HERE.
THEY SEEM TO BE LOSING INTEREST.
RUMMMMBLE!
I WONDER WHY.
WE ARE ALL DOOMED.
WELL, THAT'S COMFORTING.

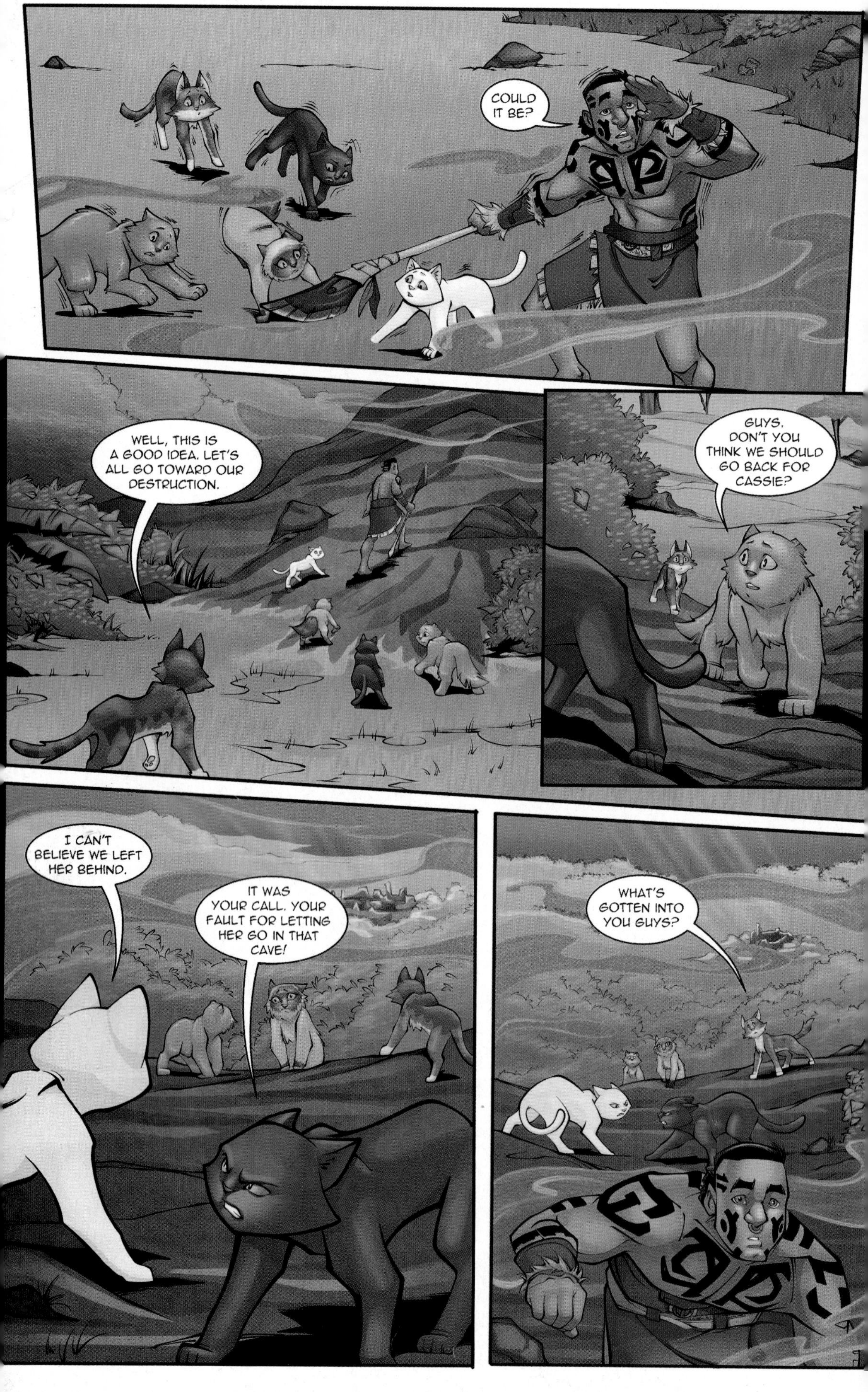
COULD IT BE?
WELL, THIS IS A GOOD IDEA. LET'S ALL GO TOWARD OUR DESTRUCTION.
GUYS. DON'T YOU THINK WE SHOULD GO BACK FOR CASSIE?
I CAN'T BELIEVE WE LEFT HER BEHIND.
IT WAS YOUR CALL. YOUR FAULT FOR LETTING HER GO IN THAT CAVE!
WHAT'S GOTTEN INTO YOU GUYS?

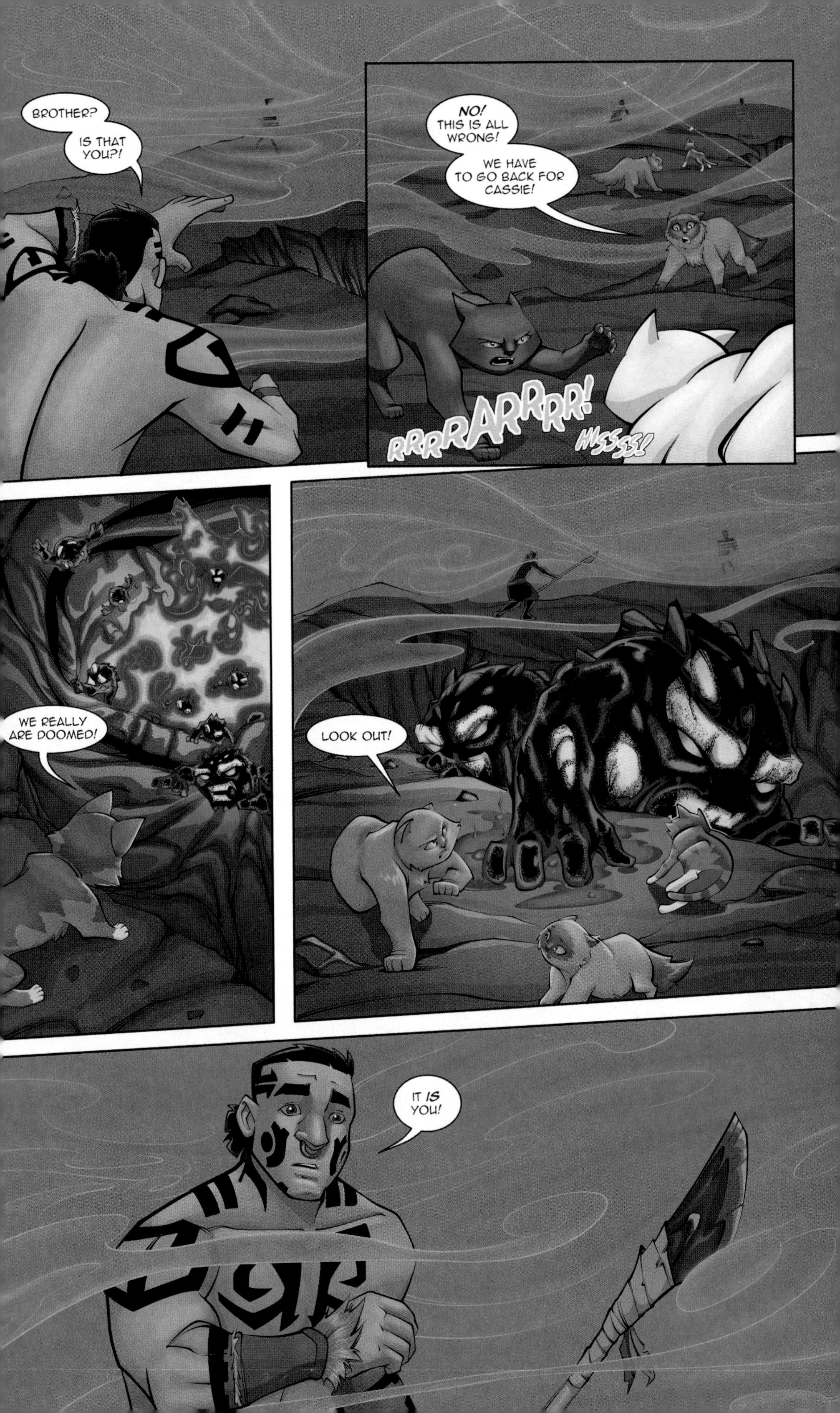
BROTHER?
IS THAT YOU?!
NO! THIS IS ALL WRONG!
WE HAVE TO GO BACK FOR CASSIE!
RRRRARRRRR!
HISSSS!
WE REALLY ARE DOOMED!
LOOK OUT!
IT IS YOU!

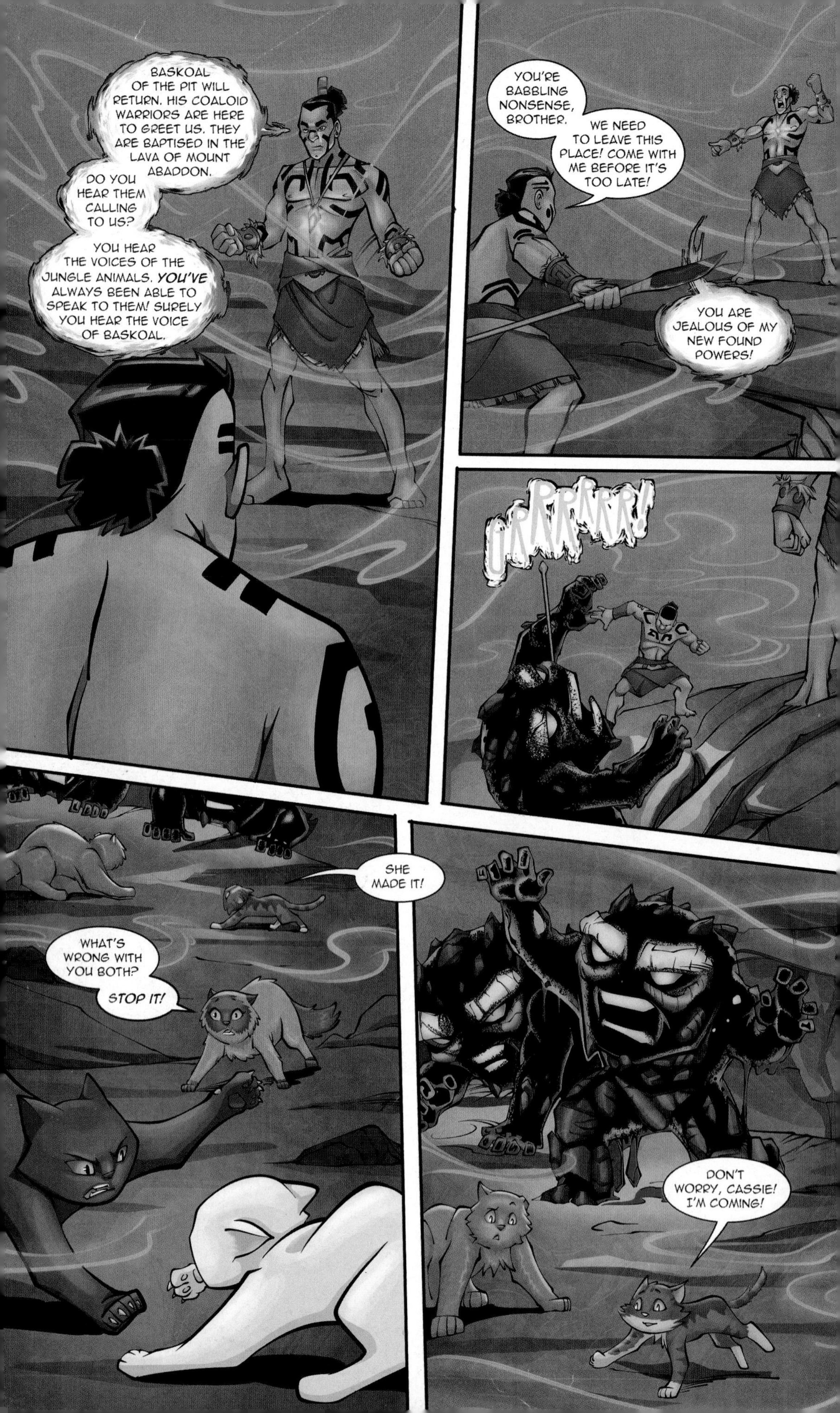

BASKOAL OF THE PIT WILL RETURN. HIS COALOID WARRIORS ARE HERE TO GREET US. THEY ARE BAPTISED IN THE LAVA OF MOUNT ABADDON.
DO YOU HEAR THEM CALLING TO US?
YOU HEAR THE VOICES OF THE JUNGLE ANIMALS. *YOU'VE* ALWAYS BEEN ABLE TO SPEAK TO THEM! SURELY YOU HEAR THE VOICE OF BASKOAL.
YOU'RE BABBLING NONSENSE, BROTHER.
WE NEED TO LEAVE THIS PLACE! COME WITH ME BEFORE IT'S TOO LATE!
YOU ARE JEALOUS OF MY NEW FOUND POWERS!
URRRRRRRR!
SHE MADE IT!
WHAT'S WRONG WITH YOU BOTH?
STOP IT!
DON'T WORRY, CASSIE! I'M COMING!

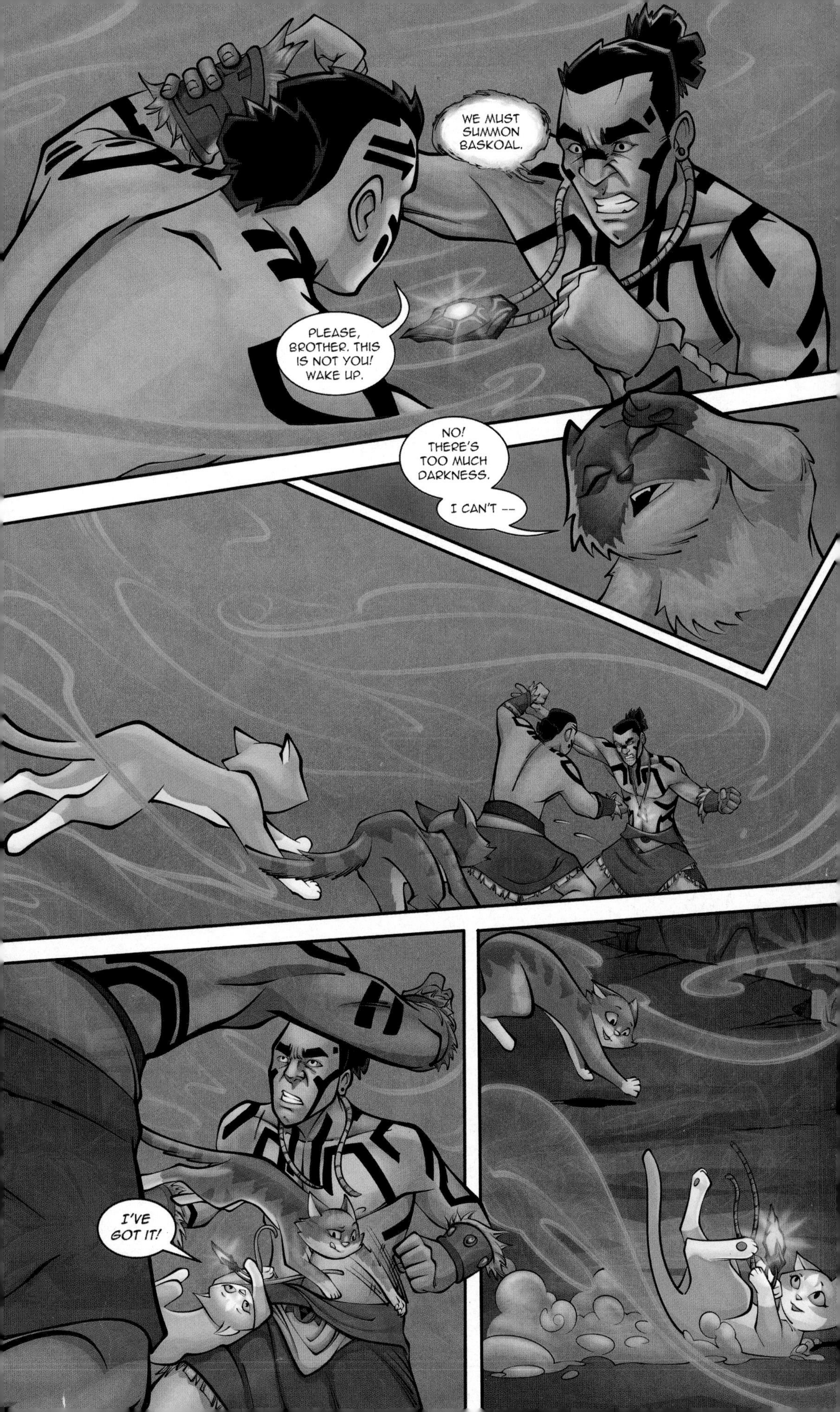
WE MUST SUMMON BASKOAL.
PLEASE, BROTHER. THIS IS NOT YOU! WAKE UP.
NO! THERE'S TOO MUCH DARKNESS.
I CAN'T --
I'VE GOT IT!

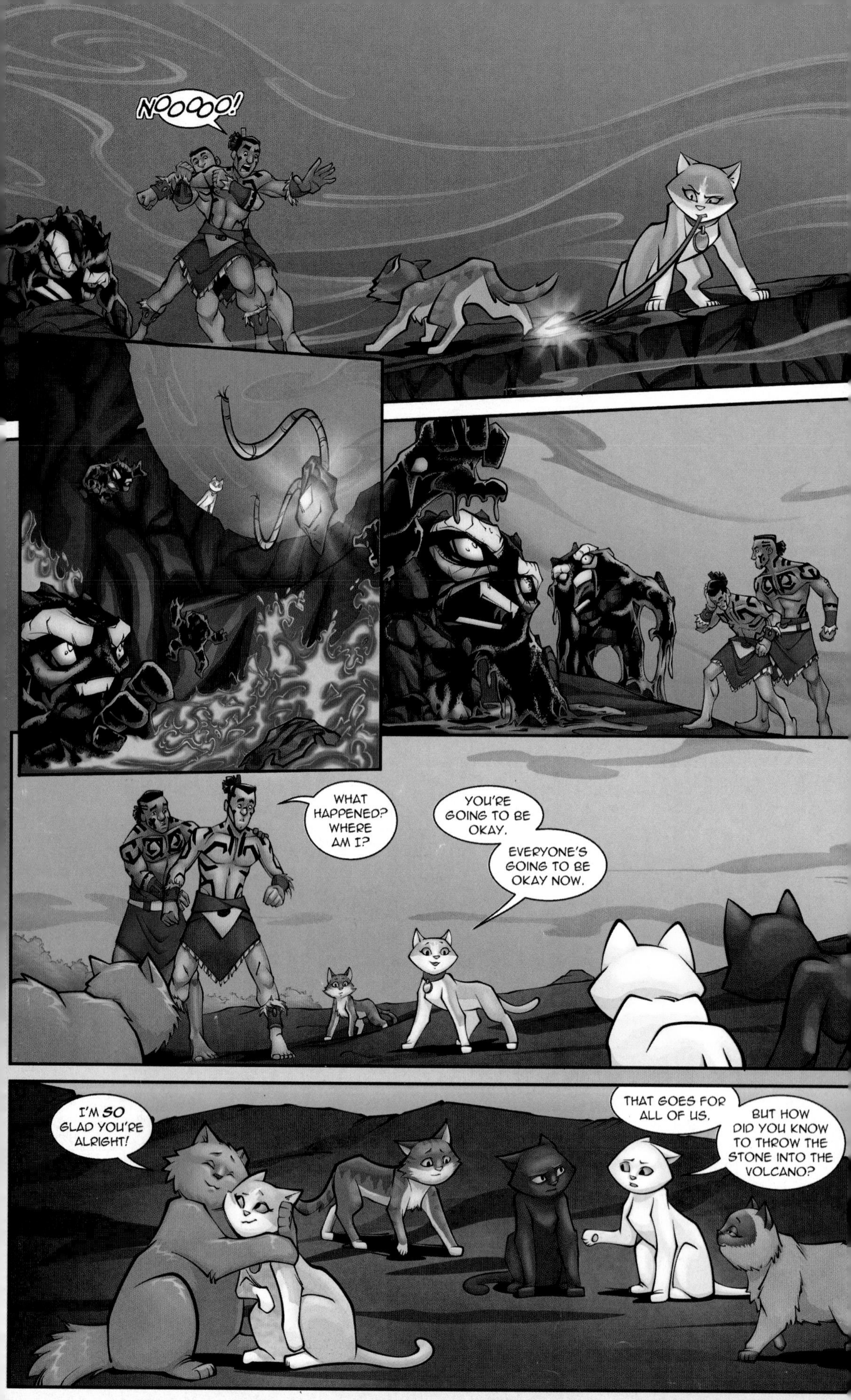
NOOOOO!
WHAT HAPPENED? WHERE AM I?
YOU'RE GOING TO BE OKAY.
EVERYONE'S GOING TO BE OKAY NOW.
I'M SO GLAD YOU'RE ALRIGHT!
THAT GOES FOR ALL OF US.
BUT HOW DID YOU KNOW TO THROW THE STONE INTO THE VOLCANO?

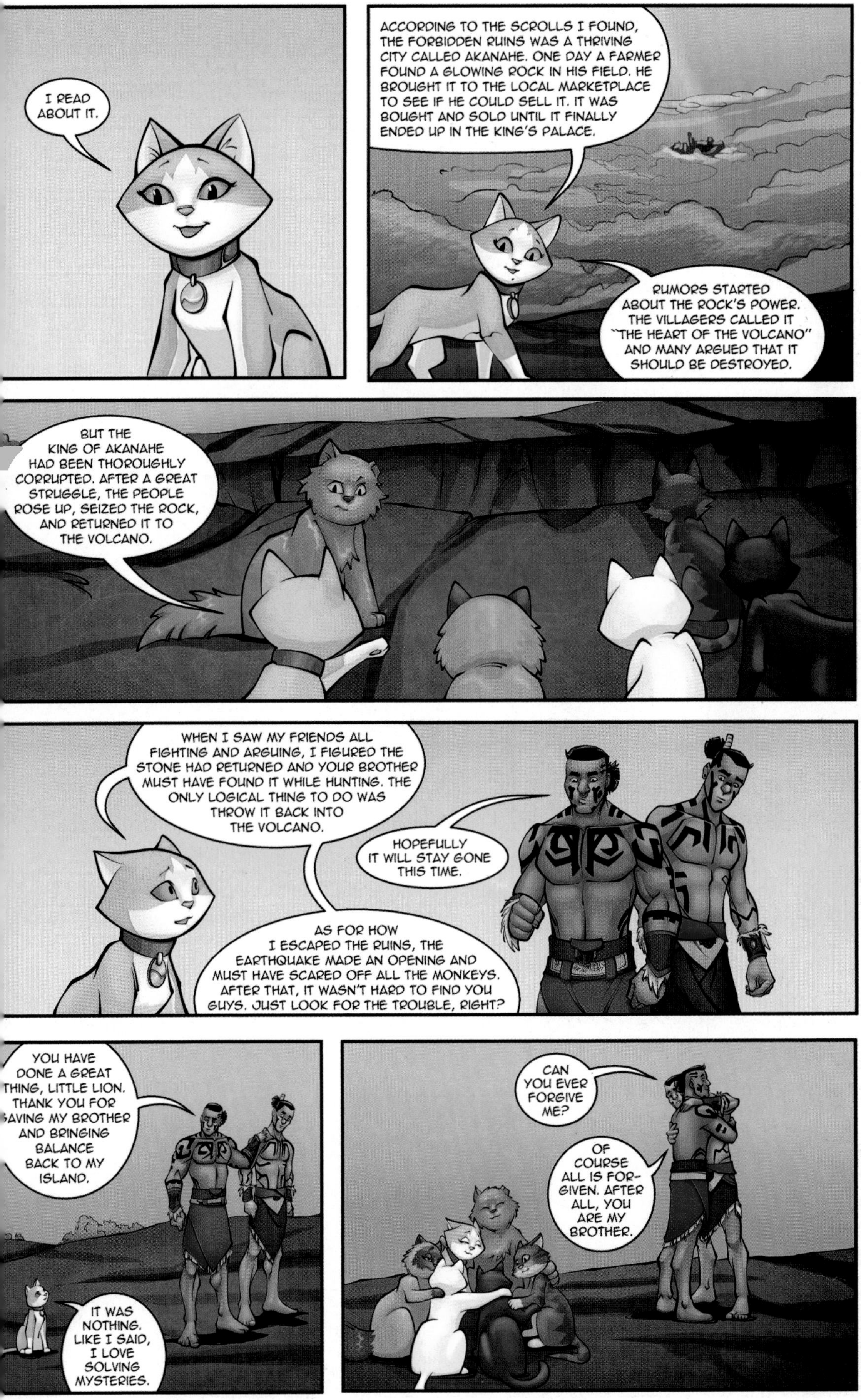
I READ ABOUT IT.
ACCORDING TO THE SCROLLS I FOUND, THE FORBIDDEN RUINS WAS A THRIVING CITY CALLED AKANAHE. ONE DAY A FARMER FOUND A GLOWING ROCK IN HIS FIELD. HE BROUGHT IT TO THE LOCAL MARKETPLACE TO SEE IF HE COULD SELL IT. IT WAS BOUGHT AND SOLD UNTIL IT FINALLY ENDED UP IN THE KING'S PALACE.
RUMORS STARTED ABOUT THE ROCK'S POWER. THE VILLAGERS CALLED IT "THE HEART OF THE VOLCANO" AND MANY ARGUED THAT IT SHOULD BE DESTROYED.
BUT THE KING OF AKANAHE HAD BEEN THOROUGHLY CORRUPTED. AFTER A GREAT STRUGGLE, THE PEOPLE ROSE UP, SEIZED THE ROCK, AND RETURNED IT TO THE VOLCANO.
WHEN I SAW MY FRIENDS ALL FIGHTING AND ARGUING, I FIGURED THE STONE HAD RETURNED AND YOUR BROTHER MUST HAVE FOUND IT WHILE HUNTING. THE ONLY LOGICAL THING TO DO WAS THROW IT BACK INTO THE VOLCANO.
AS FOR HOW I ESCAPED THE RUINS, THE EARTHQUAKE MADE AN OPENING AND MUST HAVE SCARED OFF ALL THE MONKEYS. AFTER THAT, IT WASN'T HARD TO FIND YOU GUYS. JUST LOOK FOR THE TROUBLE, RIGHT?
HOPEFULLY IT WILL STAY GONE THIS TIME.
YOU HAVE DONE A GREAT THING, LITTLE LION. THANK YOU FOR SAVING MY BROTHER AND BRINGING BALANCE BACK TO MY ISLAND.
IT WAS NOTHING. LIKE I SAID, I LOVE SOLVING MYSTERIES.
CAN YOU EVER FORGIVE ME?
OF COURSE ALL IS FOR-GIVEN. AFTER ALL, YOU ARE MY BROTHER.

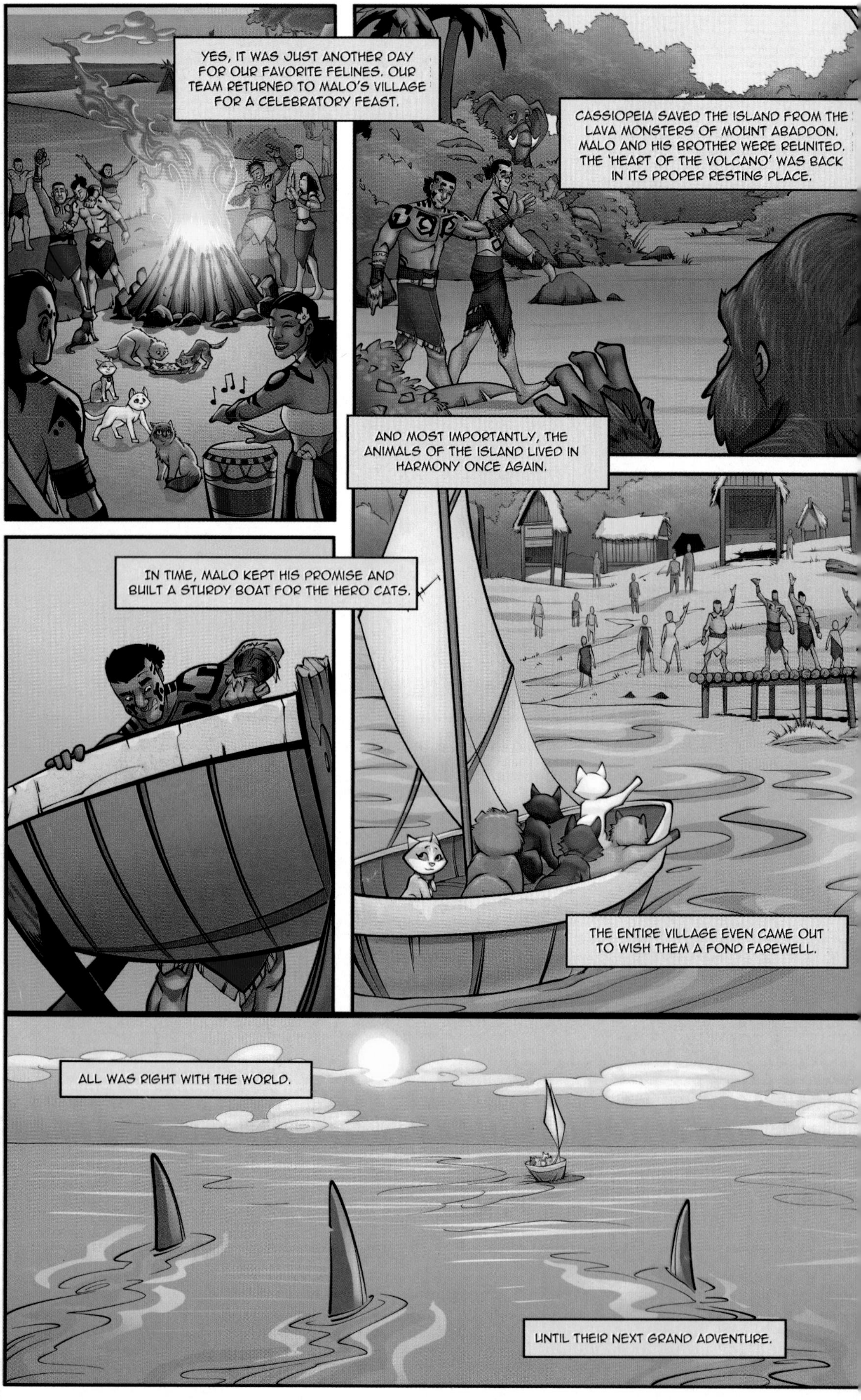
YES, IT WAS JUST ANOTHER DAY FOR OUR FAVORITE FELINES. OUR TEAM RETURNED TO MALO'S VILLAGE FOR A CELEBRATORY FEAST.
CASSIOPEIA SAVED THE ISLAND FROM THE LAVA MONSTERS OF MOUNT ABADDON. MALO AND HIS BROTHER WERE REUNITED. THE 'HEART OF THE VOLCANO' WAS BACK IN ITS PROPER RESTING PLACE.
AND MOST IMPORTANTLY, THE ANIMALS OF THE ISLAND LIVED IN HARMONY ONCE AGAIN.
IN TIME, MALO KEPT HIS PROMISE AND BUILT A STURDY BOAT FOR THE HERO CATS.
THE ENTIRE VILLAGE EVEN CAME OUT TO WISH THEM A FOND FAREWELL.
ALL WAS RIGHT WITH THE WORLD.
UNTIL THEIR NEXT GRAND ADVENTURE.

HEROCHAT

A REAL LIFE HERO CAT!

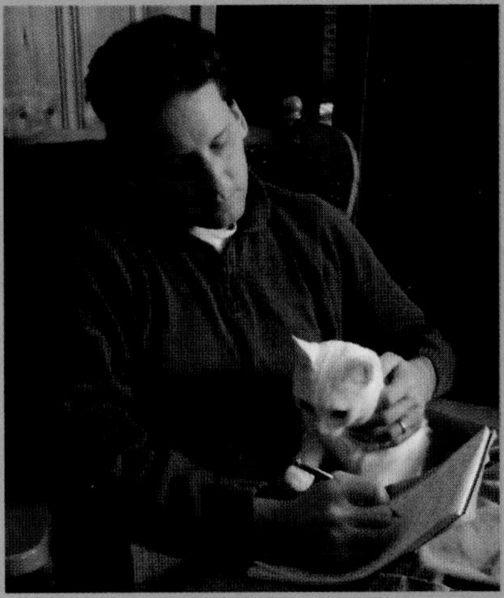

FOUR YEARS AGO MY FAMILY WAS SITTING AT THE KITCHEN TABLE AND FEELING THE STRESS OF DAILY LIFE. I KNEW SOMETHING WAS MISSING. SO I SAID FOUR SIMPLE WORDS - "WE NEED ANOTHER CAT".

MY WIFE AND CHILDREN'S EYES INSTANTLY FILLED WITH TEARS OF JOY. WE PUT UP A POST ON FACE-BOOK AND THE SEARCH WAS ON.

IT DIDN'T TAKE LONG BEFORE A CUSTOMER NAMED MATT PUCKETT BROUGHT AN ABANDONED KITTEN INTO OUR SHOP. IT WAS SMALL, BRAVE AND DIRT STAINED. MATT EXPLAINED THAT THE KITTEN WAS JUMPING INTO CARS JUST OUTSIDE OF HIS APARTMENT. A PARKING LOT DEFINITELY WASN'T A GOOD PLACE FOR HIM, SO WE TOOK HIM HOME AND WASHED HIM UP. MUCH TO OUR SURPRISE, AFTER THE GREASE AND GRIME WAS GONE HE HAD A BEAUTIFUL VIBRANT WHITE SILKY COAT.

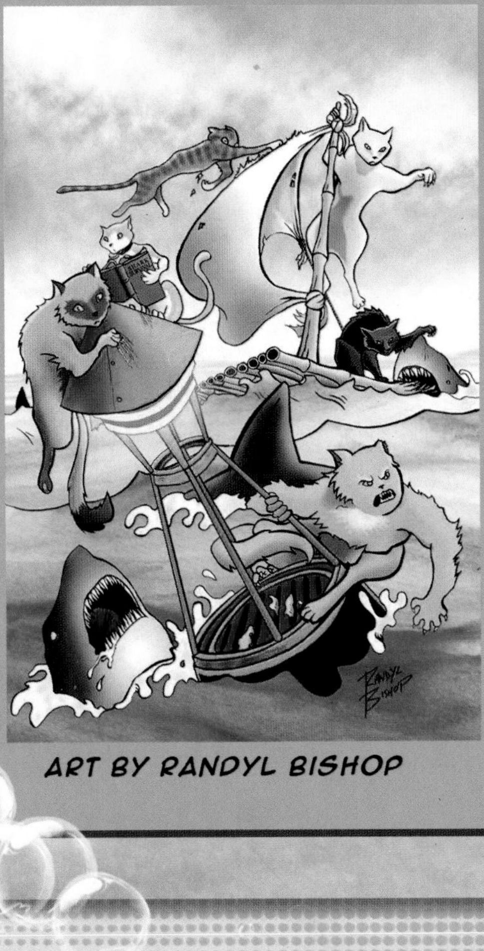
RANDYL BISHOP

ART BY RANDYL BISHOP

I HAD JUST STARTED WRITING MY HERO CATS STORIES WHEN SUDDENLY HERE HE WAS - ACE HAD FOUND US!

ACE HAS BEEN USED AS A MODEL MANY TIMES FOR OUR ARTISTS. HE'S A NATURAL. WHEN I SIT DOWN TO WRITE COMICS, HE ALWAYS JUMPS IN MY LAP TO HELP PROVIDE INSPIRATION.

HE'S OUR REAL LIFE HERO CAT.

STAY STELLAR!

KYLE PUTTKAMMER
WRITER & CREATOR

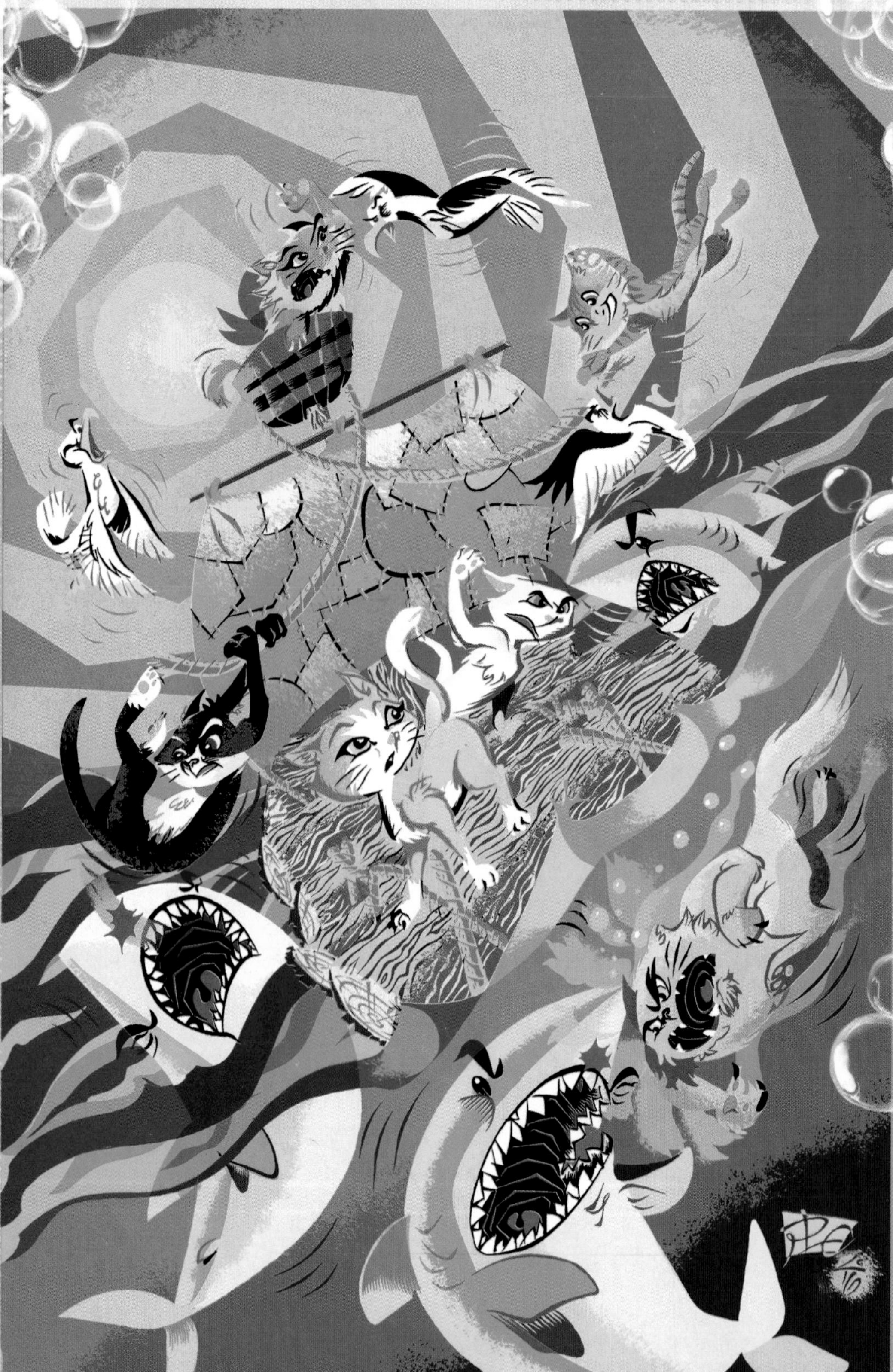

ART BY PETER CUTLER

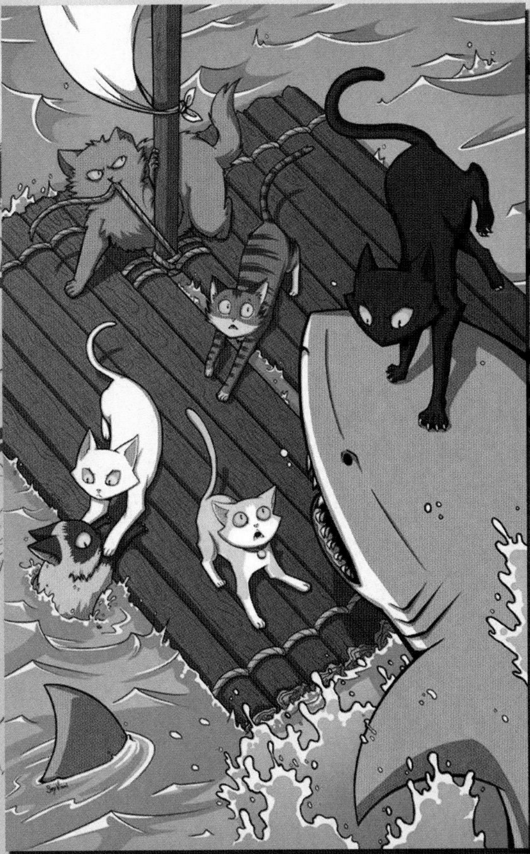

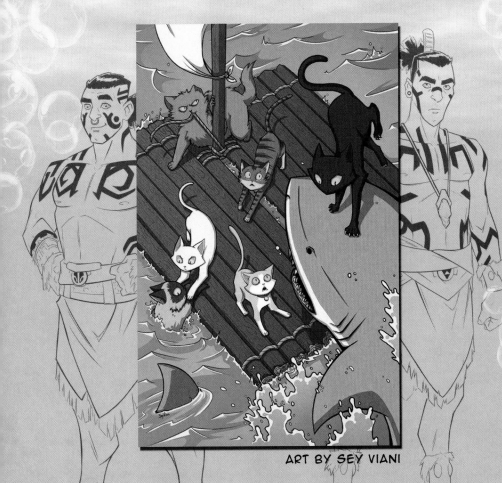

ART BY SEY VIANI

WWW.HEROCATSONLINE.COM

UP NEXT

JOURNEY TO THE FAR EAST!

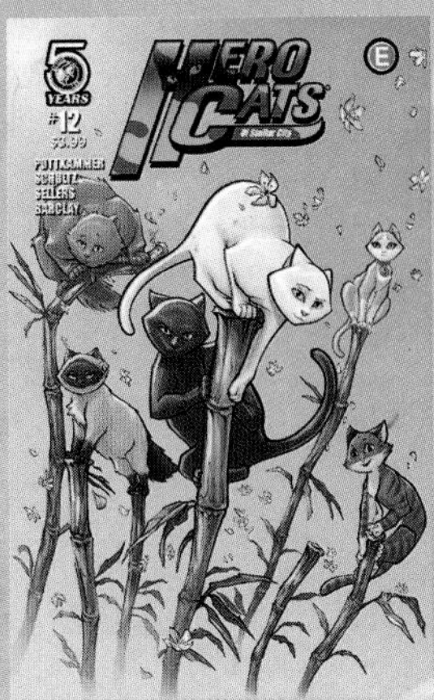
5 YEARS
HERO CATS
#12
PUTTKAMMER
SCHULTZ
SELLERS
BARCLAY

Bryan Seaton - Publisher
Dave Dwonch - President
Shawn Gabborin - Editor in Chief
Jamal Igle - Director of Marketing
Jim Dietz - Social Media Director
Jeremy Whitley - Education Outreach Director
Chad Cicconi & Colleen Boyd - Associate Editors

Herocats over Stellar City #11, July 2016

Printed in Canada.

First Printing

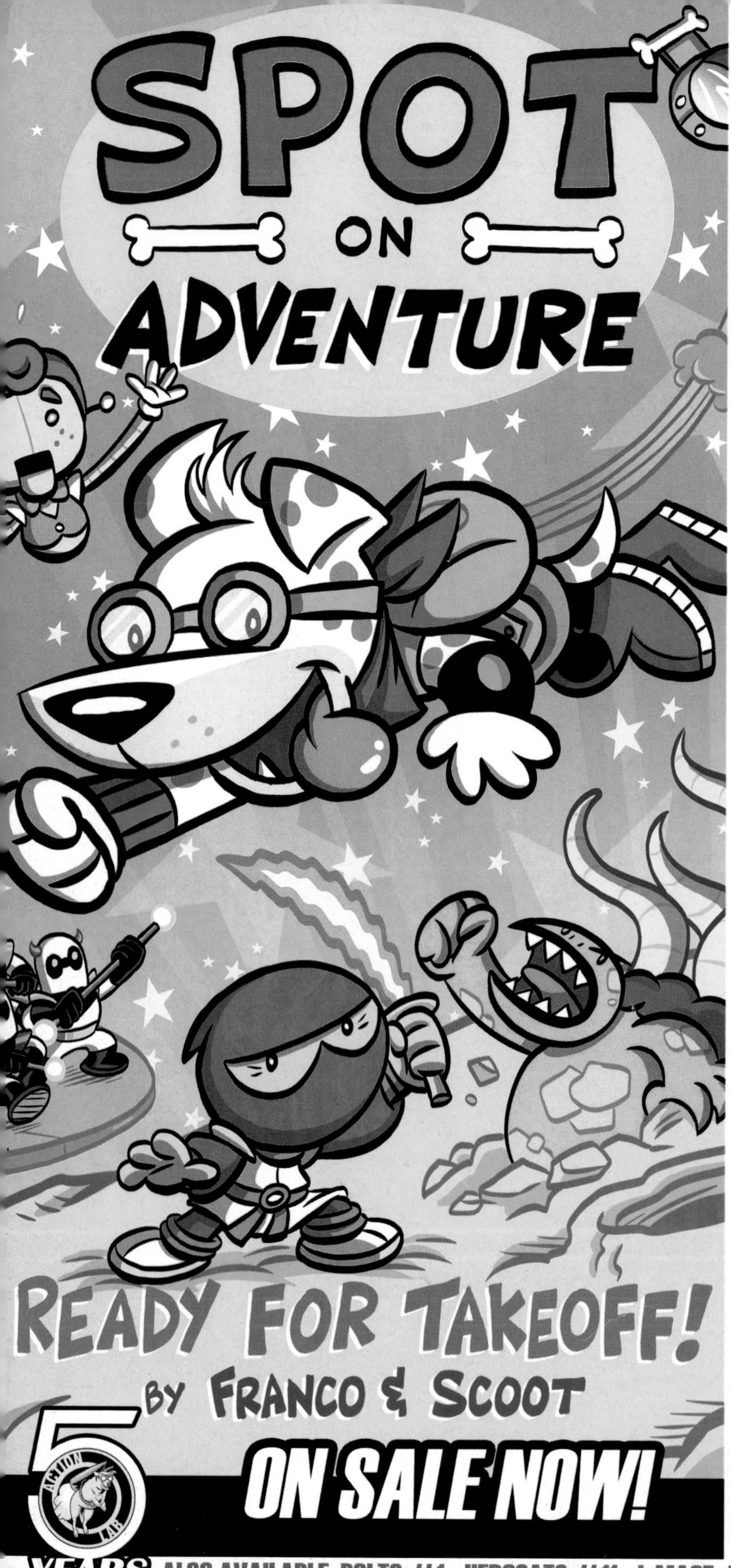

SPOT ON ADVENTURE
READY FOR TAKEOFF!
BY FRANCO & SCOOT
ON SALE NOW!
5
ACTION LAB

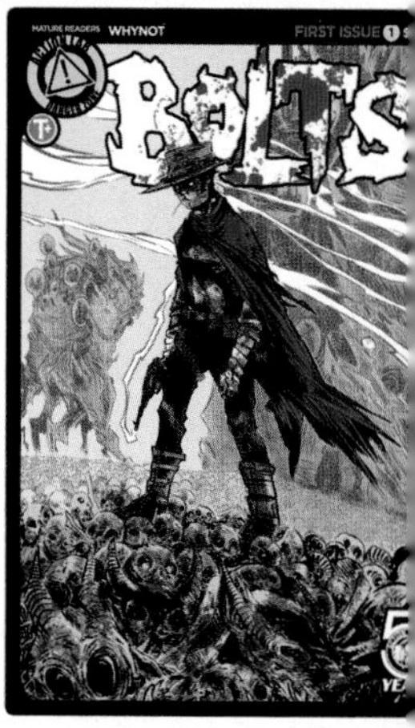

MATURE READERS WHYNOT
FIRST ISSUE 1
BOLTS

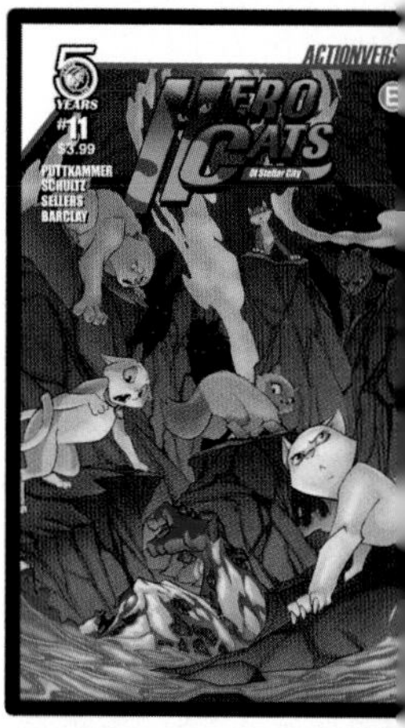

5 YEARS
ACTIONVERSE
#11
$3.99
PUTTKAMMER
SCHULTZ
SELLERS
BARCLAY
HERO CATS

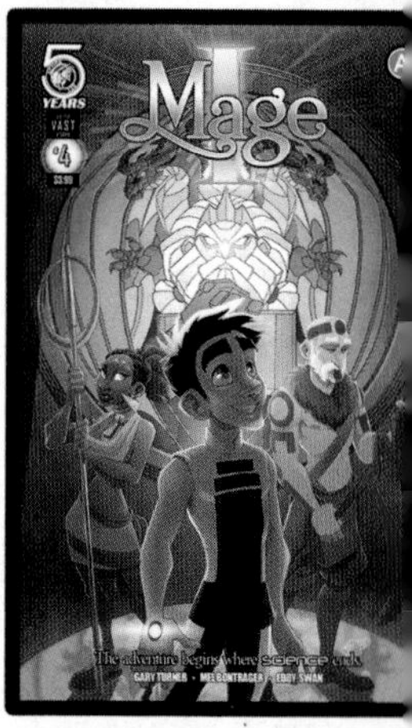

5 YEARS
#4
Mage

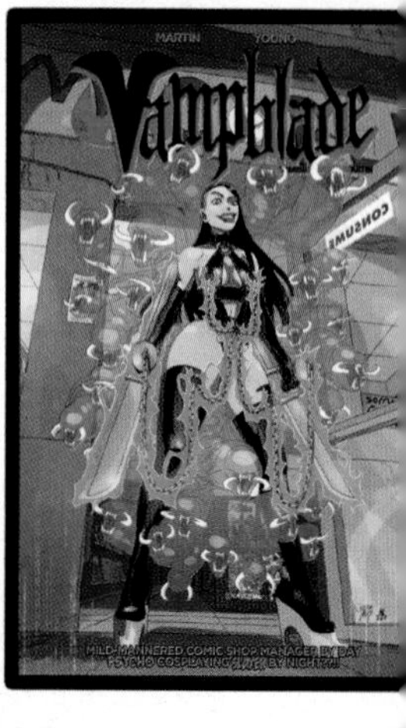

MARTIN
YOUNG
Vampblade

YEARS ALSO AVAILABLE: BOLTS #1 - HEROCATS #11 - I, MAGE #4 - VAMPBLADE VOL

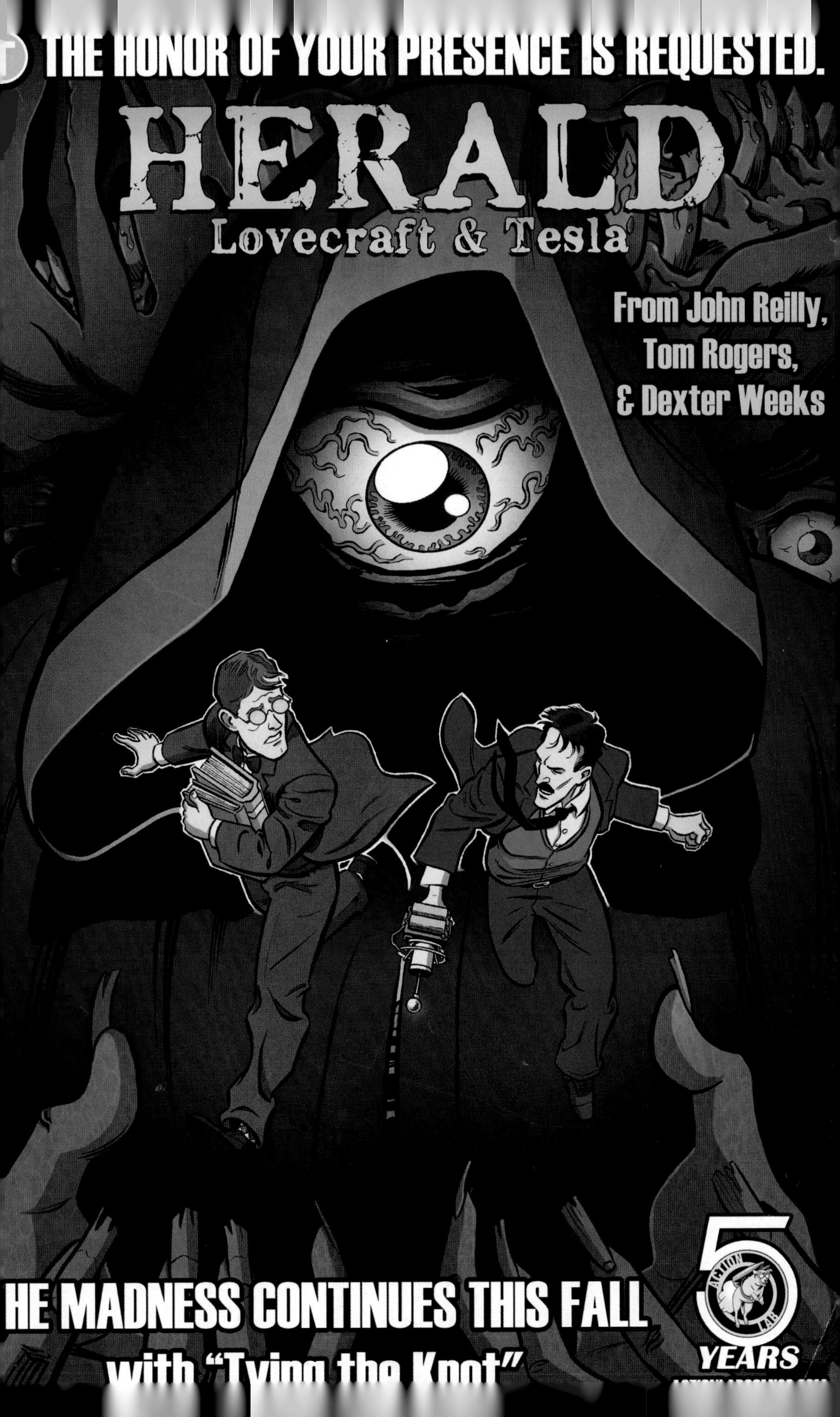

THE HONOR OF YOUR PRESENCE IS REQUESTED.
HERALD
Lovecraft & Tesla
From John Reilly,
Tom Rogers,
& Dexter Weeks
HE MADNESS CONTINUES THIS FALL
with “Tying the Knot”
5 YEARS

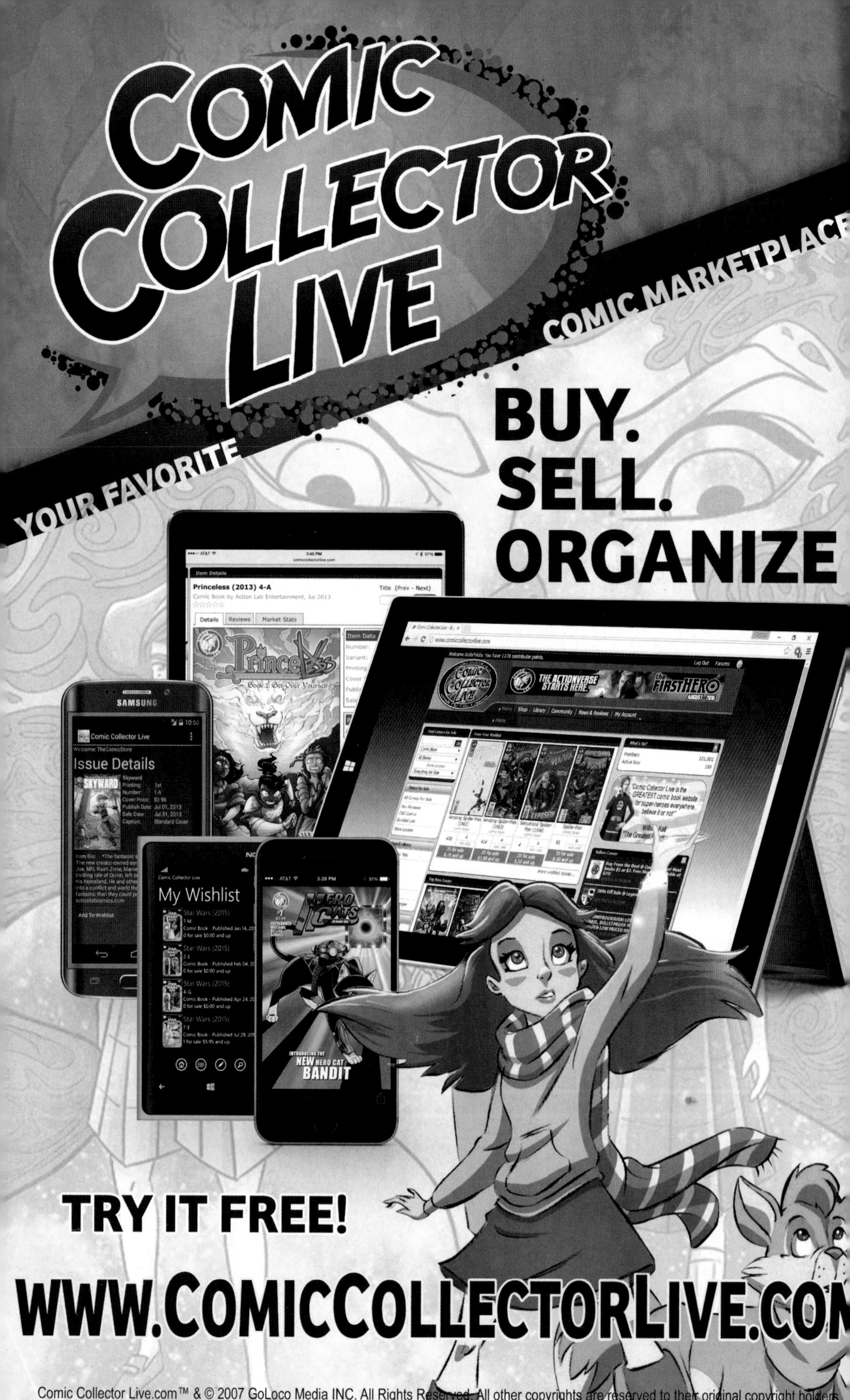
Comic Collector Live
Your Favorite Comic Marketplace
BUY.
SELL.
ORGANIZE
TRY IT FREE!
WWW.COMICCOLLECTORLIVE.COM

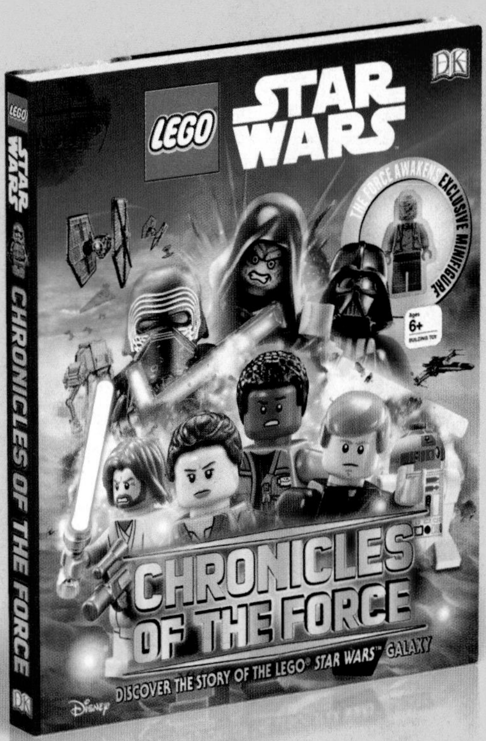
LEGO
STAR WARS
DK
THE FORCE AWAKENS EXCLUSIVE MINIFIGURE
Ages 6+
BUILDING TOY
CHRONICLES OF THE FORCE
DISCOVER THE STORY OF THE LEGO® STAR WARS™ GALAXY
Disney
STAR WARS CHRONICLES OF THE FORCE

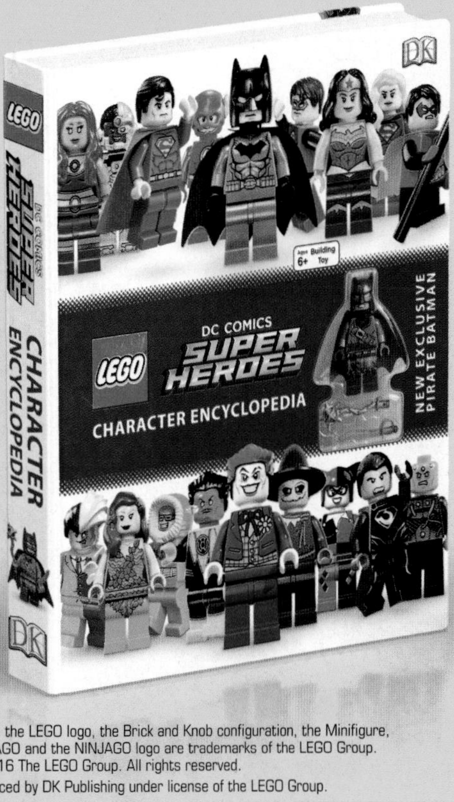
LEGO
DC COMICS
SUPER HEROES
CHARACTER ENCYCLOPEDIA
NEW EXCLUSIVE PIRATE BATMAN
Ages 6+ Building Toy
DK

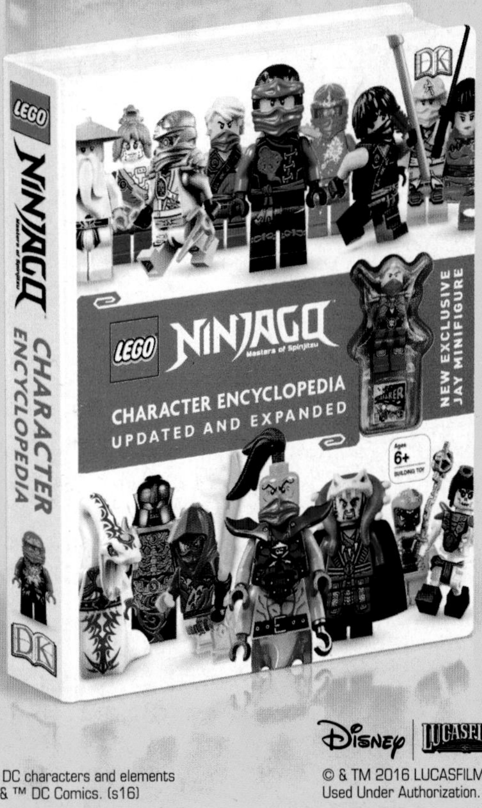
LEGO
NINJAGO
Masters of Spinjitzu
CHARACTER ENCYCLOPEDIA
UPDATED AND EXPANDED
NEW EXCLUSIVE JAY MINIFIGURE
Ages 6+
BUILDING TOY
DK

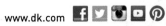

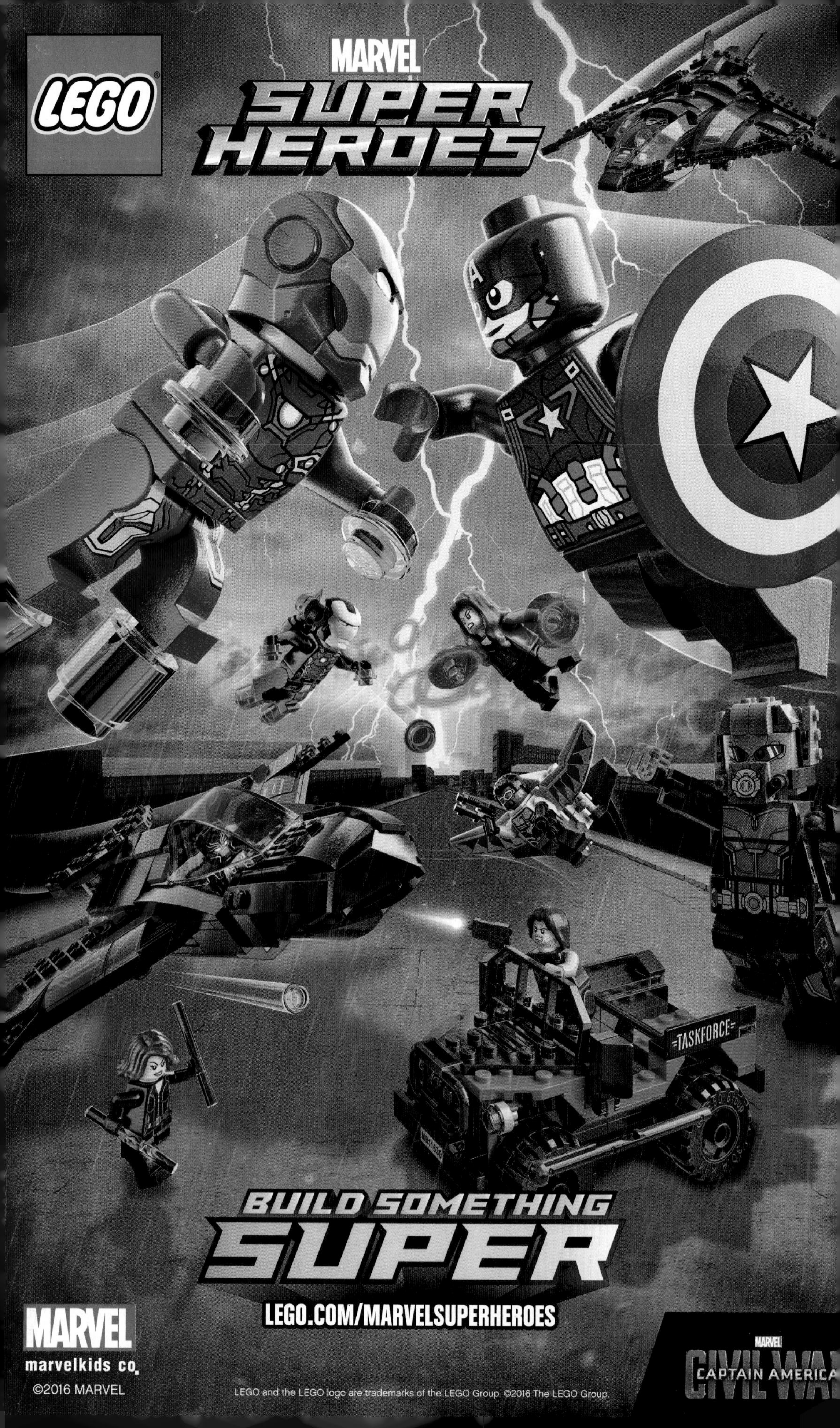
LEGO
MARVEL
SUPER HEROES
TASKFORCE
BUILD SOMETHING
SUPER
LEGO.COM/MARVELSUPERHEROES
MARVEL
marvelkids co.
©2016 MARVEL
LEGO and the LEGO logo are trademarks of the LEGO Group. ©2016 The LEGO Group.
MARVEL
CAPTAIN AMERICA

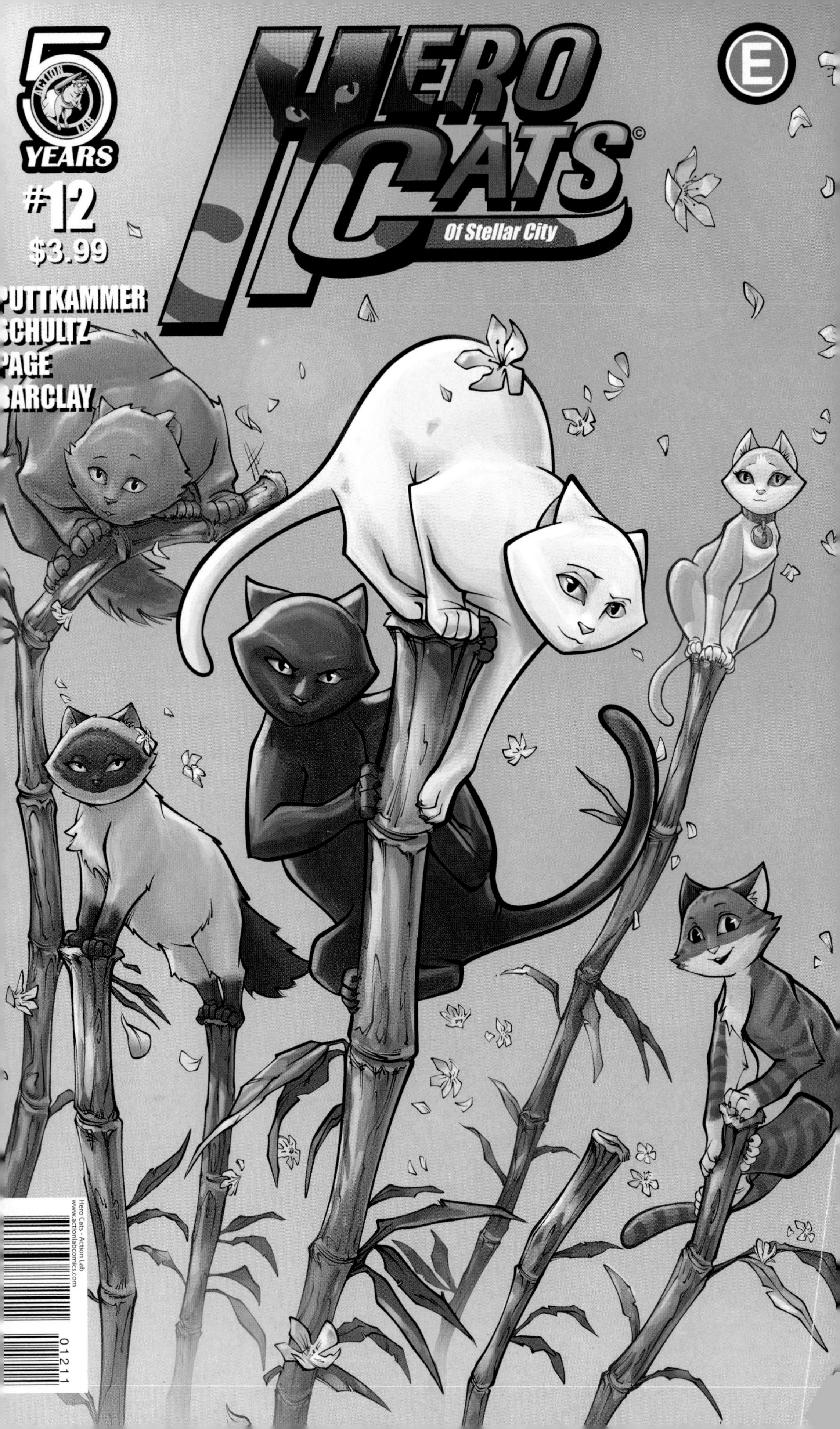
5 YEARS
ACTION LAB
#12
$3.99
PUTTKAMMER
SCHULTZ
PAGE
BARCLAY
HERO CATS©
Of Stellar City
E
Hero Cats - Action Lab
www.actionlabcomics.com
01211

FROM ALL-AGES TO MATURE READERS
ACTION LAB HAS YOU COVERED.

 **Appropriate for everyone.**

 **Appropriate for age 9 and up. Absent of profanity or adult content.**

 **Suggested for 12 and Up. Comics with this rating are comparable to a PG-13 movie rating. Recommended for our teen and young adult readers.**

 **Appropriate for older teens. Similar to Teen, but featuring more mature themes and/or more graphic imagery.**

 **Contains extreme violence and some nudity. Basically the Rated-R of comics.**

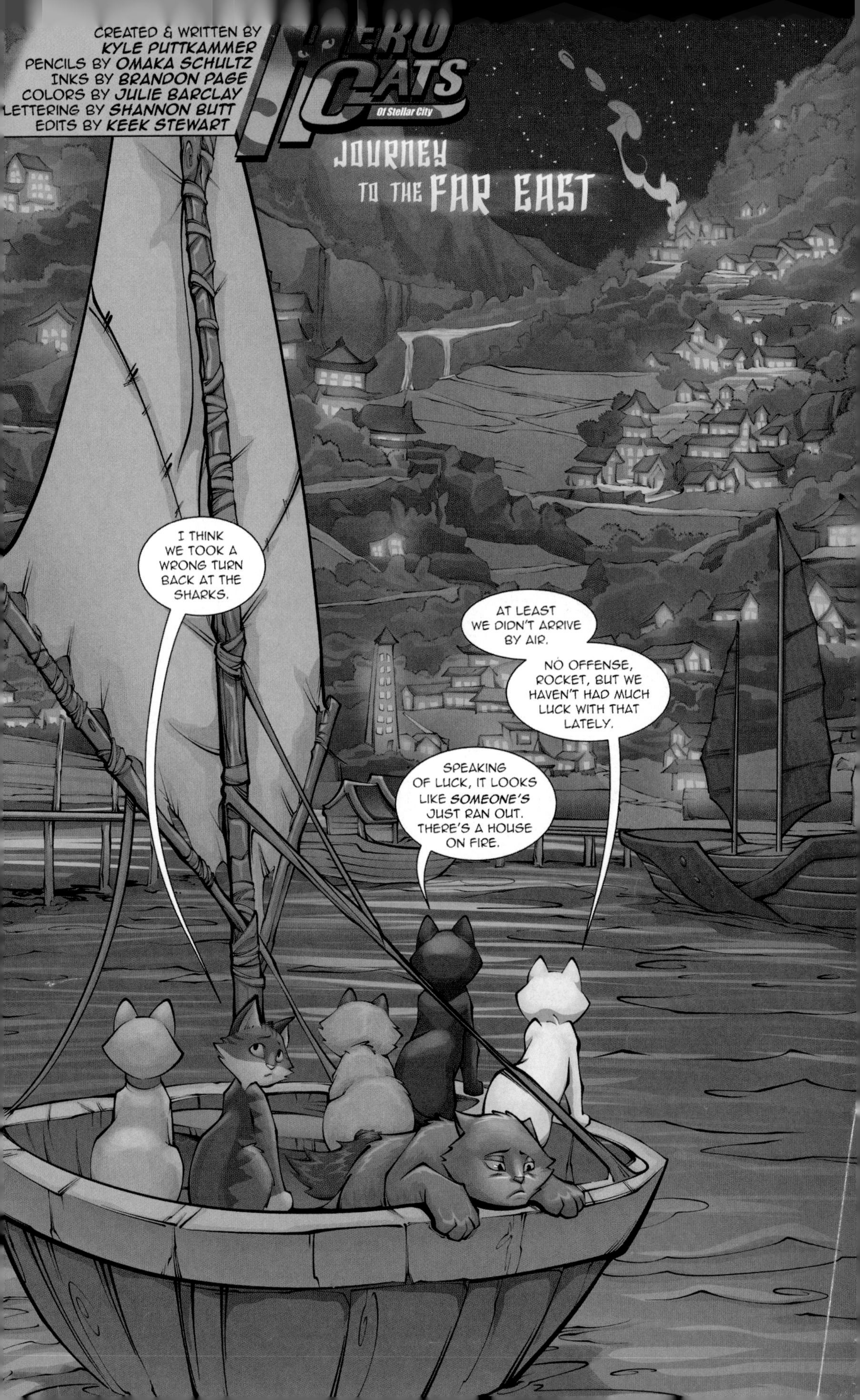
CREATED & WRITTEN BY KYLE PUTTKAMMER
PENCILS BY OMAKA SCHULTZ
INKS BY BRANDON PAGE
COLORS BY JULIE BARCLAY
LETTERING BY SHANNON BUTT
EDITS BY KEEK STEWART
CATS
Of Stellar City
JOURNEY TO THE FAR EAST
I THINK WE TOOK A WRONG TURN BACK AT THE SHARKS.
AT LEAST WE DIDN'T ARRIVE BY AIR.
NO OFFENSE, ROCKET, BUT WE HAVEN'T HAD MUCH LUCK WITH THAT LATELY.
SPEAKING OF LUCK, IT LOOKS LIKE SOMEONE'S JUST RAN OUT. THERE'S A HOUSE ON FIRE.

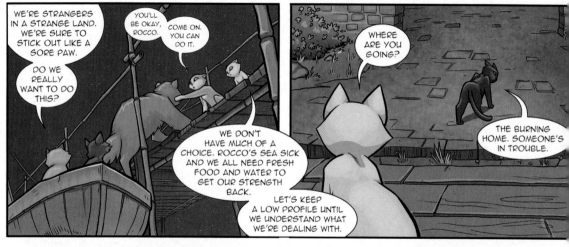

WE'RE STRANGERS IN A STRANGE LAND. WE'RE SURE TO STICK OUT LIKE A SORE PAW.

YOU'LL BE OKAY, ROCCO.

COME ON. YOU CAN DO IT.

DO WE REALLY WANT TO DO THIS?

WE DON'T HAVE MUCH OF A CHOICE. ROCCO'S SEA SICK AND WE ALL NEED FRESH FOOD AND WATER TO GET OUR STRENGTH BACK.

LET'S KEEP A LOW PROFILE UNTIL WE UNDERSTAND WHAT WE'RE DEALING WITH.

WHERE ARE YOU GOING?

THE BURNING HOME. SOMEONE'S IN TROUBLE.

I SAID WE SHOULD KEEP A LOW PROFILE, SOLDIER.

YOU CAN STAY HERE IF YOU WANT, BUT I'M GOING TO SEE WHO NEEDS OUR HELP! WE ARE HERO CATS AFTER ALL, RIGHT?

BELLE, YOU AND CASSIOPEIA TEND TO ROCCO. SEE TO IT THAT HE GETS SOME FRESH WATER AND FOOD. HE'S GOING TO NEED HIS STRENGTH. ROCKET AND I WILL CATCH UP WITH MIDNIGHT.

STAY SAFE AND WE'LL BACK UP WITH YOU ONCE WE'VE ASSESSED THE SITUATION.

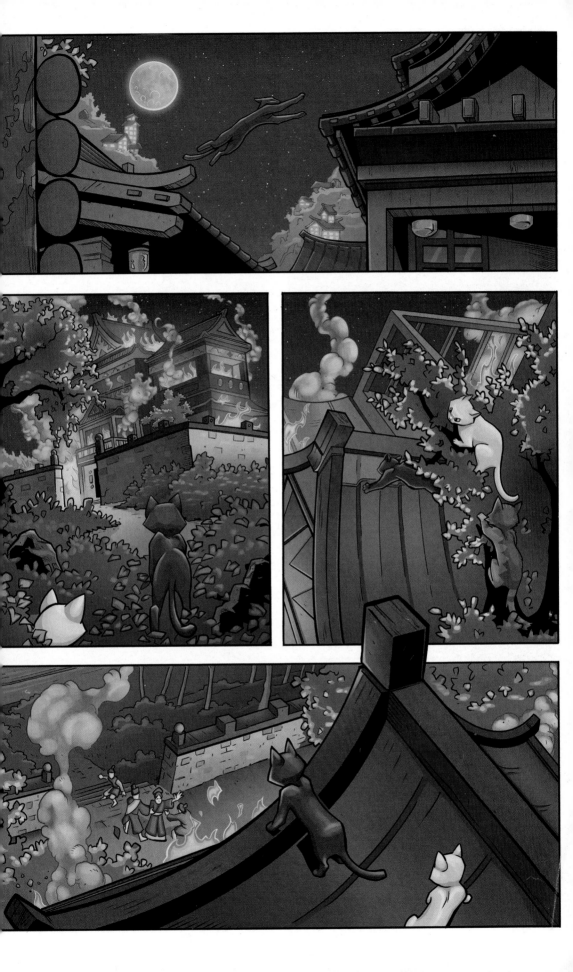

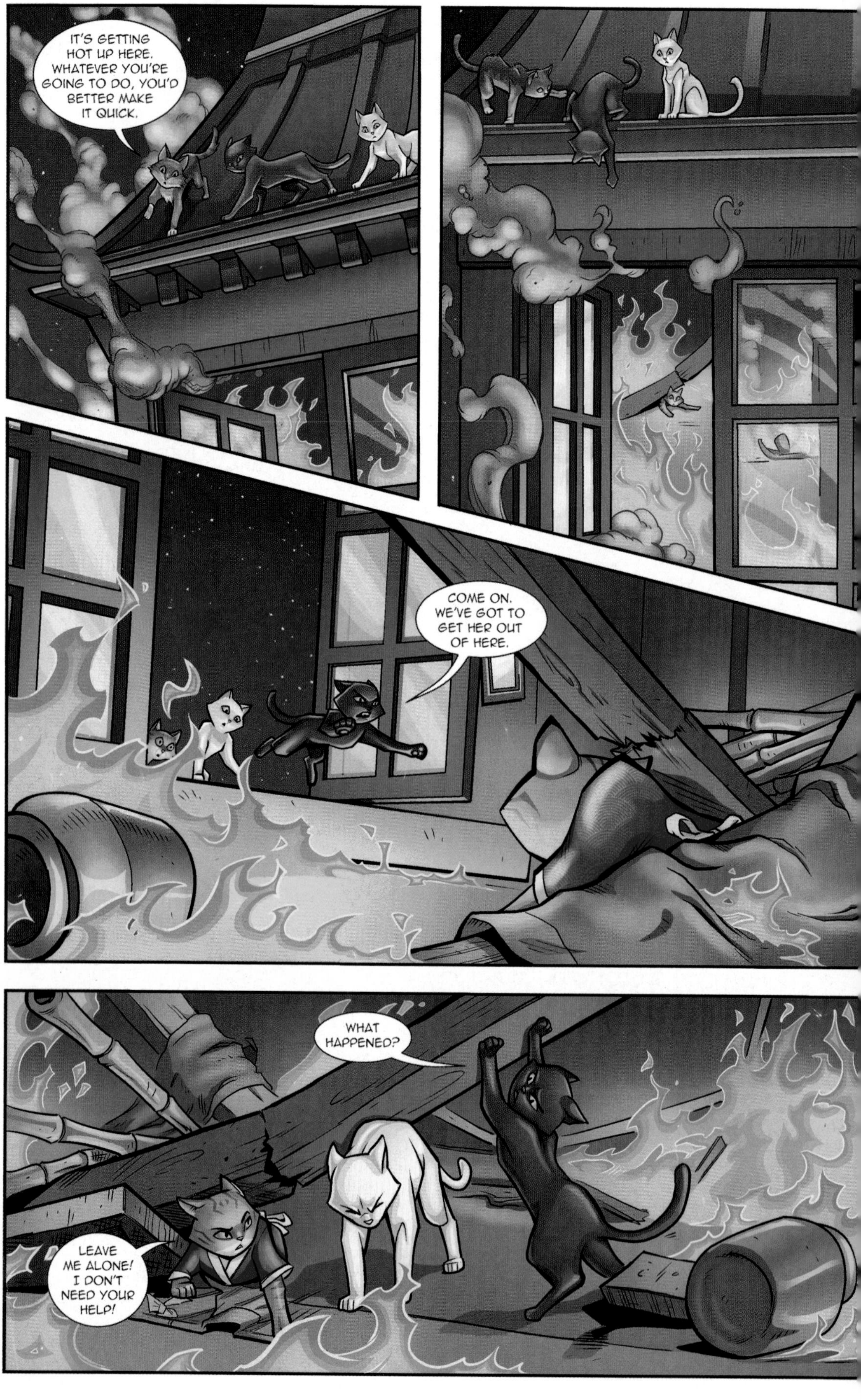
IT'S GETTING HOT UP HERE. WHATEVER YOU'RE GOING TO DO, YOU'D BETTER MAKE IT QUICK.
COME ON. WE'VE GOT TO GET HER OUT OF HERE.
WHAT HAPPENED?
LEAVE ME ALONE! I DON'T NEED YOUR HELP!

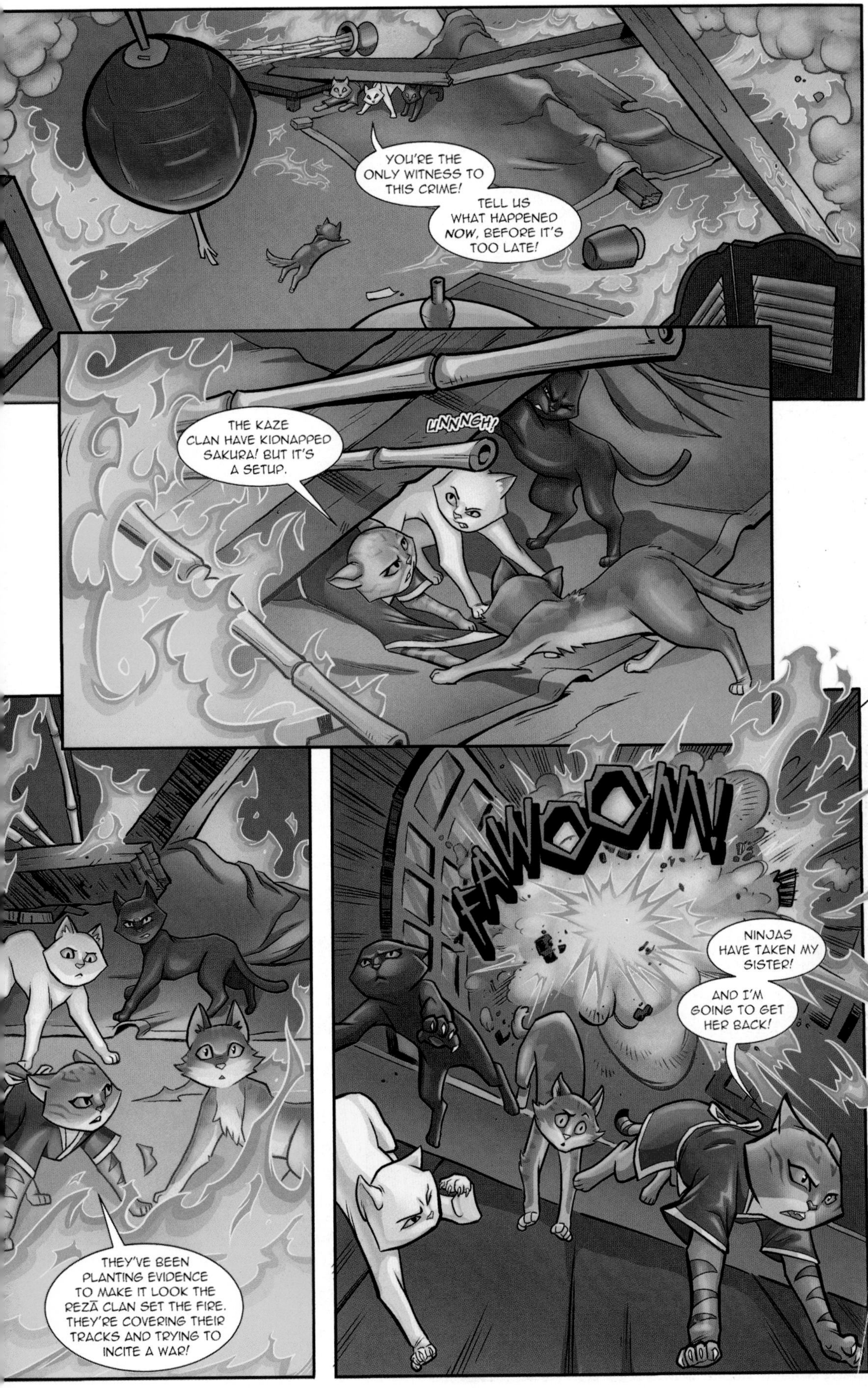
YOU'RE THE ONLY WITNESS TO THIS CRIME!
TELL US WHAT HAPPENED *NOW*, BEFORE IT'S TOO LATE!
UNNNGH!
THE KAZE CLAN HAVE KIDNAPPED SAKURA! BUT IT'S A SETUP.
THEY'VE BEEN PLANTING EVIDENCE TO MAKE IT LOOK THE REZĀ CLAN SET THE FIRE. THEY'RE COVERING THEIR TRACKS AND TRYING TO INCITE A WAR!
FAWOOM!
NINJAS HAVE TAKEN MY SISTER!
AND I'M GOING TO GET HER BACK!

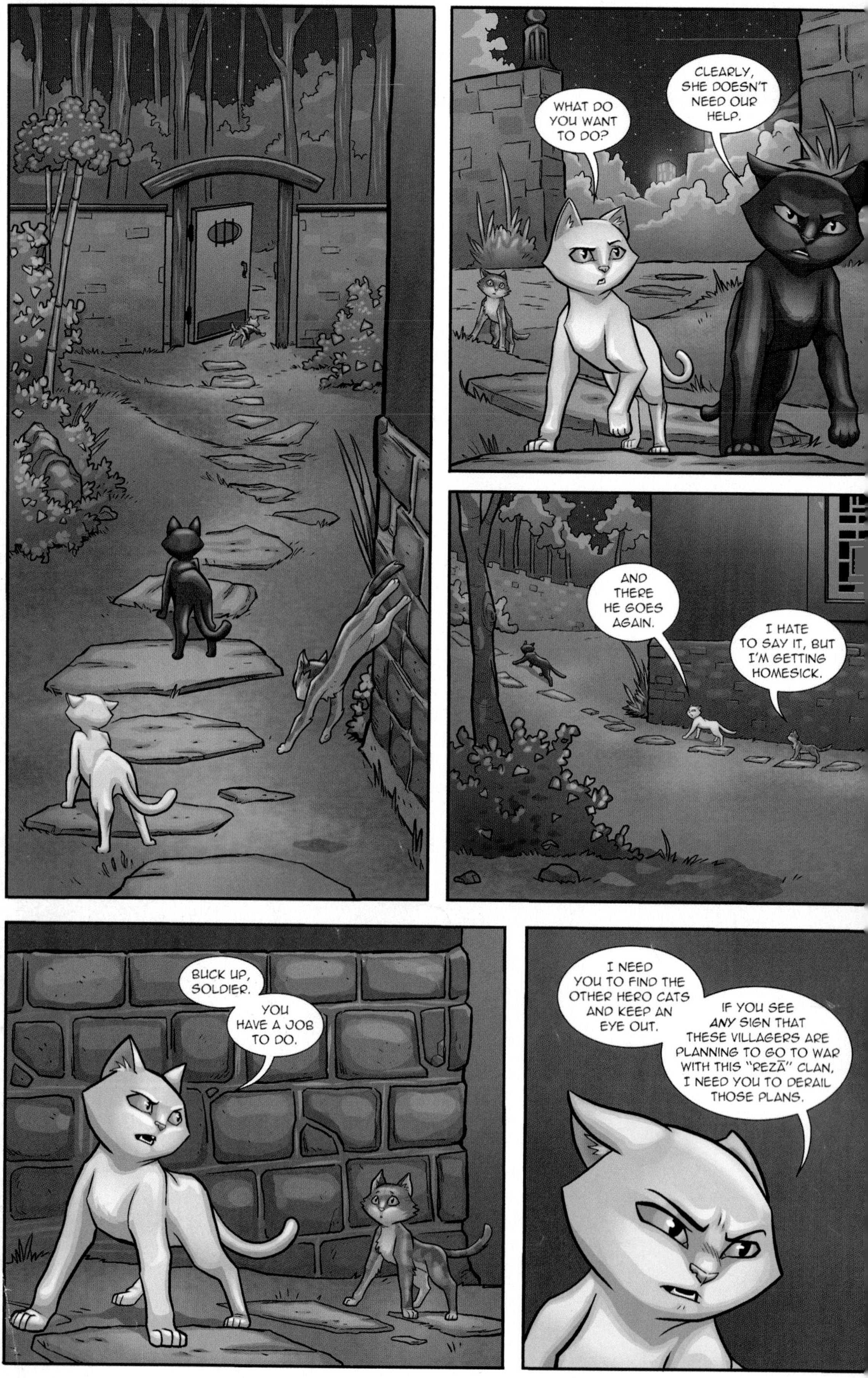
WHAT DO YOU WANT TO DO?
CLEARLY, SHE DOESN'T NEED OUR HELP.
AND THERE HE GOES AGAIN.
I HATE TO SAY IT, BUT I'M GETTING HOMESICK.
BUCK UP, SOLDIER.
YOU HAVE A JOB TO DO.
I NEED YOU TO FIND THE OTHER HERO CATS AND KEEP AN EYE OUT.
IF YOU SEE *ANY* SIGN THAT THESE VILLAGERS ARE PLANNING TO GO TO WAR WITH THIS "REZĀ" CLAN, I NEED YOU TO DERAIL THOSE PLANS.

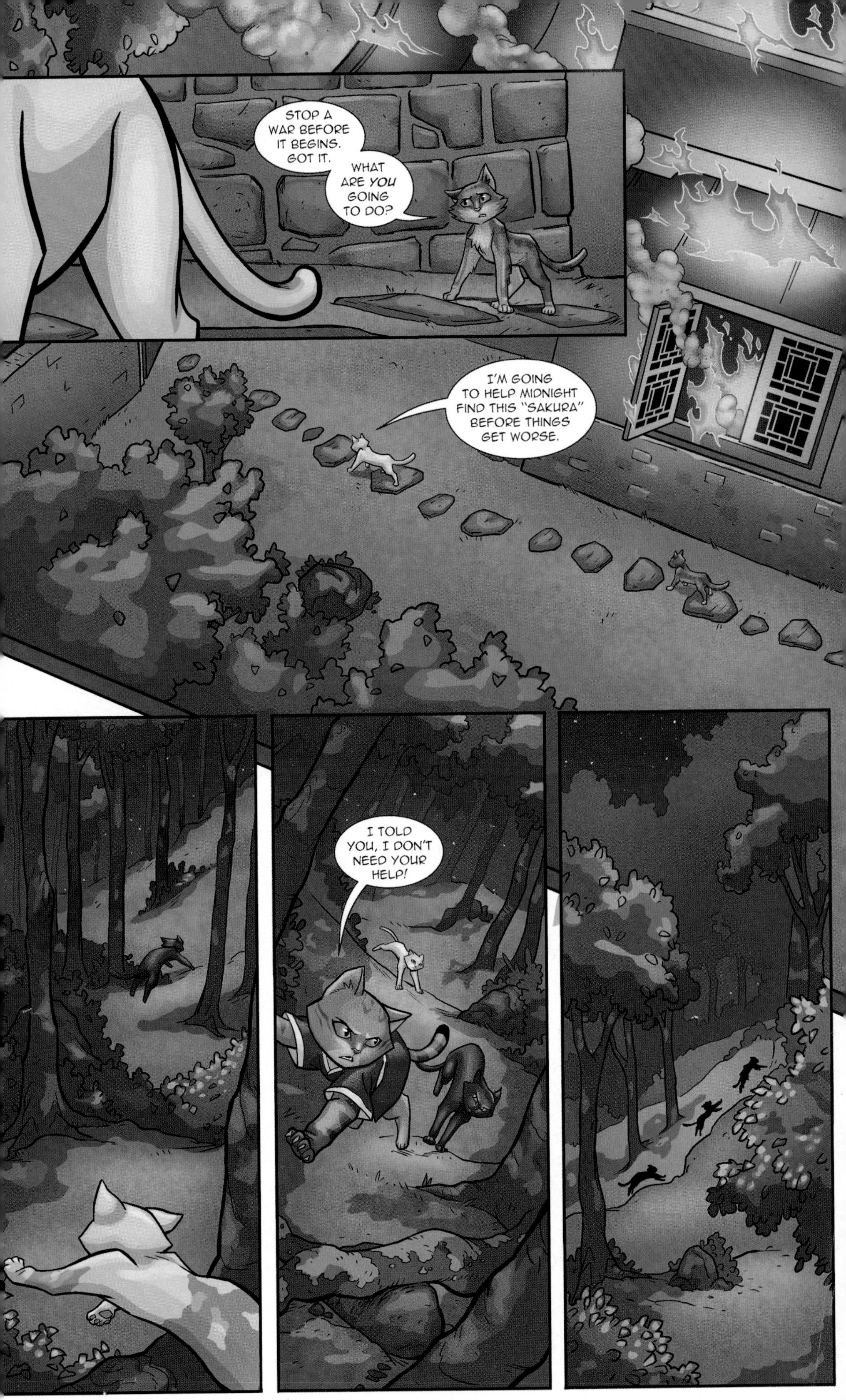
STOP A WAR BEFORE IT BEGINS. GOT IT.
WHAT ARE *YOU* GOING TO DO?
I'M GOING TO HELP MIDNIGHT FIND THIS "SAKURA" BEFORE THINGS GET WORSE.
I TOLD YOU, I DON'T NEED YOUR HELP!

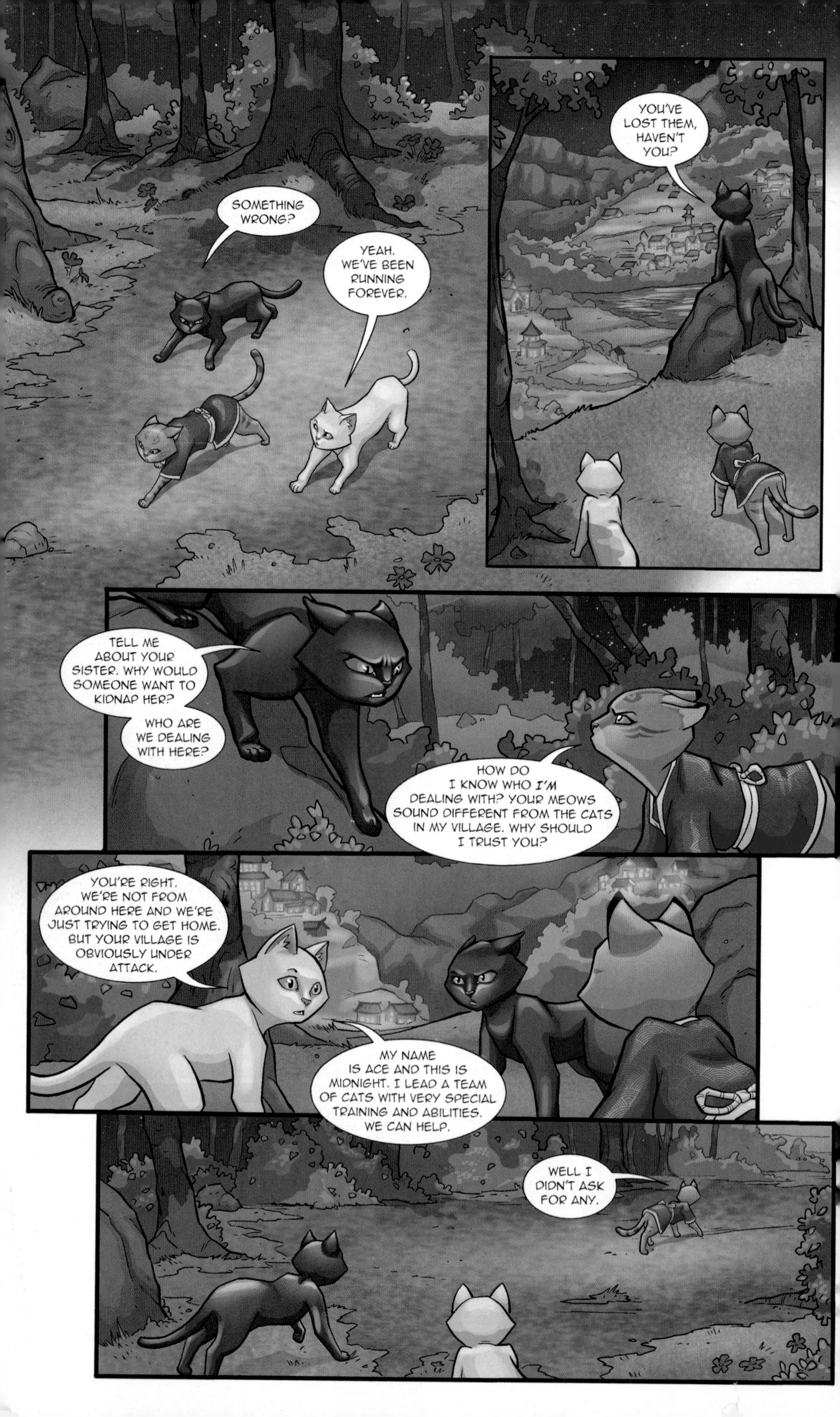
SOMETHING WRONG?
YEAH. WE'VE BEEN RUNNING FOREVER.
YOU'VE LOST THEM, HAVEN'T YOU?
TELL ME ABOUT YOUR SISTER. WHY WOULD SOMEONE WANT TO KIDNAP HER?
WHO ARE WE DEALING WITH HERE?
HOW DO I KNOW WHO *I'M* DEALING WITH? YOUR MEOWS SOUND DIFFERENT FROM THE CATS IN MY VILLAGE. WHY SHOULD I TRUST YOU?
YOU'RE RIGHT. WE'RE NOT FROM AROUND HERE AND WE'RE JUST TRYING TO GET HOME. BUT YOUR VILLAGE IS OBVIOUSLY UNDER ATTACK.
MY NAME IS ACE AND THIS IS MIDNIGHT. I LEAD A TEAM OF CATS WITH VERY SPECIAL TRAINING AND ABILITIES. WE CAN HELP.
WELL I DIDN'T ASK FOR ANY.

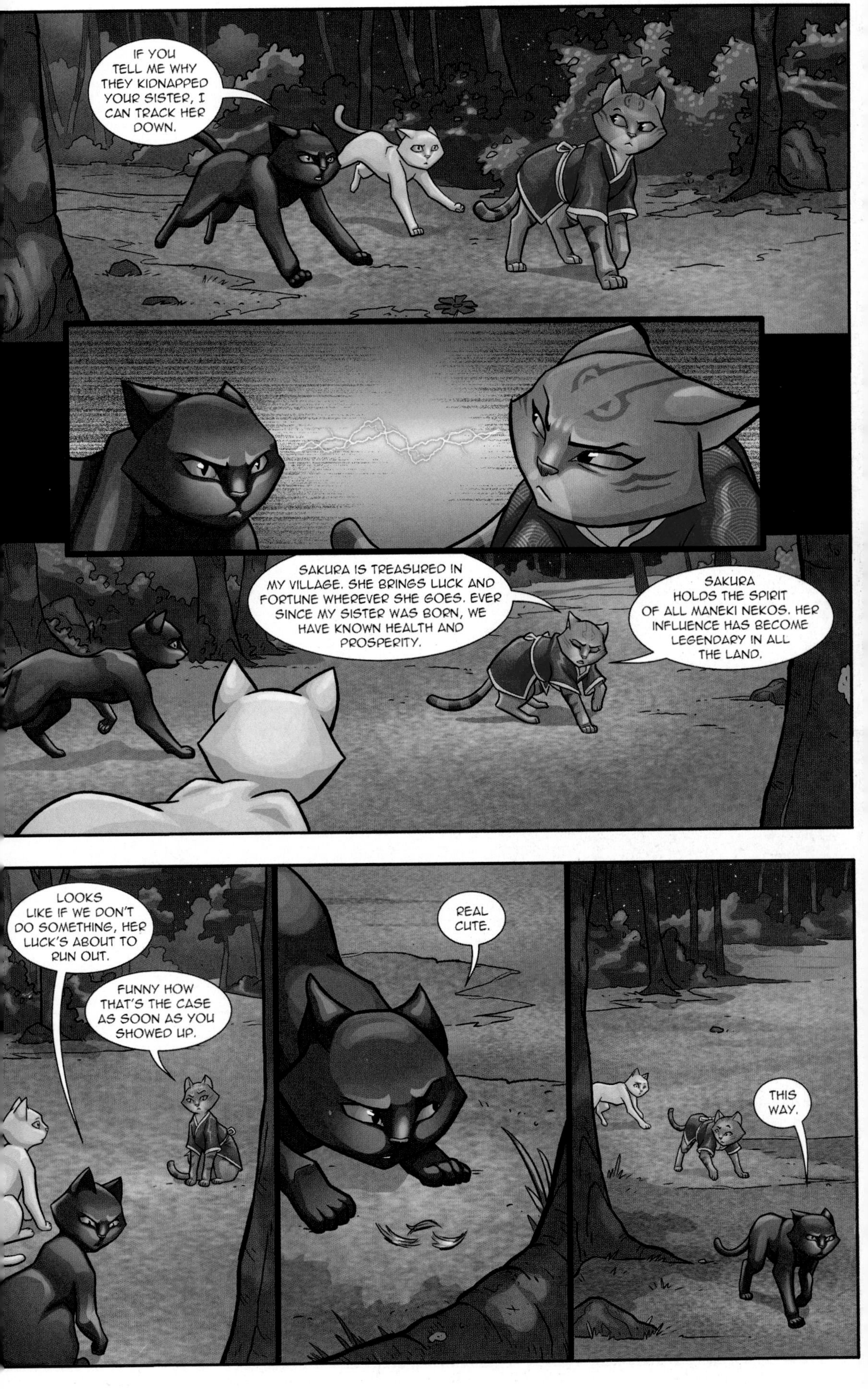
IF YOU TELL ME WHY THEY KIDNAPPED YOUR SISTER, I CAN TRACK HER DOWN.
SAKURA IS TREASURED IN MY VILLAGE. SHE BRINGS LUCK AND FORTUNE WHEREVER SHE GOES. EVER SINCE MY SISTER WAS BORN, WE HAVE KNOWN HEALTH AND PROSPERITY.
SAKURA HOLDS THE SPIRIT OF ALL MANEKI NEKOS. HER INFLUENCE HAS BECOME LEGENDARY IN ALL THE LAND.
LOOKS LIKE IF WE DON'T DO SOMETHING, HER LUCK'S ABOUT TO RUN OUT.
FUNNY HOW THAT'S THE CASE AS SOON AS YOU SHOWED UP.
REAL CUTE.
THIS WAY.

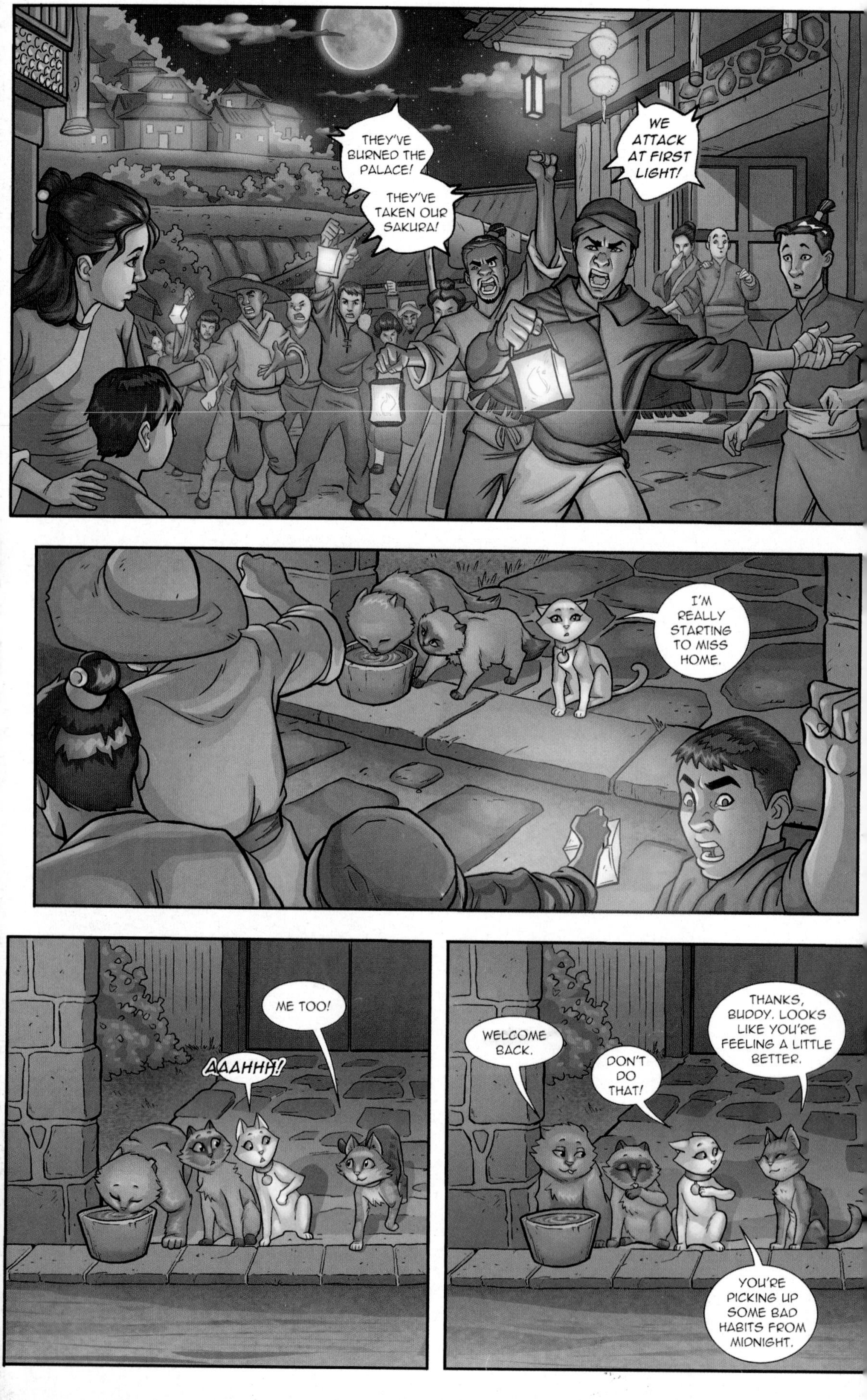
THEY'VE BURNED THE PALACE!
THEY'VE TAKEN OUR SAKURA!
WE ATTACK AT FIRST LIGHT!
I'M REALLY STARTING TO MISS HOME.
AAAHHH!
ME TOO!
WELCOME BACK.
DON'T DO THAT!
THANKS, BUDDY. LOOKS LIKE YOU'RE FEELING A LITTLE BETTER.
YOU'RE PICKING UP SOME BAD HABITS FROM MIDNIGHT.

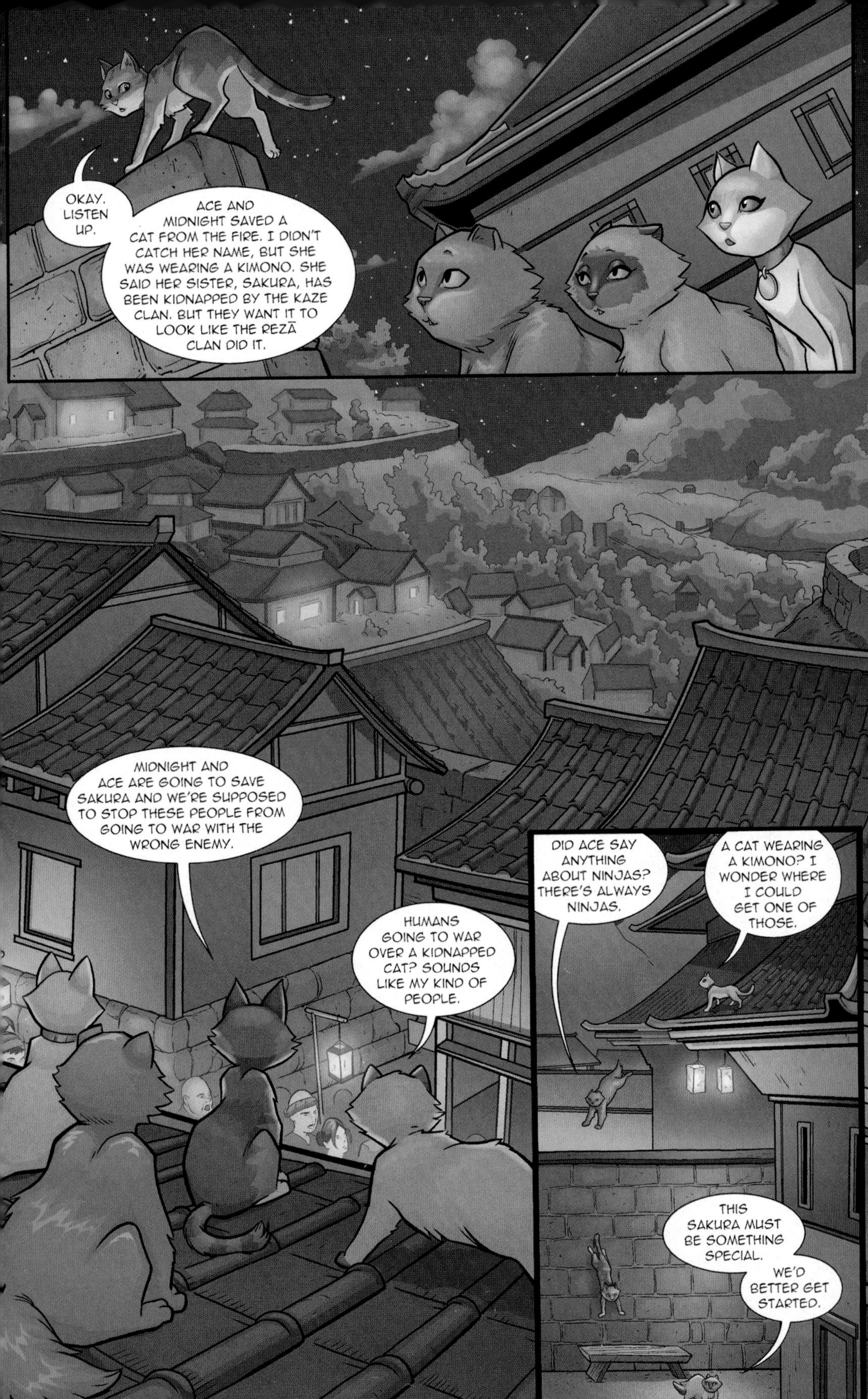
OKAY. LISTEN UP.
ACE AND MIDNIGHT SAVED A CAT FROM THE FIRE. I DIDN'T CATCH HER NAME, BUT SHE WAS WEARING A KIMONO. SHE SAID HER SISTER, SAKURA, HAS BEEN KIDNAPPED BY THE KAZE CLAN. BUT THEY WANT IT TO LOOK LIKE THE REZĀ CLAN DID IT.
MIDNIGHT AND ACE ARE GOING TO SAVE SAKURA AND WE'RE SUPPOSED TO STOP THESE PEOPLE FROM GOING TO WAR WITH THE WRONG ENEMY.
HUMANS GOING TO WAR OVER A KIDNAPPED CAT? SOUNDS LIKE MY KIND OF PEOPLE.
DID ACE SAY ANYTHING ABOUT NINJAS? THERE'S ALWAYS NINJAS.
A CAT WEARING A KIMONO? I WONDER WHERE I COULD GET ONE OF THOSE.
THIS SAKURA MUST BE SOMETHING SPECIAL.
WE'D BETTER GET STARTED.

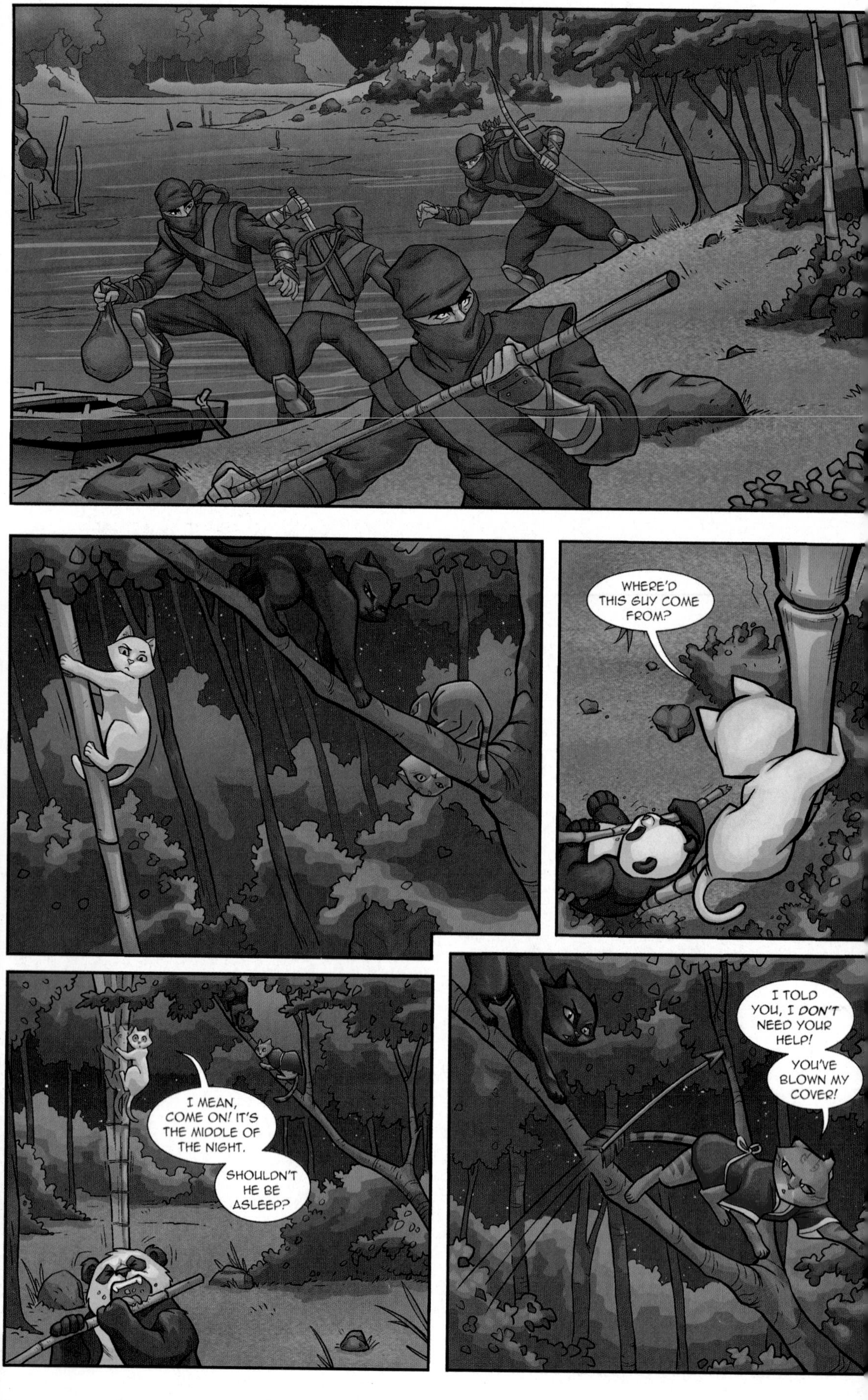
WHERE'D THIS GUY COME FROM?
I MEAN, COME ON! IT'S THE MIDDLE OF THE NIGHT.
SHOULDN'T HE BE ASLEEP?
I TOLD YOU, I DON'T NEED YOUR HELP!
YOU'VE BLOWN MY COVER!

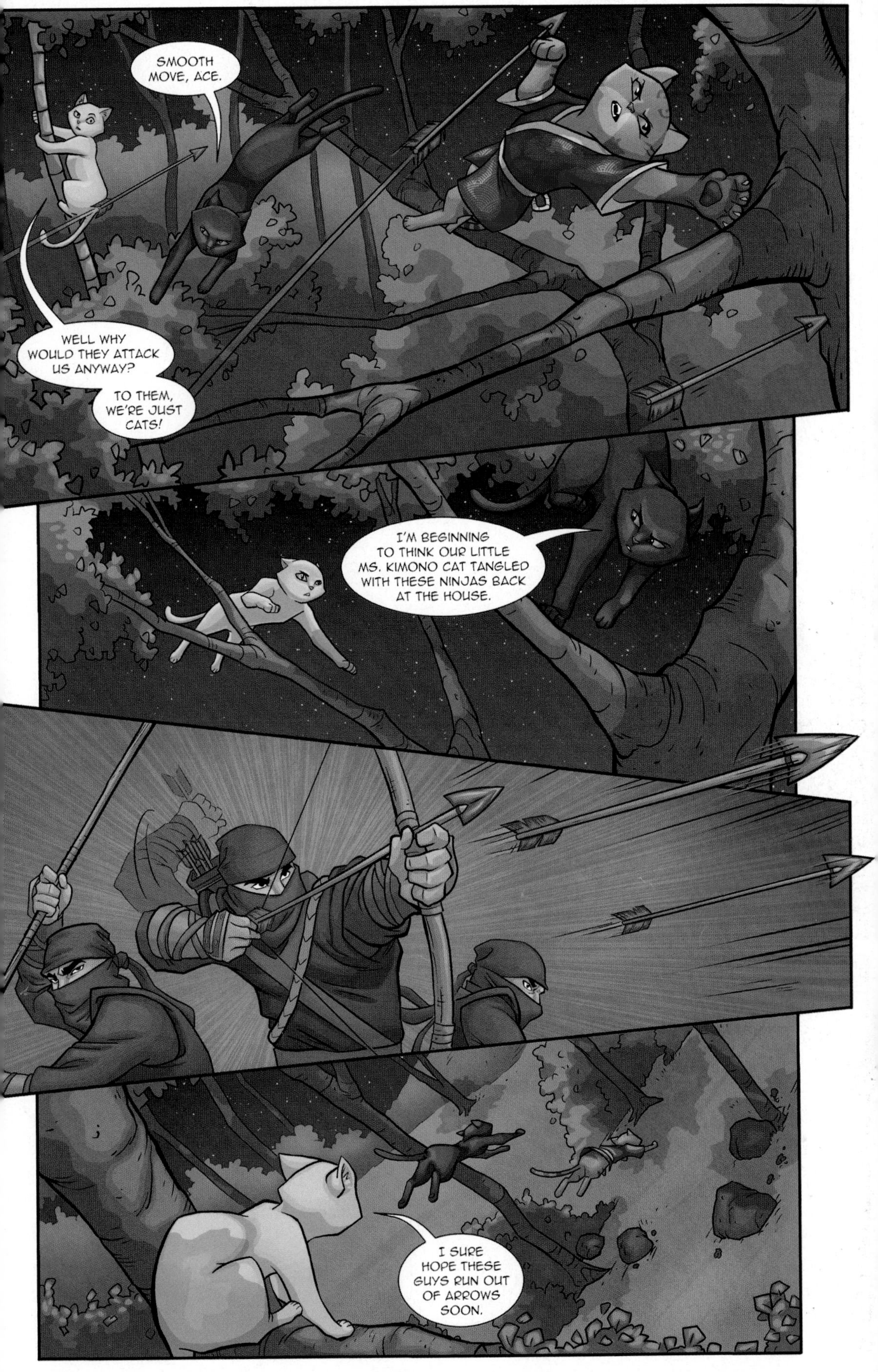
SMOOTH MOVE, ACE.
WELL WHY WOULD THEY ATTACK US ANYWAY?
TO THEM, WE'RE JUST CATS!
I'M BEGINNING TO THINK OUR LITTLE MS. KIMONO CAT TANGLED WITH THESE NINJAS BACK AT THE HOUSE.
I SURE HOPE THESE GUYS RUN OUT OF ARROWS SOON.

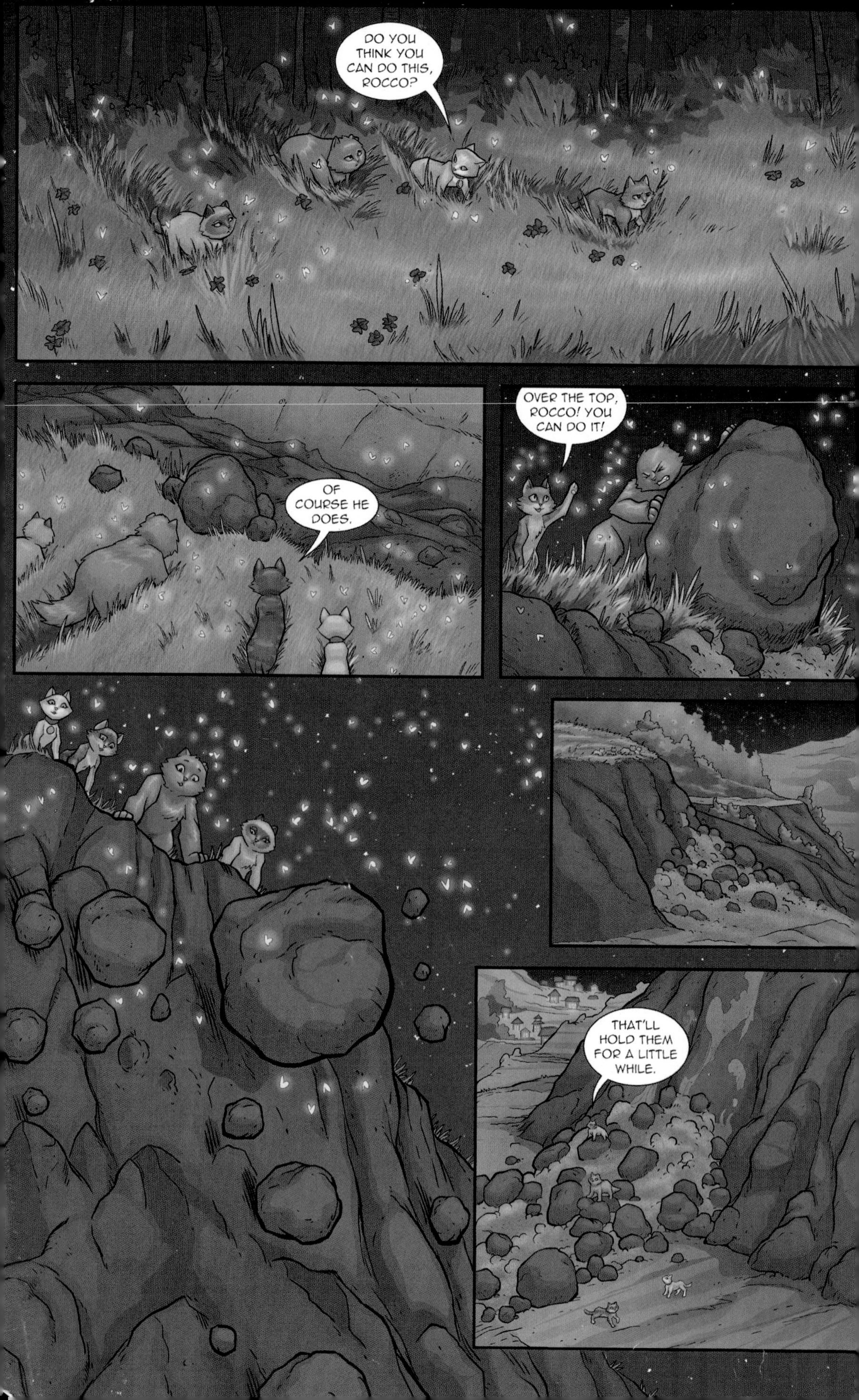
DO YOU THINK YOU CAN DO THIS, ROCCO?
OF COURSE HE DOES.
OVER THE TOP, ROCCO! YOU CAN DO IT!
THAT'LL HOLD THEM FOR A LITTLE WHILE.

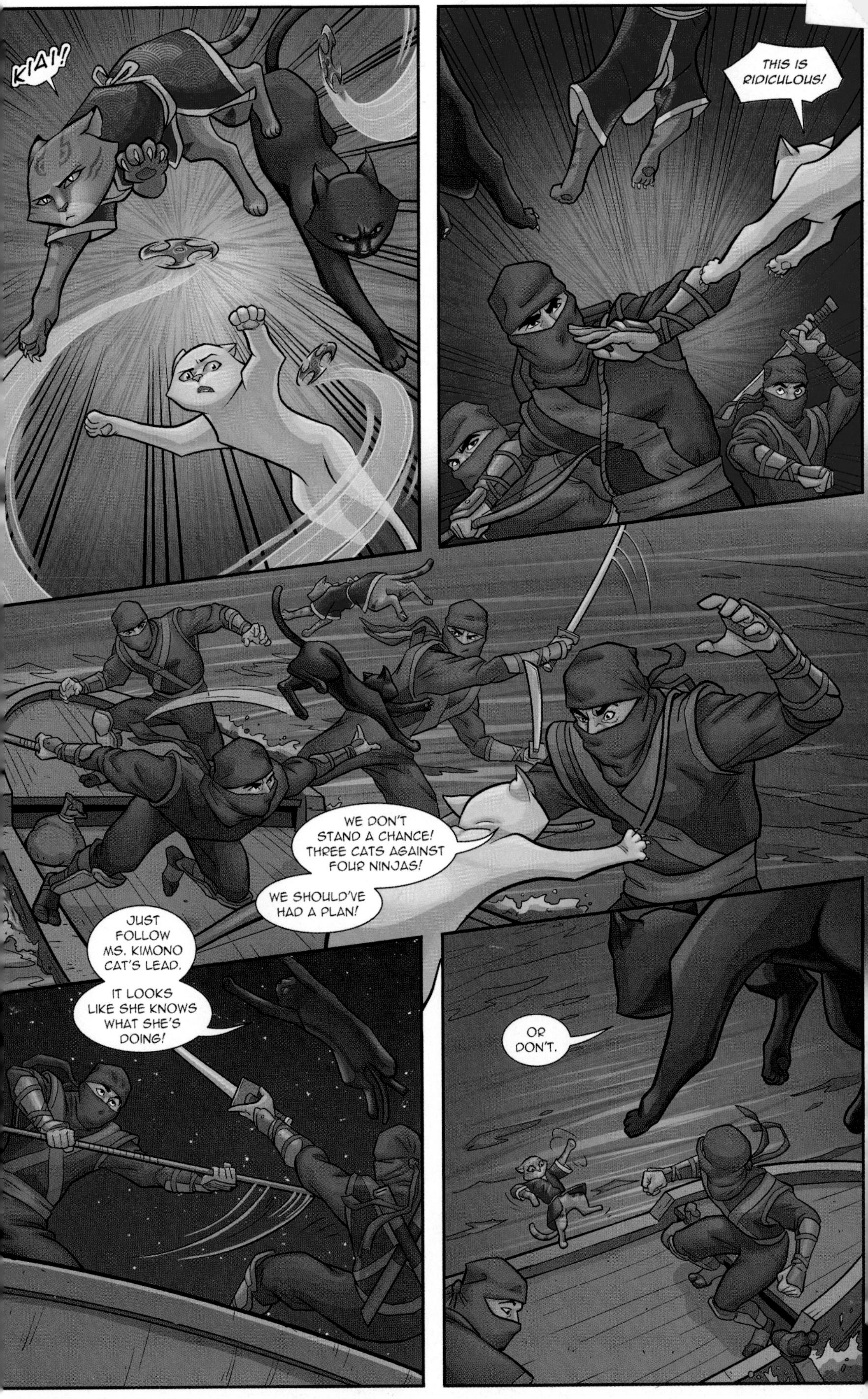
KIAI!
THIS IS RIDICULOUS!
WE DON'T STAND A CHANCE! THREE CATS AGAINST FOUR NINJAS!
WE SHOULD'VE HAD A PLAN!
JUST FOLLOW MS. KIMONO CAT'S LEAD.
IT LOOKS LIKE SHE KNOWS WHAT SHE'S DOING!
OR DON'T.

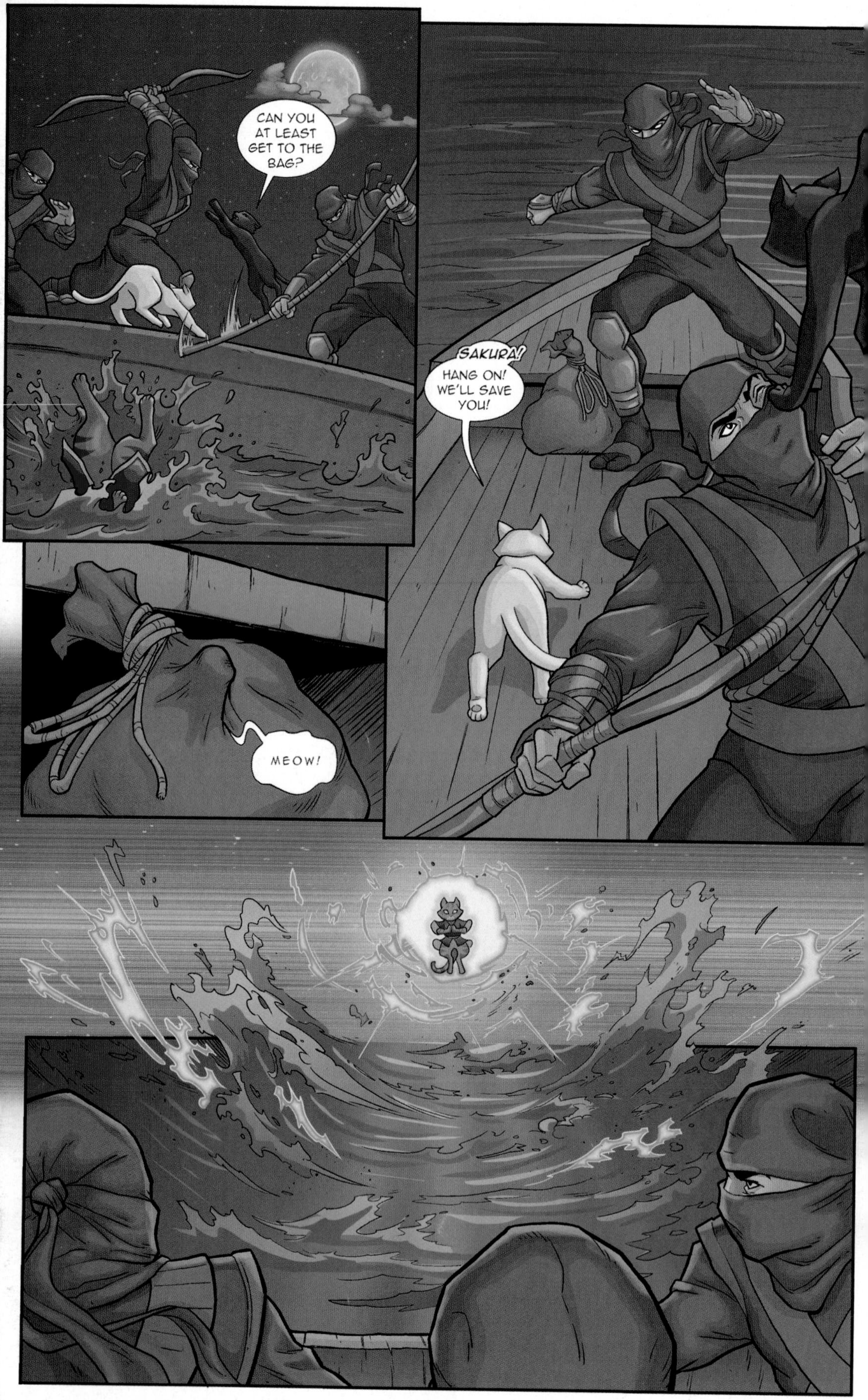
CAN YOU AT LEAST GET TO THE BAG?
SAKURA!
HANG ON! WE'LL SAVE YOU!
MEOW!

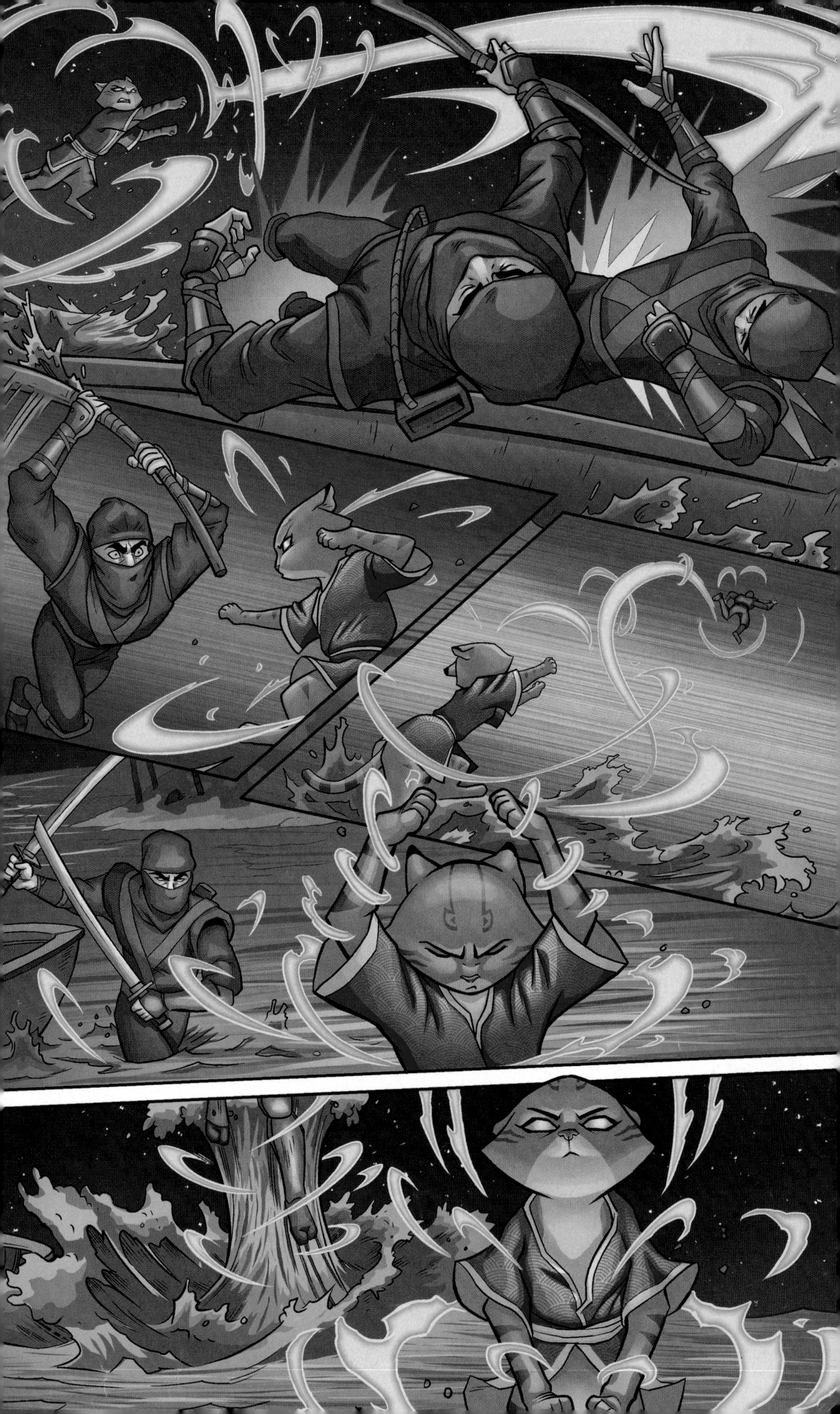

MAYBE NEXT TIME YOU SHOULD LEAD WITH THAT LITTLE TRICK, MS. KIMONO.

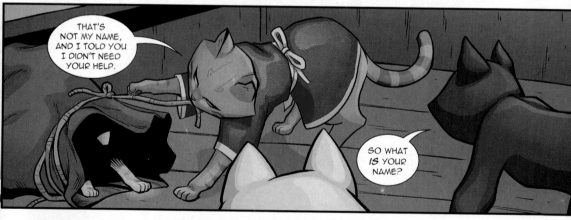

THAT'S NOT MY NAME, AND I TOLD YOU I DIDN'T NEED YOUR HELP.

SO WHAT *IS* YOUR NAME?

HER NAME IS BAMBOO. I AM SAKURA.

WE THANK YOU FOR YOUR ASSISTANCE.

NOW I FEAR WE MUST RETURN TO MY VILLAGE BEFORE IT'S TOO LATE.

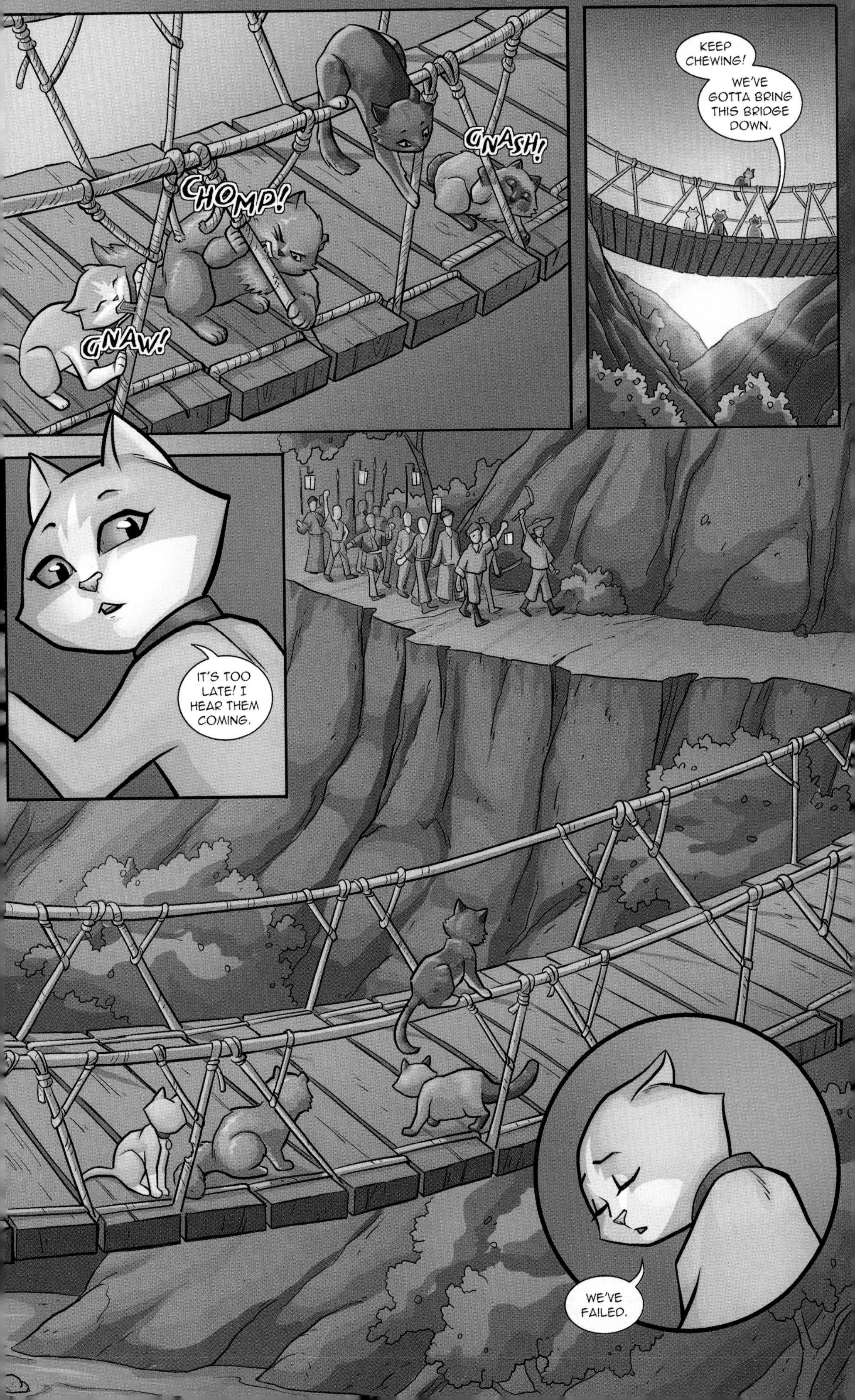
CHOMP!
GNASH!
GNAW!
KEEP CHEWING!
WE'VE GOTTA BRING THIS BRIDGE DOWN.
IT'S TOO LATE! I HEAR THEM COMING.
WE'VE FAILED.

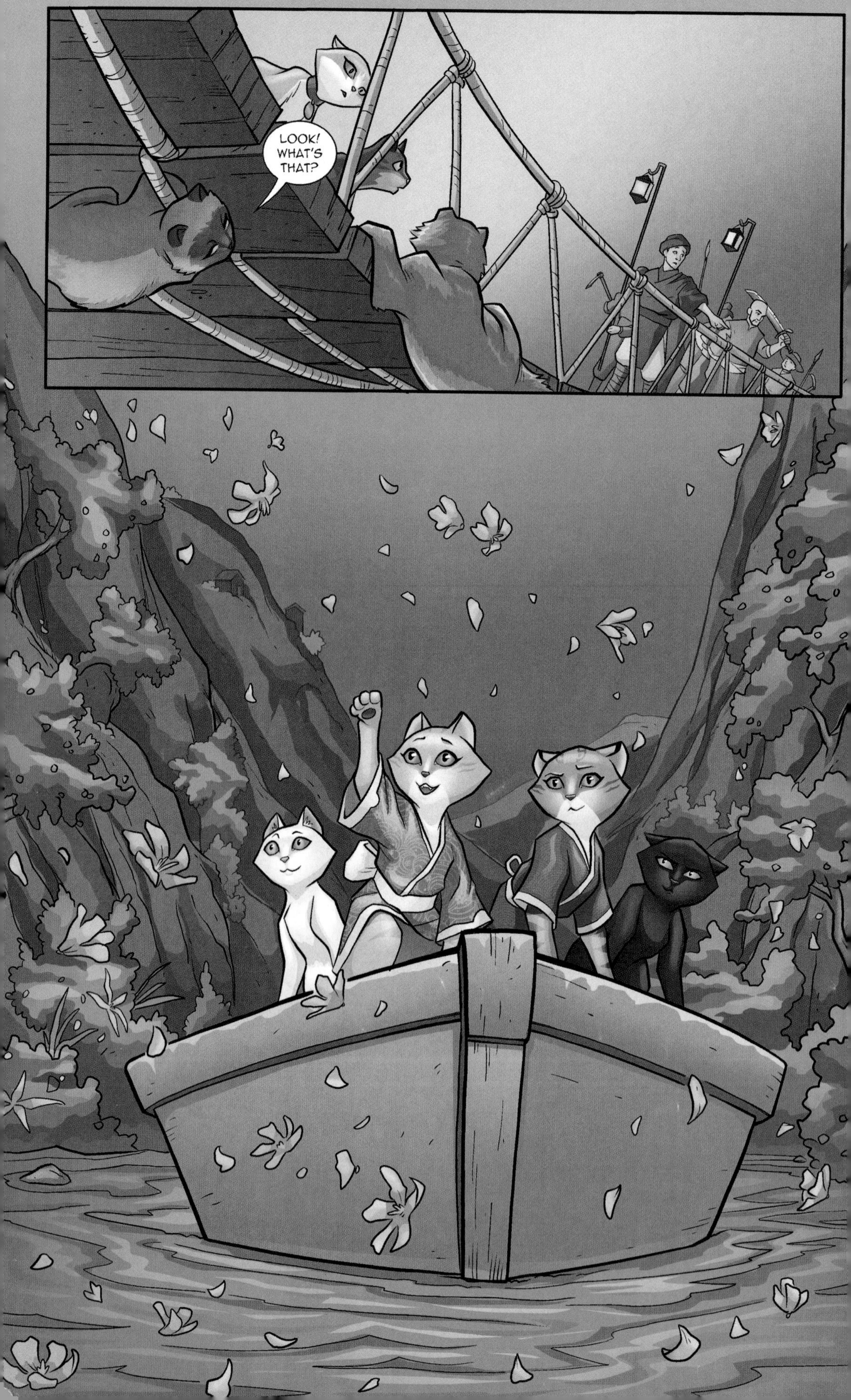
LOOK!
WHAT'S
THAT?

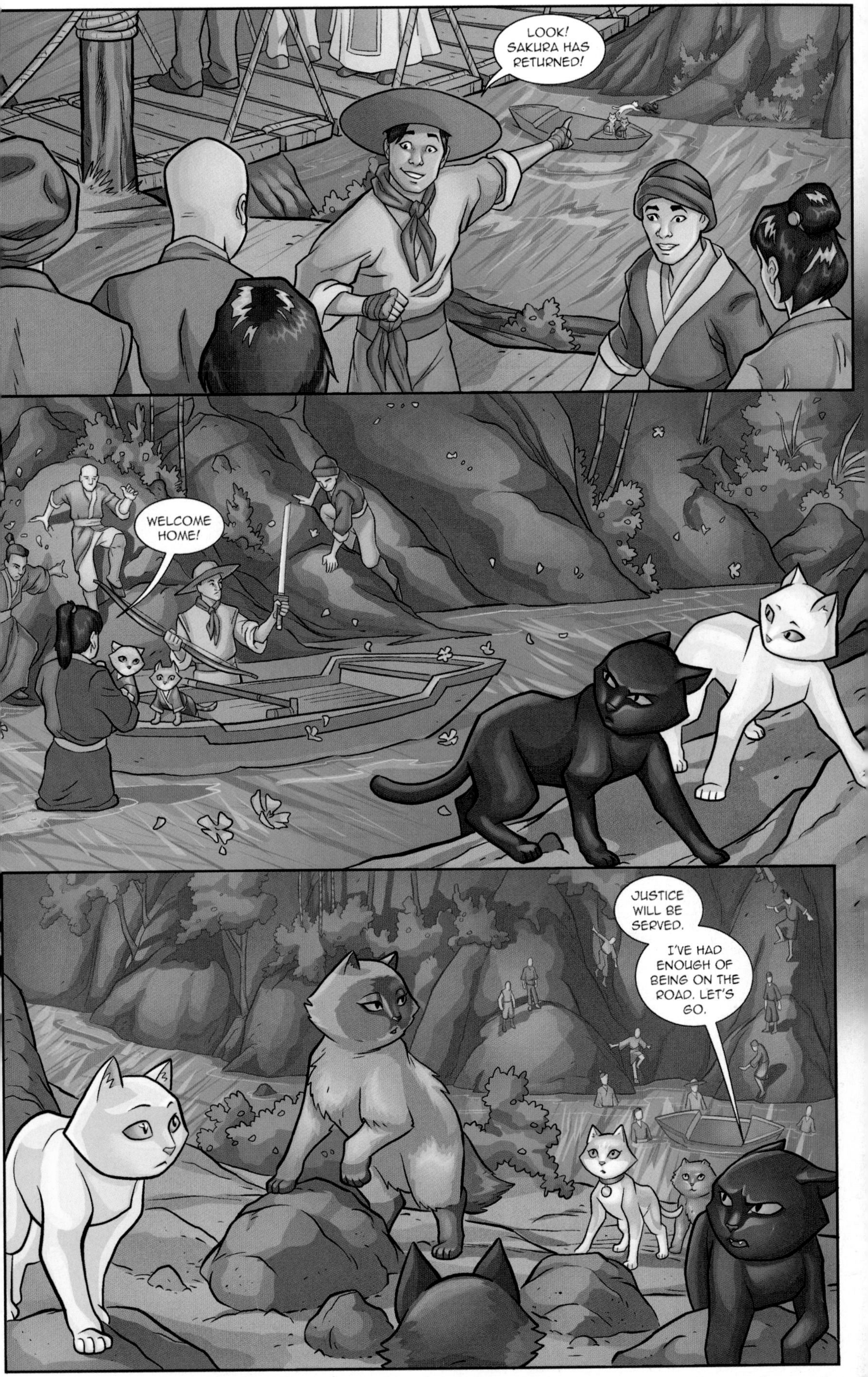
LOOK! SAKURA HAS RETURNED!
WELCOME HOME!
JUSTICE WILL BE SERVED.
I'VE HAD ENOUGH OF BEING ON THE ROAD. LET'S GO.

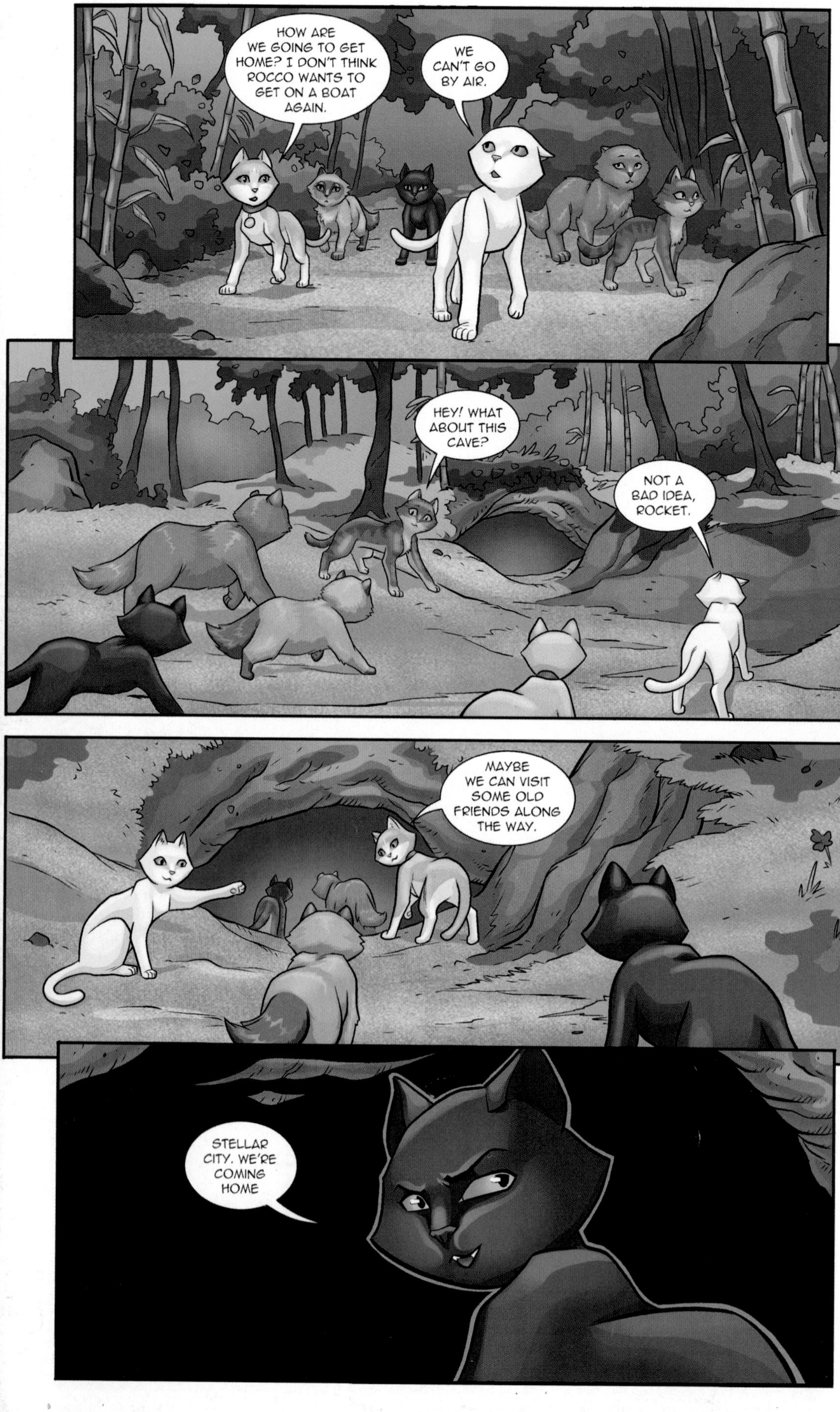
HOW ARE WE GOING TO GET HOME? I DON'T THINK ROCCO WANTS TO GET ON A BOAT AGAIN.
WE CAN'T GO BY AIR.
HEY! WHAT ABOUT THIS CAVE?
NOT A BAD IDEA, ROCKET.
MAYBE WE CAN VISIT SOME OLD FRIENDS ALONG THE WAY.
STELLAR CITY. WE'RE COMING HOME

HEROCHAT

HEY KIDS & CATS! HERE'S SOME EXCITING HIGHLIGHTS FROM OUR HERO CAT WORLD TOUR. THE CREATIVE TEAM IS STILL ON THE ROAD AND WE HOPE TO MEET YOU AT YOUR LOCAL COMIC CON OR SHOP SOON.

write to us @ kyle@galacticquest.com

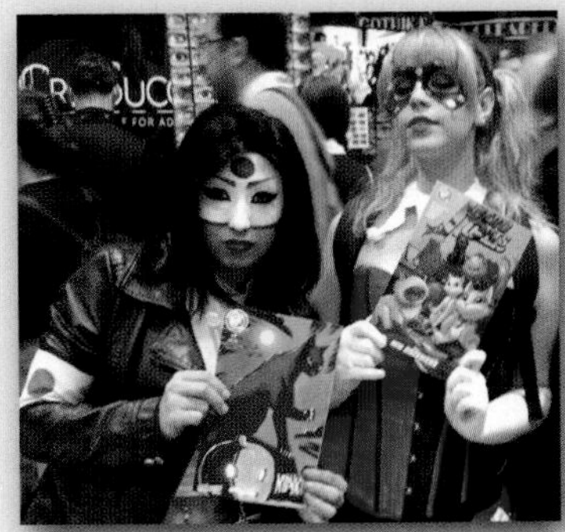

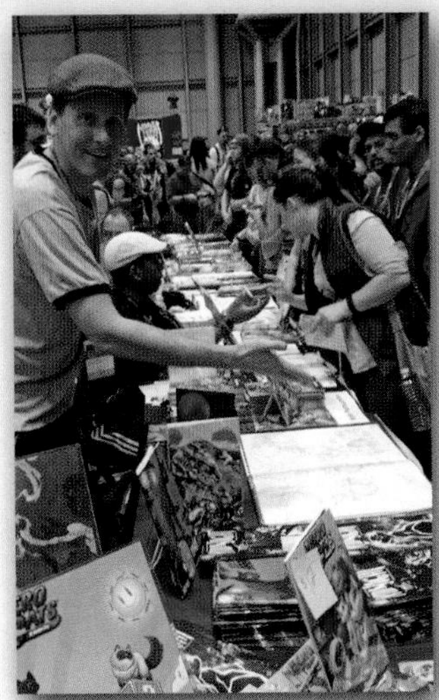

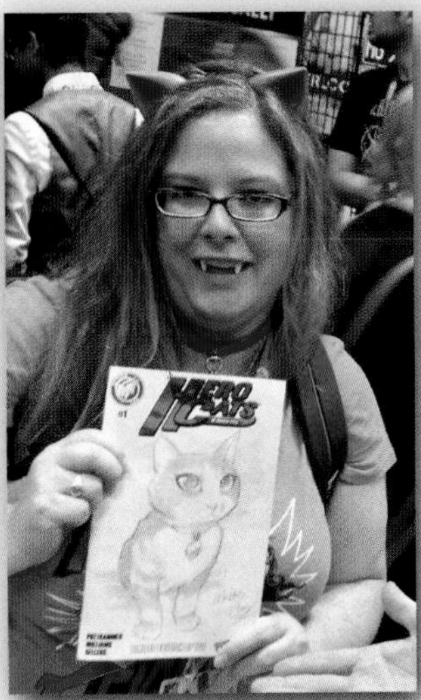
HERO CATS

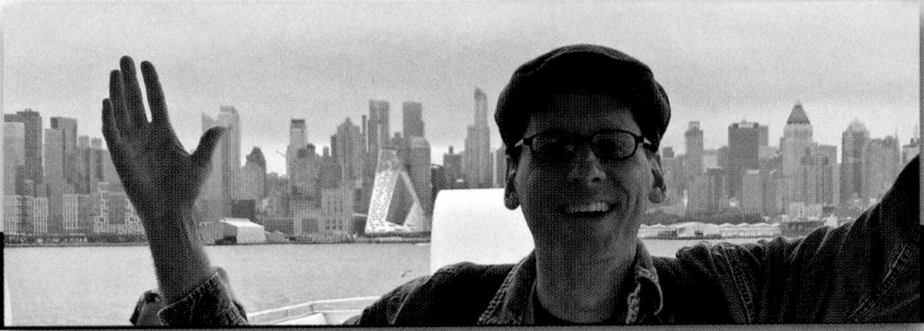

New York, NY

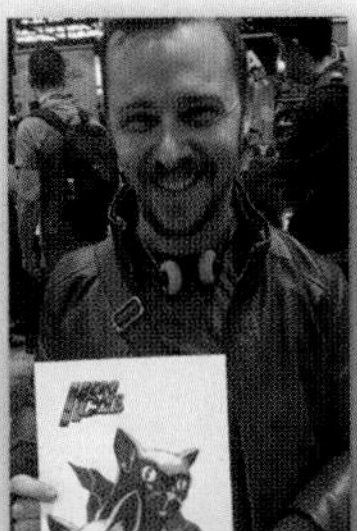

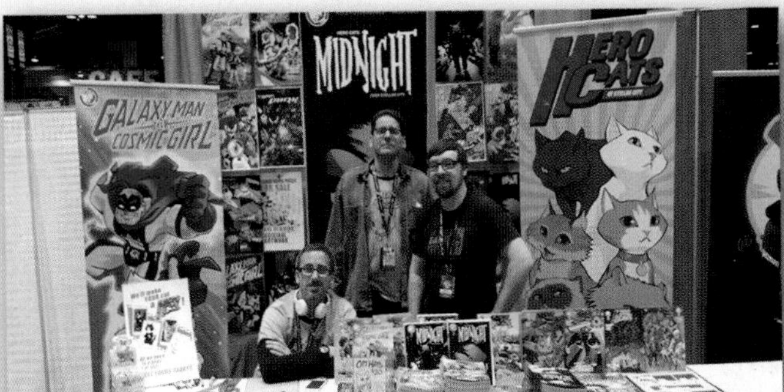
GALAXY MAN AND COSMIC GIRL
MIDNIGHT
HERO CATS
TRACY YARDLEY &
KYLE PUTTKAMMER

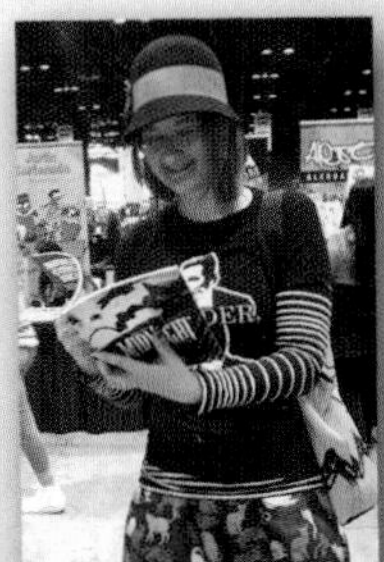

Chicago IL - Midnight Vol 1 debut

HEROCHAT

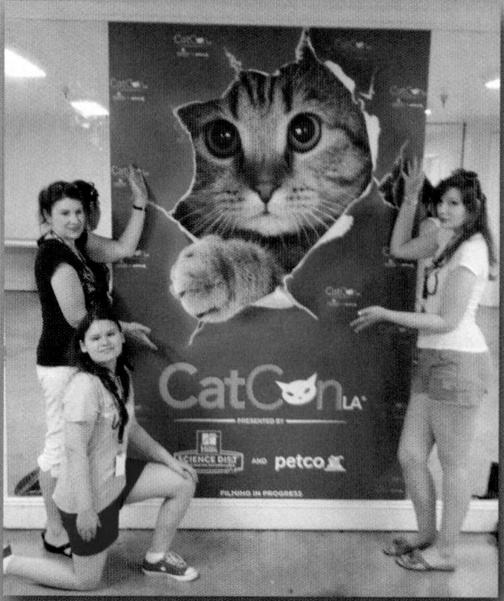
CatCon LA
PRESENTED BY
AND petco
FILMING IN PROGRESS

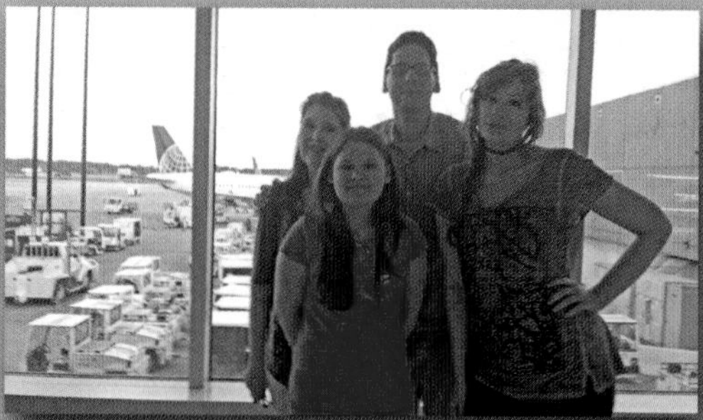

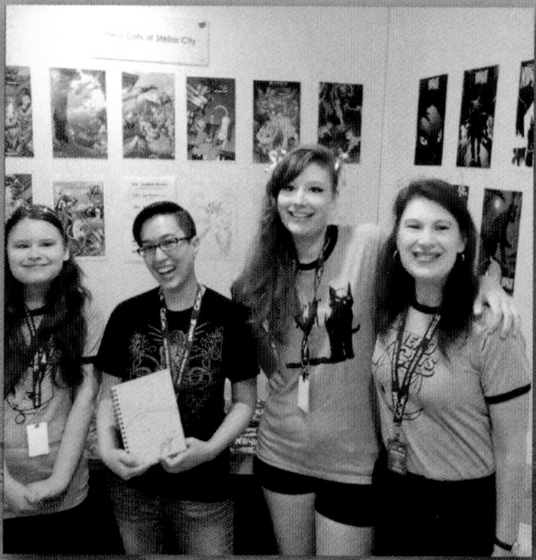

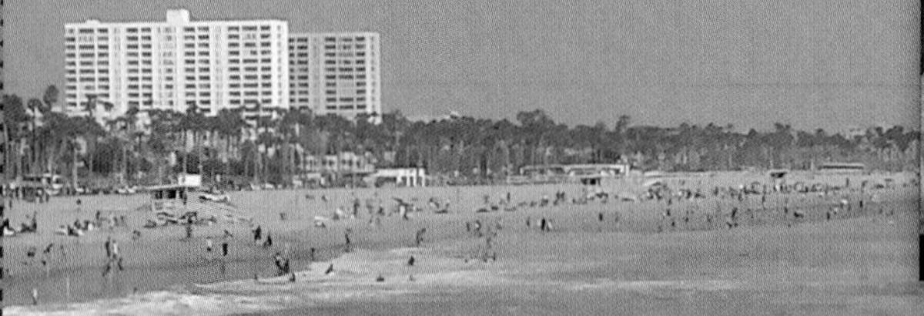

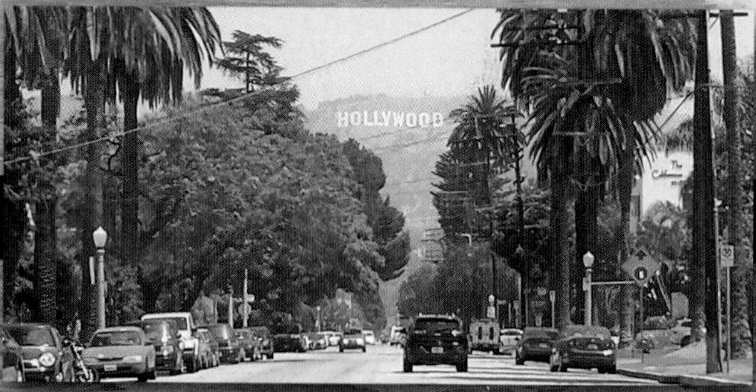
HOLLYWOOD

Los Angeles, CA

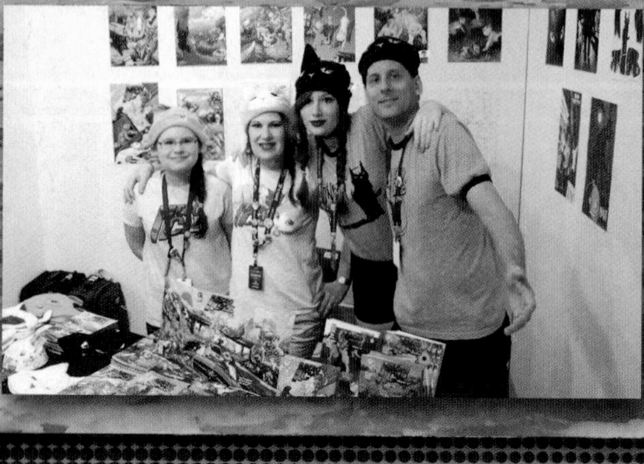

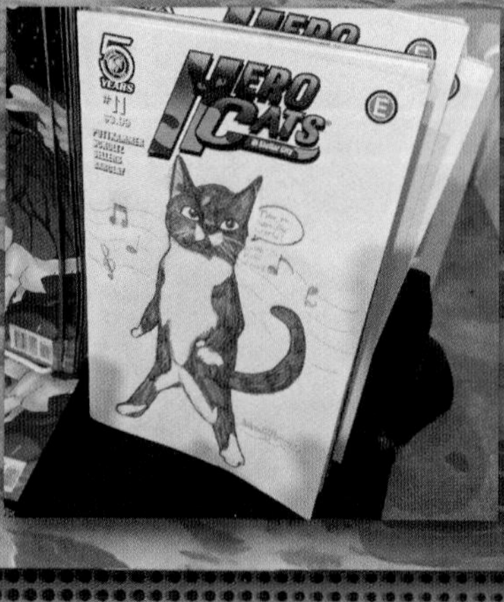
5 YEARS
HERO CATS

HEROCHAT

Portland, OR   **Greenville, SC**   **Charlotte, NC**

Atlanta, GA   **Knoxville, TN**

NEXT UP:

HERO CATS

OF THE

APOCALYPSE!

HERO CATS of the Apocalypse!

herocatsonline.com

HERO CATS #12, August 2016
Copyright Kyle Puttkammer, 2016 Published by Action Lab Entertainment.
All rights reserved. All characters are fictional. Any likeness to anyone living or dead is purely coincidental. No part of this publication may be reproduced or transmitted without permission,except for small excerpts for review purposes. Printed in Canada.

First Printing.

Bryan Seaton - Publisher
Dave Dwonch - President
Shawn Gabborin - Editor in Chief
Jamal Igle - Director of Marketing
Jim Dietz - Social Media Director
Jeremy Whitley - Education Outreach Director
Chad Cicconi & Colleen Boyd - Associate Editors

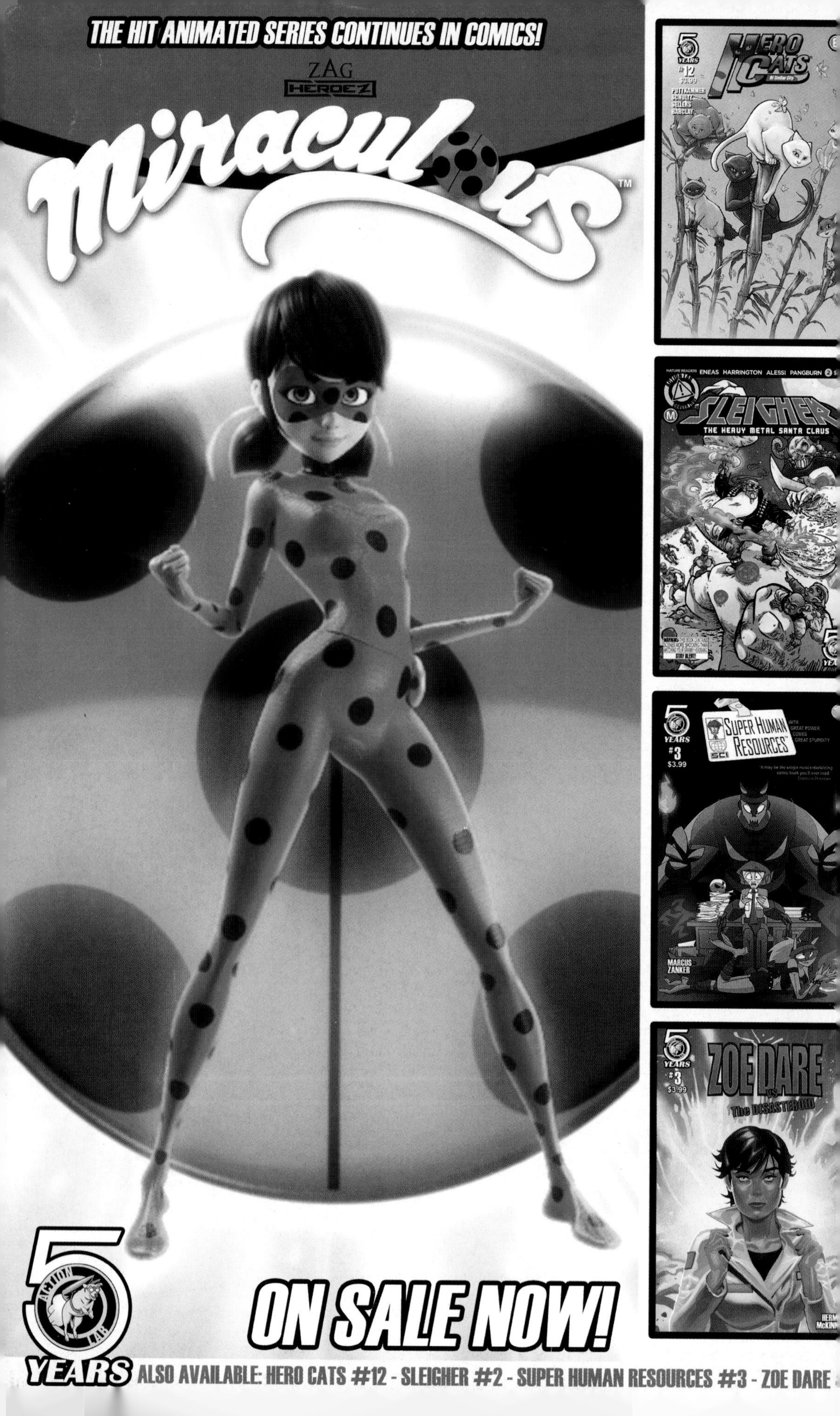
THE HIT ANIMATED SERIES CONTINUES IN COMICS!
ZAG HEROEZ
miraculous™
5 YEARS ACTION LAB
ON SALE NOW!
HERO CATS #12 $3.99
PUTTKAMMER SCHULTZ SELLERS BARCLAY
ENEAS HARRINGTON ALESSI PANGBURN 2
SLEIGHER
THE HEAVY METAL SANTA CLAUS
SUPER HUMAN RESOURCES
#3 $3.99
MARCUS ZANKER
ZOE DARE VS The DISASTEROID
#3 $3.99
ALSO AVAILABLE: HERO CATS #12 - SLEIGHER #2 - SUPER HUMAN RESOURCES #3 - ZOE DARE

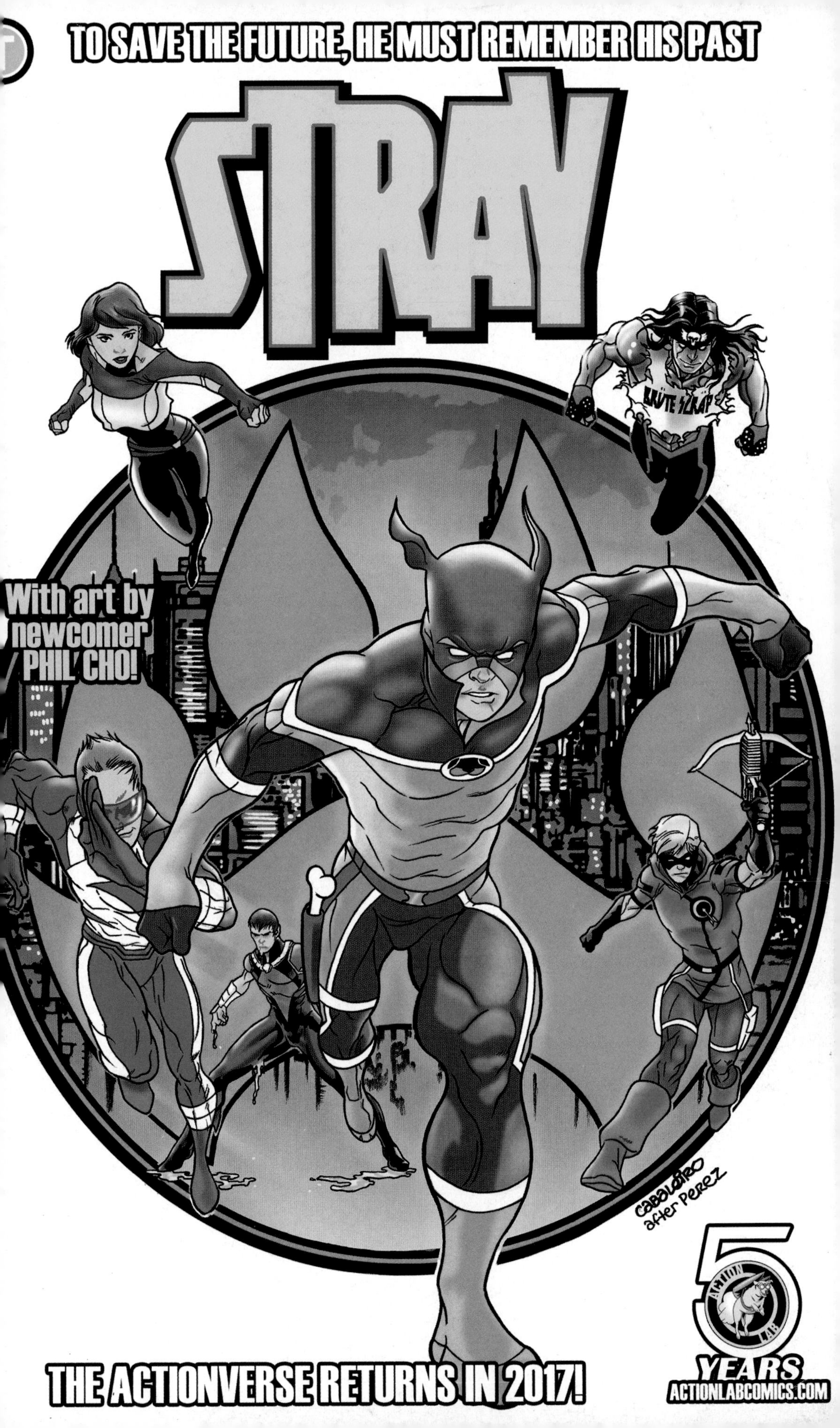
TO SAVE THE FUTURE, HE MUST REMEMBER HIS PAST
STRAY
BRÜTE SZKAP
With art by newcomer PHIL CHO!
CABALLERO after Perez
5 YEARS
ACTIONLABCOMICS.COM
THE ACTIONVERSE RETURNS IN 2017!

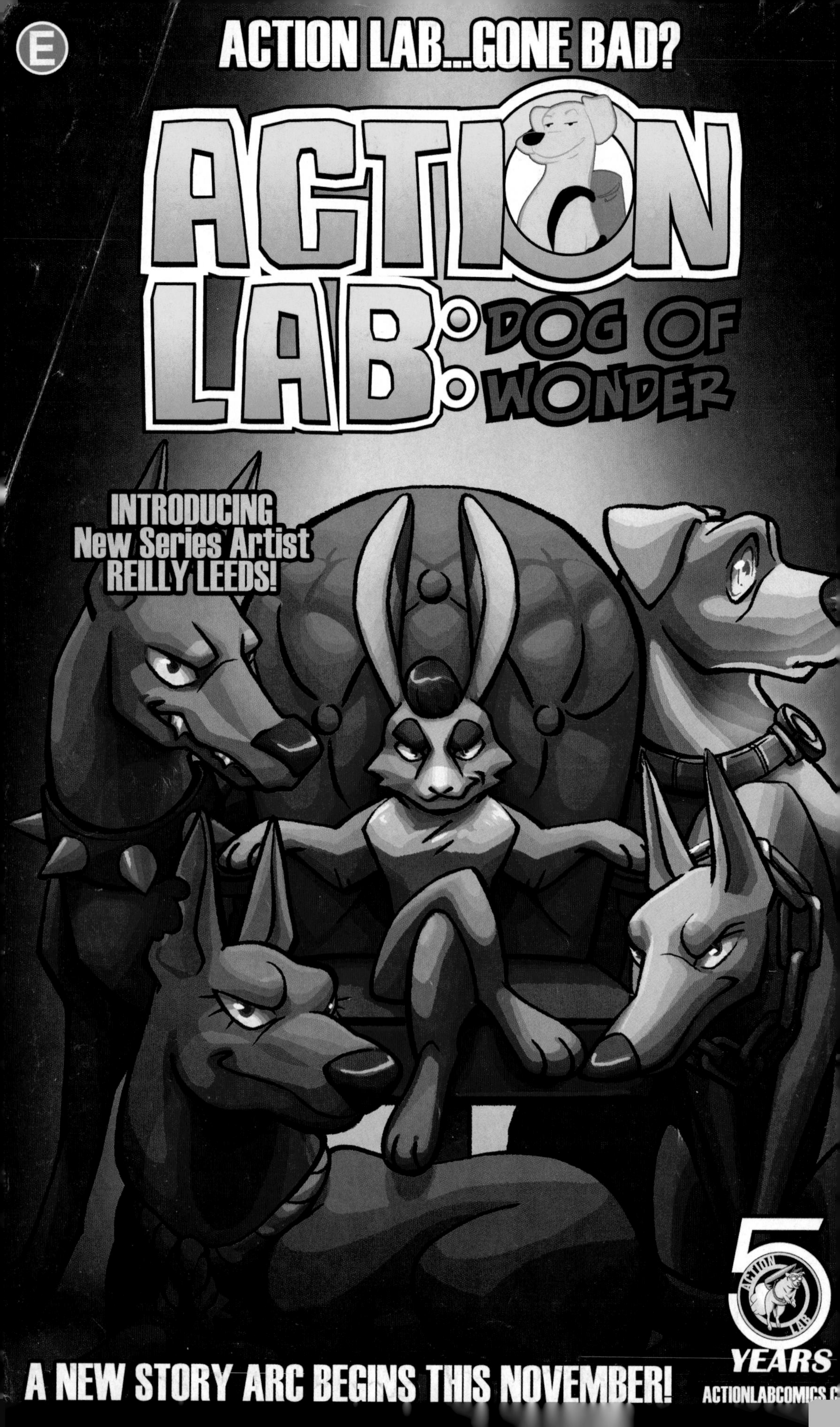
E
ACTION LAB...GONE BAD?
ACTION LAB: DOG OF WONDER
INTRODUCING
New Series Artist
REILLY LEEDS!
ACTION LAB
5 YEARS
A NEW STORY ARC BEGINS THIS NOVEMBER!